Hagar's Last Dance

Maureen Klovers

Hagar's Last Dance is a work of fiction. Names, characters, places, and incidents are either the product of the author's imagination or are used fictitiously. Any resemblance to actual persons, living or dead, or to actual events is purely coincidental.

Cover design by Josh Nuñez

For Kevin,
as we embark on the great adventure of parenthood

ACKNOWLEDGMENTS

This book would not have been possible without the assistance of numerous friends and family members.

First and foremost, I would like to thank my husband, Kevin Gormley, who is not only an indefatigable reader and editor, but also an incredibly supportive husband who continually encourages—and even pushes—me to "lean in."

My sister, Christelle Klovers, is one of my very best editors, and a wonderful sounding board when I get stuck on the plot. She is as creative as she is honest, and I gauge how improbable my plot is by the number of eye rolls she gives me. (I shoot for no more than two.)

I would also like to thank the members of my women's writing group: Maya Corrigan, author of the Five-Ingredient Mystery Series; Sherry Harris, Agatha Award-nominated author of *Tagged for Death*; Elaine Douts; Robin Templeton; and C. Ellett Logan. I am especially grateful for Sherry's willingness to "blurb" my book and provide the quote for the back cover. Maddi Davidson, another fellow Sister in Crime, provided invaluable proofreading assistance.

J.E. Coble, Assistant Fire Marshall of Guilford County, N.C., and best-selling author (and former arson investigator) John Gilstrap provided valuable insights into fire dynamics and arson investigations.

My friend John Ward, an Iraq War veteran, generously took the time to explain to me the escalation of force rules that would generally apply at military checkpoints.

Finally, many thanks to the real Zahira, my friend (and talented belly dancer) Christine Glenn. While she bears little resemblance to Jeanne Pelletier, other than their shared love of belly dance, she was an invaluable source of information on all things belly dance related and saved me from making some very embarrassing mistakes.

That said, all mistakes in this book are my own.

Chapter One

"Willamette Correctional Facility," the caller ID read. Jeanne froze and held her breath. She knew it was silly, the way she always stood silent and still, as if the caller could hear and see her from six hundred miles away. But it was some sort of guilty instinct, one she had not been able to overcome in all these years.

Her heart was pounding so loudly that she was sure Lily could hear it, but her best friend seemed completely unfazed, totally absorbed in the preparations for the royal wedding. Without even looking up from the page, Lily asked, "Well, aren't you going to answer it?"

"No." Jeanne tried to sound nonchalant, but her raspy whisper betrayed her. "We don't have time. I don't want to be late."

Jeanne stepped into her closet, a hot, airless space that did double duty as the only access to the bathroom. Rummaging around for her sword, she felt a pang of resentment towards her friend, who had the clearest, most untroubled conscience of anyone she knew. Lily seemed to glide effortlessly from one adventure to another, with no regrets, no inhibitions, no worries of any kind. Lily was sensual, impetuous, blunt, and loud. She once gave three days' notice before moving to Istanbul to be with her Turkish lover. The relationship only lasted two months, but Lily had no regrets. "I learned to make amazing baklava from his grandmother," she had announced upon her return. "I studied belly dancing with one of the great teachers of the Middle East and unearthed a four thousand-year-old pot while tagging along with some archaeology students. I had a great life experience."

Jeanne, on the other hand, was one of those people with whom fortune would not be lenient. She knew she would get caught the first time she smoked pot and be kidnapped and sold into white slavery the first time she hitchhiked. All of the rules applied to her, and none of them applied to Lily.

Peeking out from behind a gray sweater was the sheath of her long, curved sword. She flung it in a battered old golf club bag. Spotting a flash of iridescent green and blue sequins, she reached out to grasp her bra top and then snatched a long peacock-blue chiffon skirt and a matching bead-encrusted belt.

When she emerged from the closet, she walked through her cramped "living room/bedroom"—really just a small square of cheap parquet floor crammed with second-hand furniture—to the galley kitchen. She leaned down and patted Scarlett, her one-eyed, three-legged Golden Retriever, who was lurking hopefully by her bowl. "Now be good, Scar," Jeanne admonished her as she dropped a treat in her bowl.

She turned to Lily. "I guess I'm as ready as I'll ever be."

At first, Jeanne and Lily made good time on the drive from Glover Park to Northeast, sailing through every light in Lily's Crown Vic, an old cop car she had purchased from a sleazy used car salesman in Baltimore. When they reached U Street, however, they were greeted by a sea of red tail lights that stretched as far as they could see.

Panic rose in Jeanne's chest. Why had she ever agreed to this? It was one thing to shimmy across the bare wooden floor of the Arabian Nights Dance Studio after a long day of legal temp drudgery at the soulless Higgins, Higgins, and Applebaum. That was freeing, even empowering. Rehearsals distracted her from the reality that, at the tender age of twenty-eight, the Great Recession had already crushed her dream of being some crusading non-profit's legal beagle—fighting for compensation for ex-miners with black lung disease, ensuring deaf children had access to interpreters in school, maybe even saving a few whales—and converted her into an underpaid, overworked, and extremely bored mercenary.

It was quite another to perform in front of a crowd of two hundred at Algiers, the city's premier Middle Eastern restaurant and nightclub.

She looked longingly out the window at Ben's Chili Bowl and imagined herself ensconced in one of Ben's deep red vinyl booths, totally anonymous, devouring a half-smoke smothered in chili and slurping a chocolate milkshake.

"If you're nervous," Lily said, "just imagine the audience naked."

Jeanne laughed. "Easy for you to say. Your size-two Filipina ass will be in the audience, fully clothed, while my pasty white flesh is jiggling about."

"Not jiggling. Rippling in a highly sensuous and artistic manner. And besides, pasty white is in. Fake tans, looking all orangey, risking skin cancer—that's so last year."

Smiling, Jeanne started to relax a little. Lily always had a way of making her feel better. In fact, it was Lily who had coaxed Jeanne into taking up belly dancing in the first place, and Jeanne had never regretted it, not for a minute. She loved its grace and sensuality, its embrace of women with belly fat, stretch marks, and cellulite. The twenty extra pounds she carried were actually a help, not a hindrance.

But she did not consider herself to be especially good. Not like Lily, who could effortlessly layer a belly roll on a shimmy. Why had Yasmina picked her, of all people, to open tonight's performance at Algiers? She was about to ask Lily this very question. But then Lily popped in an ABBA CD, cranked up the volume, and began singing "Dancing Queen" at the top of her lungs, all while pointing emphatically at Jeanne. While she didn't particularly feel like a queen, Jeanne was comforted nonetheless by Lily's faith in her.

Twenty minutes later, they were navigating Northeast D.C.'s industrial wasteland, one of the very few corners of the city that had resisted the wave of gentrification. The parking lots were empty, ringed with barbed wire, and the warehouses stood vast and silent. Discarded needles glinted beneath the occasional lamplight.

When they came to a screeching halt in front of Algiers's windowless façade, Jeanne jumped out and rushed up to the ornately carved oak door, driver's license in hand. Already ten minutes late, she tapped her foot impatiently until the security guard finally nodded and handed it back to her. Algiers took its security very seriously.

As the door opened, Jeanne caught an intoxicating whiff of cardamom, roses, and roasted lamb. For a moment, she forgot that she was going to be performing. Instead, she stood mesmerized by the colored lanterns; the exquisitely beaded and embroidered jewel-toned pillows; and the hundreds of Oriental carpets covering every conceivable surface, their curlicues and tendrils swirling across the floor and the walls, the tables and the benches, until it seemed as though every right angle had disappeared. The interior was exactly the way she had always pictured a sultan's palace.

"Jeanne!"

Her sister Vivienne stretched out on a crimson and emerald green carpet, her kitten heels dangling over the edge of the divan. To Jeanne's everlasting irritation, Vivienne always managed to look like she was in a modeling shoot, and tonight was no exception. She was ravishing in a sapphire wrap-dress, her long strawberry blonde locks pulled into a loose chignon. Everett, her two-year-old, lay straddled across her midsection, giggling as she bounced him up and down.

"Hey, Viv. Glad you could come."

"I wouldn't miss it for anything!"

Mitch, her husband, looked less excited. He paced in the corner, barking orders into his cell phone. "Don't say anything. Not where you went, not whom you were with. Don't spit, don't drink, don't sneeze. Don't even piss." Jeanne watched the vein in his forehead throb each time he said "don't," and hoped all of that frowning and sneering would unglue his toupee and send it flying.

He shoved his phone in his pocket and planted a hurried kiss on Vivienne's cheek. "Sorry, sweetheart. I've got to go. Duty calls."

Jeanne snorted. "What? You're going to spring another thug so he can continue to be a menace to society?"

"Everyone deserves a good defense, Jeanne."

"Spoken like a true mercenary."

"Very funny. I guess you have time to think up lines like that when you are a paralegal."

"Contract attorney."

"Oh, yes...contract attorney."

Vivienne wrinkled her nose. "Enough, you guys. I'll see you at home, honey." She turned to Jeanne once he was out of earshot. "I thought you agreed to a truce."

Jeanne sighed. She had always detested Mitch. She found him smarmy, condescending, greedy, and vain, but more than anything, she hated the way he had taken all of the fire and spice out of her sister. She hadn't had a real conversation with Vivienne in years. They only talked about Vivienne and Mitch's beach house, their stock portfolio, Everett's teething and walking and talking, the raw foods diet, the Atkins diet, the flat belly diet. Jeanne never realized there were so many diets in the world until Vivienne met Mitch. But she supposed

15

that Vivienne was happy, and she should try to like Mitch for her sister's sake. If only he didn't make it so damn hard.

"Sorry," Jeanne mumbled. "I need to get ready."

When Jeanne entered the makeshift dressing room—a storage room in the basement—Yasmina was doing a split on the cracked linoleum floor, her back to the door. She cradled her cell phone against her ear, her tone almost a whisper. "Yes, I understand," she murmured.

For some reason, Jeanne felt as though she were intruding. Slipping out the back door, she spent a few minutes loitering by the dumpsters, mentally reviewing her routine while staring up at the stars. Every time she opened her mouth, her breath froze into a thousand little ice crystals. Her teeth chattered. Even for someone from Maine's North Woods, it was cold.

When she re-entered the dressing room, Jeanne noisily cleared her throat. Yasmina's expression quickly turned to a smile and she motioned for Jeanne to put her things next to the mirror. "He's here," she said quickly into the phone, then snapped it shut.

"Is your family coming?" Jeanne asked before she could help herself. She didn't know why she said that, since she knew perfectly well that Yasmina's mother and sister were in Houston and the rest of her family was in

Jordan. She remembered how they had stayed up late, drinking hot sweetened mint tea, talking about their families, their girlfriends, their careers, and their love lives—well, Yasmina's love life anyway. There really wasn't much to say about Jeanne's. Yasmina had shown her family photos, full of handsome bearded men and full-figured women with bright, lively eyes and shiny dark hair poking out from their headscarves. And Jeanne had confided too much. Much too much.

Yasmina frowned, and Jeanne turned red. Yasmina was no doubt wondering how someone who had spent two months on her couch as a refugee of D.C.'s affordable housing crisis could have forgotten all of the details of her personal life. "No, not family. They've seen me a hundred times. Just a few friends—well, acquaintances actually. All my friends are at the studio—I don't have time for a social life outside of it."

From what Jeanne had seen in her two months of living with Yasmina, that certainly seemed to be true. Except for the occasional paramour, belly dancing was her life. Her idea of a good time was to rehearse with some of the other instructors or watch videos of the great Egyptian cabaret artists of the fifties and sixties.

Yasmina hopped up from the floor, crossed the room, and an affectionately patted a large wooden trunk. "My family's here in spirit, though. I brought some of my grandmother's old costumes."

17

Jeanne squeezed into her costume and pulled out her makeup case. Out of the corner of her eye, she watched Yasmina. There was something different about her today. Yasmina's svelte arms and torso glistened as usual, she wore all of the same bangles, and she hummed the music as she always did. Yet Jeanne sensed that, for once, Yasmina was not thinking about her performance. Something else was occupying her thoughts; something else was causing her lips to tremble slightly as she pouted into the mirror to apply her lipstick.

"Did Vivienne and Mitch come?" Yasmina asked.

"Yes," Jeanne said as she squirted some glue on a set of false eyelashes, lifted it to her eyelid and tried not to blink. "And, surprisingly, they brought Ev—shit!"

She wiped frantically at her eye, trying to get the glue out. It seemed like an ominous omen. She was such an amateur that she couldn't even get ready without hurting herself. Why hadn't Yasmina picked Lily instead? Lily would have been so much more polished and confident.

"Let me see." Yasmina's voice was gentle and calm as she dabbed at Jeanne's eye.

Jeanne sighed. "I've never been good at any of this."

Yasmina deftly wiped a few clumps of glue off of the fake eyelashes and re-applied a thin strip of glue. "Close your eyes," she murmured and then pressed them gently against Jeanne's eyelids "There—all done."

Blinking, Jeanne felt the unfamiliar brush of plastic against her eyelids. "Do you ever get used to this?"

18

"Of course. The eyelashes, the makeup, the costumes, the props—they're all part of the spectacle. Remember, the performance is not just about the steps. It's also about your expression, how you interact with the audience, how much fun you seem to be having. Trust me, if you're doing it right, the energy's infectious."

"What was your first time like?"

"Horrible." Yasmina laughed, revealing two slightly crooked front teeth. "I slipped on some couscous, tore my costume—the most expensive I had ever bought—and embarrassed myself in front of my crush. Pout," she said, and Jeanne obeyed. "But your first time will be much better. For two reasons: one, I made sure they won't be serving couscous until after you're done with your dance and two, you are a much better dancer than I was."

Jeanne could not imagine that to be the case. In her mind, Yasmina had never been a nervous beginner. She'd always been confident, self-assured, beautiful. Yasmina made it all look effortless, as though she'd emerged from the womb dancing. But all Jeanne managed to say was, "I really doubt that."

Yasmina shook Jeanne gently by the shoulders. "You need to give yourself some credit. You are smarter, prettier, and more talented than you think you are. Now go out there and make me proud. Remember, tonight you're not Jeanne. You're Zahira," Yasmina said, invoking Jeanne's stage name with a mischievous smile, "Middle Eastern dancer extraordinaire."

19

Chapter Two

Dum dum, tek-a-tek, dum, tek-a-tek. The familiar *beledi* rhythm sent tingles up Jeanne's spine. She pictured Sayed's calloused palm striking the *tabla* to create the deep, resonant *dum*, his bony fingertips strafing the surface to create the sharper, higher-pitched *tek*. Now she heard the wail of Marwan's *oud* and finally Yousef's sibilant *ney*. The beat was driving and urgent, the melody hypnotic. She remembered this magical moment from when she had been on the other side of the curtain—how the crowd had held its breath in anticipation, hanging on every note, waiting for the moment when Yasmina, laden in gems and sequins, emerged from a darkened doorway like a butterfly emerging from its chrysalis. With her exquisite sense of drama, Yasmina had made the most of the situation, whirling into the spotlight with her golden Isis wings.

Jeanne knew that this was her opportunity to create such a moment, and yet she just stood there, immobile. Her feet felt as though they were encased in lead. "*Yela, Zahira, yela!*" Yasmina hissed into her ear. "Go!"

Stepping into the spotlight, Jeanne was pleasantly surprised to find that she could not see the audience at all, which was strangely empowering. Just concentrate, she told herself. Pretend that you are rehearsing all alone. She could hear the crowd stir as her arms began undulating in thrall to the *oud*'s lament. Her bare feet brushed the floor each time Sayed's palm struck the *tabla*. Relaxing, she moved her hips in time to the *ney* and gently placed the sword on her head. The crowd murmured as the sword swung to and fro, but as precarious as it looked, she knew it would not fall. As Yousef's fingers fluttered over the notches, she swung her hips in an exaggerated figure-eight pattern, matching her speed to his rhythm. The energy spread to her shoulders, which shook as though possessed by some incredible demon, even as her hips continued to swing in their own intricate patterns. Her breasts vibrated gently with each shake of the shoulders, and she suddenly felt sexy, exotic, and even playful. While keeping her head perfectly still, she used her neck muscles to tilt it from side to side, and the crowd roared.

At last, the drumming began to crescendo. Faster and faster she turned, each beat jolting through her

21

shoulders, chest, arms, or hips. And then her great shimmy began, waves upon waves of energy like a slowly building earthquake. The audience whistled, clapped, and ululated in amazement. And still the *tabla* did not fall silent. Sayed was testing her, she knew, and she rose to the challenge. Each time he sped up, she did too.

Then, with a final *dum*, the shaking and the drumming were over.

Jeanne changed her clothes quickly, snuck back into the dining room through a side door, and slid onto the divan next to Vivienne. She hoisted Everett into her lap and pulled him close.

"You were magnificent," Vivienne whispered. "With talent like that, I don't know why you bothered with law school."

From across the table, Lily gave Jeanne a thumbs-up. "You're going to be number one on YouTube," she mouthed as she turned the video camera on Yasmina, who was now midway through her hair-raising wineglass routine.

Even though she had seen it a thousand times, Jeanne held her breath during Yasmina's dance. It was nerve-wracking to watch her teacher arrange three wine goblets on the floor, stem side up, and then step gingerly onto the shimmering surface. The crowd let out a collective gasp as Yasmina thrust her right foot to the side, tracing a long, graceful arc across the floor, with the wineglass gliding beneath her, and then did the same with the left foot. She caught the stem of a wineglass between her toes, raised it with her foot, and balanced it on her head. As she shook her head for dramatic effect, the glass wobbled, sending jitters through the audience. Unperturbed, Yasmina smiled, snatched the other two glasses with her feet, and nestled each one against her shoulder blades.

For her next dance, Yasmina brought out her veil. She began with the silk draped over her face, as though she were a demure virgin bride. As the music began to swell, she flung the veil over her shoulders and began to twirl. The veil concealed and then revealed her various undulating body parts, transforming the veil from an object of modesty and repression into one of seduction and power. She beckoned to a young man in the audience, and his friends coaxed him onto the dance floor, the crowd roaring its approval.

Although Yasmina danced with a number of customers, Jeanne noticed that she paid particular attention to one guest. He was a portly Middle Eastern man, around fifty, in a white button-down shirt and brown polyester pants. Dark, beady eyes darted lecherously beneath his bushy black brows, and his cheeks flushed crimson. He quivered with pleasure as Yasmina twirled her veil over and around him. When

Yasmina playfully dropped the veil on his head, the crowd chuckled.

Yasmina was midway through her sword dance when Lily poked Jeanne in the arm and nodded towards the back of the room. At first, Jeanne was perplexed; she noticed nothing out of the ordinary. But as her eyes drifted upwards, she glimpsed a haze hugging the low-slung ceiling.

The kitchen was to the left but, to Jeanne's surprise, the smoke was no thicker by the kitchen door than anywhere else. In fact, the smoke seemed to be coming from the basement stairwell, and it was growing thicker by the second.

"Fire! Fire!" Jeanne shouted just as the fire alarm sounded. Her lungs filled with acrid smoke as she thrust Everett into Vivienne's outstretched arms. It tasted as though she had swallowed an ashtray. "Go!"

Jeanne had a vague memory of the fireman in her third-grade fire safety class reminding them that smoke tended to rise. She was lowering herself to the carpet when she spotted Yasmina out of the corner of her eye. To her amazement, Yasmina was running in exactly the opposite direction of the rest of the crowd—towards the stairwell.

Towards the fire.

Jeanne leapt up, pushing and shoving her way through the crowd. A woman's bracelet scraped her elbow, and a heavy torso slammed into her hip. "Idiot," she heard a man's voice mumble, "you're going the wrong way."

"Yasmina! You've got to get out!"

Yasmina spun around to face Jeanne. She was coughing, waving her hands in front of her face in a futile attempt to push away the smoke. Her eyes were bloodshot, and her veil hung limply over her arm. "The costumes," she shouted, pointing towards the stairwell. "I can't let them burn! One of the skirts was worn by my grandmother when she used to perform in Amman."

Jeanne stared at her. Was she serious? No family heirloom was worth running into the inferno. "The costumes are replaceable," Jeanne pleaded with her. "You're not."

Their eyes met, and it seemed as though time stood still. Jeanne felt her pulse racing violently. Yasmina had to realize it was hopeless, right?

Yasmina took a step towards her, and Jeanne thought she was coming to her senses. But then she suddenly spun around and headed towards the back of the room.

Jeanne watched, dumbfounded, as her teacher disappeared into the smoke, her crimson skirt and bodice swallowed up by the haze. Her sequins glinted for a moment and then disappeared. Jeanne's mouth was dry. She wanted to run after her, to be like the heroine of her daydreams, strong and fearless, but the truth was that she was neither brave nor stupid enough to follow.

Jeanne got down on her knees and headed towards the exit, which was becoming more obscured every second. There were names being frantically called, obscenities being hurled, and prayers being recited loudly. At that moment, Algiers was easily the most religious and most profane place in town. A pair of thick, veiny ankles blocked her field of vision for a moment, followed by a pinstripe pants leg. "Move, you fat cow!" a deep voice bellowed, and suddenly she felt a deep, throbbing pain as a table came crashing down on her right leg, tiny shards of glass grazing her hands and ankles. Jeanne yelped in pain, her mouth filling with smoke, her eyes burning. She caught a glimpse of a few rivulets of blood streaking down her limbs, seeping into the carpet, and fought a wave of nausea. She had always hated the site of blood, especially her own. But she knew that she had to endure, to press on in spite of the pain, the smoke, and the chaos. The smoke was intensifying too fast; Algiers would be nothing but a hulking ruin by the time the firemen arrived.

If only she could rest a moment.

Lifting her head slightly, she reached up to massage her neck. Through the black haze, she caught a glimpse of the man that Yasmina had lavished attention on during her veil dance. He was slumped over in his chair, and his arm hung limply by his side. But no one seemed to notice or to care. They ran right past him, tripping over the chair legs. The survival instinct had taken over.

She crawled as fast as she could to him, put one hand on the arm rest, and, wincing, pulled herself up until she was staring at the top of his head. She lifted his chin for a better look.

His eyes were partially open, but they did not seem to see her at all. They were glassy, immobile. She shivered. Could he have succumbed to smoke inhalation already? She shook him gently at first, then more roughly. She slapped him across the face. Bristles of his mustache grazed her fingers.

There was still no response.

There was a glass of water on the table behind him, and she threw it on his face.

Still no reaction. The smoke was grower thicker; she was running out of time.

Slinging an arm underneath him, she began dragging him towards the exit. But he was too heavy and she sagged under his weight. Her mouth filled with smoke and she coughed as she tugged at the arm of a broad-shoulder young man rushing past. "You!" She motioned silently at the limp figure, and the man flung him over his shoulders.

A few moments later, they crossed the threshold to the welcome sound of sirens wailing in the distance. Jeanne could feel the intense heat at her back, the cold February air stinging her face. She took deep, greedy breaths, her pulse racing violently.

27

When they reached the safety of the chain link perimeter, she motioned towards an empty patch of sidewalk. "Here, put him down over here."

Resting her throbbing forehead against a lamp post, she thought that while her first solo performance had certainly been dramatic, it was not in a way she hoped ever to repeat.

"Jeanne!"

She looked up to see Vivienne and Lily running towards her, Everett bouncing up and down on his mother's hip. Never had she been so happy to hear her sister's voice.

"I was so worried about you," Vivienne babbled. "We couldn't see you. I didn't know where you went."

"I'm fine. I went back to help Yasmina, and then I saw this man and he was overcome by smoke and he—" Jeanne broke off mid-sentence as she noticed Lily's stricken expression. Lily's hand was over her mouth and she looked as though she were about to vomit. "Lily, I'm okay. Really, I—"

"I know, but I don't think he is." Lily turned away.

Jeanne and Vivienne realized what Lily meant at precisely the same moment. "Oh, my God," Vivienne gasped, clutching Everett closer.

Jeanne staggered, fell to the ground and stared in disbelief at the blood soaking the man's shirt. Numb, she reached into her pocket and pulled out her cell phone. A curt female voice answered. "Operator, 9-1-1."

Jeanne's voice came out in a hoarse whisper. "I'm outside Algiers in Northeast D.C."

"Yes, I heard about the fire, ma'am. The fire department should be there any second."

"We're going to need the police as well. I have a middle-aged male with a chest wound." She brushed her fingers against his neck. "And I don't feel a pulse."

Chapter Three

Detective Walker flashed her badge and dismissed the others to talk to Jeanne alone. Tall, with dark skin and intelligent, searching eyes, she jotted notes as Jeanne recounted the evening's events.

"So you're the one who found him." It came out more as a question than a statement.

"Well, I saw him in the haze," Jeanne said weakly, glancing at the roof. Flames shot out of it, sending golden embers sailing into the night like errant firecrackers. From where Jeanne stood, she could see the silhouette of a single fireman. He looked so precarious perched on the ladder, pointing his hose down into the inferno, but she supposed he was used to it. "I thought he was overcome by smoke and so I pulled him out of the club."

"What's his name?"

"I don't know. I don't know anything about him, really, except that he was in the audience and that I noticed him slumped over."

"When did he slump over?"

Jeanne shrugged. "About two minutes after the alarm went off, I saw him hunched over. But I have no idea how long he was like that."

"When did you notice that he had a chest wound?"

"On the sidewalk. When I saw the blood rushing out."

"You didn't notice this inside?"

"No." Jeanne sighed. "Like I said, it was very smoky in there."

The heat from the fire was so intense that Jeanne's face was warm to the touch. She saw a single bead of sweat form on Detective Walker's forehead, then begin to slide down her temple.

Detective Walker brushed it away. "Let's go over this again. Where was he sitting in relation to the dance floor?"

"At a table next to the dance floor."

"To the right of the floor, or to the left?"

"Right."

"And where were you when the fire started?" The detective raised her voice to be heard over the roar of the engines and the crackle of the radios. Wailing sirens filled Jeanne's ears; it seemed as though they had called in every fire truck in the city.

"At a table on the left side of the dance floor, more or less directly across from him."

"So why didn't you discover him until two minutes after the fire alarm went off? And more to the point, why had you only moved a few feet since the alarm went off?"

Jeanne clenched her fists and swallowed hard, trying to keep her voice as even as possible. "Like I keep telling you, I was very worried about my belly dance instructor, Yasmina, who was going in the direction of the fire. Please," Jeanne pleaded, "the firemen should be looking for her. She's missing, and may be trapped inside." The red flashing ambulance lights were off to the right, and she could make out the man's body on the stretcher, draped with a sheet. "And I'm guessing he's beyond hope."

"Ma'am, trust me, the firemen are doing everything they can to locate anyone trapped inside. I promise we'll get to your friend in a moment. Now," Detective Walker said, "did you see anyone carrying a firearm at any time this evening?"

"No."

"Did you see anyone with any unusually large purses, bags, or packages?"

"No."

"Did you see anyone wearing unusually bulky clothing that could have been used to conceal a weapon?"

"No, but it is kind of the middle of winter." As soon as she said it, Jeanne wished she could take it back. Her sarcasm would not be appreciated, and it wouldn't do anything to speed up their search for Yasmina. But she was just so frustrated. Why spend so much time on a dead man when there was a living woman inside?

Detective Walker looked up at her sharply. "Meaning?"

"Everybody had a heavy winter coat."

Detective Walker clenched her jaw, but said nothing. Out of the corner of her eye, Jeanne could see Lily shouting at a group of firemen. Hopefully they had already radioed in a description of Yasmina.

"Now, about your friend."

Jeanne breathed a sigh of relief. "Yes?"

"Can you provide a description?"

"Five-foot-seven, slim but curvy, maybe one hundred thirty-five pounds, wavy black hair, brown eyes. She was wearing a crimson belly dance costume."

"And where was she headed when you last saw her?"

"The stairs to the basement."

For a moment, Detective Walker's impassive mask slipped, and Jeanne glimpsed a fleeting look of concern. She knew what the detective was thinking: the fire started in the basement. Or at least that's where the smoke seemed to be coming from. Detective Walker relayed the description over her walkie-talkie and then took a few more notes.

After a few more questions about the fire, Detective Walker handed Jeanne her card. "In case you think of anything." Her official persona suddenly melted away, and she became almost maternal. "Now, child, I suggest you go home and get some rest."

Jeanne did not sleep at all that night. She did not even try.

Curled up on her futon, she thumbed through old photo albums of Yasmina and the rest of her dance troupe. In every picture, Yasmina's skin glistened. Her smile was luminous, her hair dark and lustrous. She looked so happy and carefree.

So alive.

Tears welled up in Jeanne's eyes and she felt a lump in her throat. She wanted to believe that Yasmina was alive, but with each passing hour, hope ebbed away. No one from their troupe had been able to reach her, and none of the local hospitals would admit to her being a patient.

She tried to brush away the awful thought that she had contributed to Yasmina's death, or at least failed to prevent it. It nagged at her conscience. Maybe there was something she could have said or done to make Yasmina turn back. She could have tried brute force and dragged

Yasmina with her. Or perhaps even guilt—what if she had refused to leave unless Yasmina went with her?

Scarlett dozed at her feet, her three legs tucked underneath her. Jeanne had rescued her from the pound, so she never knew what happened to the other leg, nor could anyone tell her why Scarlett had only one eye. But she could tell that Scarlett was one scrappy, savvy survivor, and that was good enough for Jeanne. Leaning forward, she ran her fingers through Scarlett's thick fur.

If only Yasmina turned out to be a scrappy, savvy survivor.

She had told Detective Walker that Yasmina was her teacher and her friend, but in truth, Yasmina was not so much her friend as her idol. She admired her grace and fluidity on the dance floor, and her dedication to her craft, of course, but her loyalty and gratitude went much, much deeper.

Yasmina had liberated her from being Jeanne, just Jeanne, and given her a new identity, a new name, and an inner voice, an inner hope, that could not be extinguished no matter how many crushing setbacks she suffered. She had always had a wildly interesting and eccentric internal life, which she chronicled in musty notebooks that no one had ever seen, tucked away in an old Barbie's playhouse box at the bottom of her linen closet. Fantastic, extravagant, and utterly pointless adventures unfurled across these pages, all documented in her slanted left-handed script, which always seemed to creep upward, ever upward, as if threatening to fly off the page. She always wrote in green ink. In these stories, she trekked across Africa, smoked hookahs with Iranian revolutionaries, and served as the Dalai Lama's tai chi instructor. The characters in her notebook did not do anything useful; they did not plod along on a continuous set of stepping stones to self-improvement. They did not study hard in high school in order to go to a top college in order to go to a top law school. They just were, and they just did. They did things because they wanted to, not because they needed to. And never because they should.

By day, she was—and had almost always been—Jeanne the good, Jeanne the wise, Jeanne the prudent. But under Yasmina's tutelage, she had developed a whole new identity as Zahira. She was now Jeanne, the boring, mousy legal temp by day, and Zahira, the exotic, fearless performer by night.

To Jeanne, Yasmina represented power and beauty, hope and light, passion and confidence. She did not think of Yasmina as a mere mortal, really. In the two months they had lived together, Yasmina had never gotten cross with her for drinking the last of the milk, or having her alarm go off for fifteen minutes at a stretch. She had never nagged Jeanne about her housing search, or suggested that Jeanne move into Lily's loud, rat-infested communal living experiment. Yasmina never got a pimple, her hair was never greasy, and she never seemed to gain a pound despite joining Jeanne in her nightly ice cream binges. Jeanne was in awe.

As the first rays of sunlight peeked over the horizon, Jeanne opened the freezer and grabbed a pint of Ben and Jerry's New York Super Fudge Chunk. Ben and Jerry were the two most important men in her life—besides, perhaps, her nephew Everett—and she considered their ice cream medicinal. Particularly New York Super Fudge Chunk. Her favorite flavor contained calcium, antioxidants (the chocolate), and protein (the nuts), and it normally did wonders for her mood. Every time she discovered a hidden dark chocolate chunk, she felt a jolt of satisfaction.

She shuffled back to Flaca, her avocado and tangerine paisley loveseat, circa 1972, which she had acquired from a Bolivian woman with a mutt named Flaca. While she gorged on ice cream, Jeanne channel-surfed, searching for any news at all about the fire. The morning news shows were obnoxious. The news anchors marveled at a cat that survived ten days trapped in drywall. "We're glad our fine feline friend has eight more lives ahead of her," the blonde cracked. Then they cut to a series of ads for erectile dysfunction and arthritis medications.

"And we're back," the blonde's darkly handsome co-anchor said. "We're now going live to Northeast, where our own Scott Daniels is at the scene of a horrific crime that occurred last night. Scott?"

"Sam, I've been talking to folks all night and no one can recall a more bizarre or tragic end to a wonderful evening of Middle Eastern food and entertainment. It all began inside Algiers, a Northeast D.C. institution." He gestured behind him. "At approximately eight-fifteen yesterday evening, Yasmina Hariri, a well-known fixture in the local belly dancing scene, was in the middle of her routine when the fire alarm went off. The restaurant soon filled with smoke. When the smoke had cleared, Ibrahim Abu Ali, a non-managing partner of Algiers, was dead of a gunshot wound."

So that's why she paid special attention to him, Jeanne thought. He was an owner.

An old photo of Yasmina flashed on the screen. "Ms. Hariri is missing and may have been injured or killed in the fire."

"Scott, is there any word on a motive?"

"Well, Sam, I'm not allowed to reveal my sources, but I can tell you that evidence left at the scene has led police to investigate this as a hate crime."

The remote control slid out of Jeanne's hand and skittered across the parquet floor.

*   *   *   *

"Jeanne Pelletier?"

She looked up from the mound of files in her cubicle to see Detective Walker flashing her badge. "Coffee break time. Investigator Balistreri"—she jerked her thumb towards a pot-belled man in his forties—"and I need to ask you a few more questions."

Jeanne grabbed her coat and purse, and they headed across the street to Starbucks. Seated at a small table in the back, she eyed them warily over her double skim peppermint latte. She noticed that Investigator Balistreri and Detective Walker drank their coffee black.

The investigator opened his notebook and regarded her intently. "Ms. Pelletier, I'm a fire scene investigator. It's my job to determine the cause and origin of the fire. If I determine that this was an arson attack, this information will help Detective Walker and her team determine who the perpetrator might be. I know that Detective Walker already took your statement, but I have some additional questions for you about the fire."

He seemed to expect a response, so she nodded.

"Now," he continued, "I understand that you were in the dressing room before the show."

"That's correct. I was opening for Yasmina."

"How did you enter the building?"

"Through the front entrance."

"And you never went in or out the rear entrance?"

"Just for a moment. Yasmina was on the phone, and it seemed to be a private conversation, so I slipped out the back for a few moments."

"This is the back entrance by the dumpsters, correct?"

"Correct."

He jotted a few notes. "Did you notice any graffiti on that rear exterior wall by the dumpsters?"

Jeanne frowned. Given that the media was reporting it as a possible hate crime, she could only imagine what sort of graffiti had been found. Try as she might, however, Jeanne could not recall anything. But it was not exactly as through she had been looking for anything, either.

"No," she said slowly. "But of course it was dark. And I was more than a little preoccupied."

He looked up at her sharply. "Preoccupied?"

"Just stage fright. It was my first solo."

He nodded sympathetically and then asked, "Did you see any accelerant, either in the dressing room or immediately outside? Containers of gasoline, kerosene, paint thinner, turpentine, that sort of thing?"

Jeanne sighed. "Everything was stored in the basement. I suppose they could have had paint, turpentine, all kinds of cleaning supplies. And anything could have been hidden in the dumpsters."

"Did you notice anything out of the ordinary?"

"No." She decided to put their poker faces to the test. "Has Yasmina been found?"

"We can't release this type of information, ma'am, until the next of kin is notified. So I can neither confirm nor deny that your friend has been found dead, or found alive, or that she's still missing." He was giving her the standard response, but she thought his eyes looked sad. Her heart sank. Somehow it did not seem as though Yasmina's family would be receiving good news.

Feeling as though all of the oxygen had been sucked out of the room, Jeanne dug her fingernails into the table and breathed as deeply as she could.

To Jeanne's surprise, Detective Walker placed her hand on Jeanne's arm. "You were close, huh?"

"Last year, I spent two months living with her when I got kicked out of my old apartment. They decided to turn the building into high-end condos."

Detective Walker nodded sympathetically.

"She was like an older sister to me."

"You an only child?"

Jeanne shook her head, but no words came out.

"That's all right, honey. I know what you mean. Sometimes the family we create is better than the family God gives us." Detective Walker took a swig of coffee. "Now, do you know why anyone might hold a grudge against the club or one of its owners?"

"No."

"Maybe an employee who thought they'd been treated unfairly? Unpaid wages, discrimination claims, sexual harassment, that kind of thing?"

"No," Jeanne said. "But honestly, I've only performed there once, and I've probably been in the audience a dozen times. I don't really know much about the inner workings of the business."

Detective Walker made a few notes of her own. "Okay," she said. "Now there are some questions that I need to ask you. Please don't be alarmed, but given that you were in the area where the fire started, and that you reported the murder, we have to ask you the standard questions."

Jeanne swirled her latte and stared at the table. "Okay."

"Do you own, or have access to, any accelerant?"

"No."

"What about candles?"

"Of course." Jeanne was confused. What did candles have to do with anything? "Everyone has candles. During the last storm, my building lost power for two days."

Detective Walker laughed. "Aren't you lucky? My neighborhood was out for five. Okay, next question: do you own, or have access to, any type of firearm?"

She put her hands under the table so they couldn't see them shaking. "Yes." Her voice came out squeaky.

Jeanne detected a flicker of surprise in Detective Walker's face. "What kind?"

"I have a hunting rifle registered to my name in Maine."

Jeanne swallowed hard as Detective Walker wrote that down. She sensed that a rifle was not the murder weapon, because the detective did not seem particularly interested in this admission.

Which was a very good thing, since Jeanne would have to lie about where it was now. It would be unwise to volunteer that it was at the bottom of an old well by a rotting barn on old Paul Thibault's property.

Or that she had considered using it to kill a human.

Chapter Four

The interview concluded, Jeanne raced back across the street, flashed her badge at security, and sprinted into the first open elevator. Jeanne jabbed the ninth floor button eight times. She could not get there fast enough.

The doors opened, and Jeanne ran down the corridor to the accounting office. Whenever she saw a partner approaching, she shouted, "Sorry. I'm on a deadline." She figured that they could appreciate that. Maybe she'd even get brownie points. That Jeanne Pelletier, they would think. She isn't idle for even a second.

She arrived at Lily's desk quite out of breath.

"What's wrong?" Lily said.

"What's wrong? The guy that I rescued has died of a gunshot wound—Nine News Now confirmed that in their report this morning—the police are investigating the incident as a hate crime, and based on my conversation with Detective Walker and Investigator Balistreri this morning, I get the sinking feeling that Yasmina is dead."

Lily's eyes filled with tears. "Oh, my God."

"Can we go somewhere private to talk?"

Lily motioned for Jeanne to follow, and they made their way to the women's restroom. Finding it empty, they slipped inside the handicapped stall.

After a few minutes of stunned silence, Jeanne finally spoke. "What do you make of the news claiming it might be a hate crime?"

"It's probably nothing," Lily said. "You know how those reporters are. They want to make you think they have some big scoop, but really they just want off the kitty rescue beat." She lowered her voice. "I searched the District property records this morning. Algiers owes two years of back taxes and the building has been put up for sale twice in the past two years."

"Were there any takers?"

"Nope."

"So someone's got serious financial problems."

"My thoughts exactly. And who benefits from a massive fire? Yousef."

Jeanne thought back to her estate planning class. At the time, she had found it so boring, so useless. But now it might actually come in handy. "If the police and fire department are investigating it as arson—and based on my conversation with them this morning, they most definitely are—the insurance company won't pay out until the beneficiaries have been ruled out as suspects."

"Apparently Yousef thought he could cover his tracks."

"But why kill Ibrahim?"

"So he could keep all the money himself. Why split it when you can have it all?"

Jeanne shook her head. "He won't keep it all. The insurance payment will go to the business, which is— was—jointly owned by Yousef and Ibrahim."

"Yeah, but Ibrahim's dead."

"Which means his share of the business will go to his heirs," Jeanne said. "Unless Ibrahim's will says that his interest in the business passes to Yousef upon his death, Yousef will be splitting it with someone."

The door swung open, and Lily hopped up on the toilet seat, one leopard print spike heel teetering on the edge. Jeanne pointed frantically at Lily's head, and Lily crouched just in time. Another second and the woman would have come face to face with the world's tallest Asian woman.

When the woman finally left, Lily whispered, "What if Yousef doesn't realize that's how it works? What if that is what Ibrahim's will says or that's what Yousef thinks his will says?"

"Then he's got a very strong motive," Jeanne agreed.

"We're going to need to size up Yousef."

"And how do you propose to do that?"

"Simple," Lily said. "You and I are going to attend our first Islamic funeral this afternoon."

"You know I can't take off."

"You have the flu, Jeanne," Lily said. "And so do I. In fact, your sister Vivienne has been sick with the flu for three weeks."

"What? You think the partners of Higgins, Higgins, and Applebaum have suddenly become great humanitarians who care about their contractors?"

"Of course not. They wouldn't care if you died. But they do not, under any circumstances, want everyone to get the flu. That would bring productivity to a halt."

"I think I feel a chill coming on."

"And a cough."

"Oh, yes," Jeanne said. "A horrible, horrible cough."

"*Allahu akbar. Allaahumma salli alaa muhammadin wa alaa muhammadin kama sallayta alaa ibraaheema wa alaa aali ibraaheema innaka hameedun majeed...*"

The imam's deep, resonant voice crackled with emotion. Jeanne found it both thrilling and somber. The rich, melodious tones echoing through the vast carpeted hall, ricocheting off exquisitely patterned tiles and swirling calligraphy, seemed infinitely more appropriate for such an occasion than the tired platitudes, delivered in a flat, world-weary American accent, that Jeanne had heard at many a funeral. The voice was commanding, yet pleading, calling out to Allah in a strong, confident voice that crescendoed towards the middle of each phrase and then tapered off into a respectful yet anguished whisper.

Her toes sank deeper into the plush Persian carpets, and she tugged her headscarf—an old purple Pashmina she had dug out of her closet—tighter. "*Allahumma baarik alaa muhammadin wa alaa aali muhammadin kamaa baarakta...*"

Jeanne and Lily stood in the first row of women, behind four rows of men. Jeanne kept one eye on Yousef. His shoulders were hunched forward, and she noticed that he was always a half second behind when the mourners switched from standing to kneeling. She wondered how observant a Muslim he really was.

She kept the other on Aisha, his wife. Aisha stood perhaps fifty feet to her left, her corpulent form enveloped in a black hijab so very unlike the flowing, embroidered dresses she normally wore. Her lips moved ever so slightly, and Jeanne noticed that she glanced every now and then at her husband.

"*Allaahumma ighfir lihayyinaa, wa mayyitinaa, wa shaahidinaa, wa ghaa-ibinaa, wa sagheerinaa, wa kabeerinaa, wa dhakarinaa wa unthaanaa...*"

From time to time, Jeanne twisted around to scan the women's section for other dry eyes, and she noticed that Lily was doing the same. There were only a handful:

two wizened old women, hunched over and clad in
black, who watched the proceedings with dark, piercing
eyes; a broad-faced, green-eyed woman in a dark blue
skirt who smiled serenely throughout the proceedings
(whether from bliss that Ibrahim was dead or simply a
good-natured belief that he was in paradise, Jeanne could
not tell); and a stunning young woman who stared stone-
faced ahead. Jeanne kept the latter's elegant profile—
sweeping eyelashes, a long, aquiline nose, and full, pouty
lips—in her sights. Not once did the woman move. Her
lips never parted to recite the prayers, and she never
reached up to readjust her sky blue headscarf, which
slipped slowly backwards to reveal glossy, dark chestnut
brown locks. Jeanne could not tell if she was numb with
grief, in shock, or simply refusing to take part in the
proceedings.

"*Allahu akbar!*" the imam shouted. "*Assalumu
alaikum wa rahmatullah,*" he continued, turning his head
to the right and then the left.

Repeating after him, the crowd turned their heads to
the right and then to the left. The men in the front row
picked up the funeral bier and the mourners began to
process out of the mosque. Jeanne and Lily followed
them, out of the sanctum, out into the blinding
sunshine and the rumbling traffic along Massachusetts
Avenue.

The beautiful young woman fell in with a clutch of
middle-aged and older women, their faces stained red

with tears, and disappeared into a phalanx of hijabs and headscarves that surged onto a residential side street and squeezed into old Buicks and off-duty cabs headed to the burial.

"Zahira." An unfamiliar voice with a thick Middle Eastern accent hissed into her ear, and Jeanne looked down, startled. There, at her elbow, was Aisha, grasping at her arm with arthritic, calloused fingers that felt like sandpaper. "Keep walking and don't give away that I'm talking to you," Aisha whispered. "It's rude to talk during Islamic funerals. But I couldn't miss this opportunity to thank you for trying to save Ibrahim. He was a friend, not just a business partner."

"I'm sorry I couldn't do more," Jeanne murmured in a low voice.

But Aisha wasn't in the mood for condolences. "I came to this country to escape prejudice, discrimination, and hatred," she said. "But it has followed me. How could this happen? Arson, murder, the total destruction of a club my husband and I spent twenty-five years building—this is the worst kind of hate crime. All because we are Arabs." She pressed her cell phone into the palm of Jeanne's hand. "See for yourself."

Jeanne struggled to make sense of the image: jumbled objects devoid of context, dark shapes. But slowly her eyes began to focus on familiar, if oddly distorted, objects. She saw twisted metal rods, a few lonely metal springs, and puddles of water, a sheen of ash floating on top. On the right hand side of the photo, she saw a gaping hole where the stairs had been. She remembered how they had creaked beneath her feet, how she had clutched the bannister in terror upon hearing the first strains of the oud.

Aisha reached over and flipped to the next photo. "And look what they left behind." She spit on the ground. "Pigs."

It was the exterior brick wall of Algiers, the one Inspector Balistreri had questioned her about. Jeanne recognized the sturdy metal doors and the large green dumpster. With mounting dread, she enlarged the image. Her lips trembled as she read the words, scrawled in angry red letters: "Hagar...was a whore."

She felt Aisha's nails digging into her arm and she looked down to see the older woman's eyes covered in a thin film of tears. "Yasmina was like a daughter to me," Aisha whispered.

Jeanne feared she knew the answer, but she had to ask anyway. "Has she been found?"

Aisha nodded, and then she began to weep.

Chapter Five

Jeanne yearned to weep, to shout, to curse, to bear some sort of witness to her friend's passing. But tears were elusive, and her lips remained set in their firm, determined line. She had long suspected that her reservoir of tears had run dry eleven years ago, and now she had proof.

She bid a hasty good-bye to Aisha and Lily and headed off through the dark, silent woods of Rock Creek Park. Twenty minutes later, she emerged by the tennis courts in Montrose Park, turned onto R Street, and beat a path to the Georgetown Public Library, where she ensconced herself in a corner as dark as her mood and thumbed through a dog-eared copy of *Hate Groups of America*. A shiver ran down her spine as she realized just how many hands had turned its pages. She hoped it had been consulted purely for research purposes, and not in the way that one might peruse *Fiske Guide to Colleges*.

The sheer variety of hate groups was bewildering to Jeanne. There were anti-Semites, white supremacists, black separatists, border vigilantes, homophobes, neo-Nazis, eco-warriors, vegan terrorists, skinheads, neo-Confederates, and even reactionary ultraconservative Catholics and communists. There were anti-Muslim groups and radical Islamic groups. And then there were groups that defied all attempts at categorization and were labeled by the author as "general hate groups." It was hard to tell whom they didn't hate.

As she perused the chapters on anti-Muslim groups and radical Islamists, there were three local groups that caught her eye. The first, Islam Al-Ulaama, was led by Sheikh Al-Ulaama, a one-armed imam who was fond of issuing fatwas. He called for the restoration of the worldwide caliphate, the forced conversion of all Jews and Christians to Islam, and the removal of the "infidels" from the Holy Land. Irate over the participation of Miss Turkey and Miss Malaysia in a recent international beauty pageant, he had accused the pageant organizers of putting "Islamic harlots on display." Jeanne surmised that belly dancers might fall under his definition of "Islamic harlots" too.

Crusaders Against Sharia were busy exhorting their followers to boycott Kentucky Fried Chicken, which they believed was foisting halal chicken on unsuspecting customers as a way of introducing sharia into American law. They pointed to Colonel Sanders' long beard as

53

evidence of a pro-Islamic management attempting to brainwash America's youth with subliminal messages. A few of their members had been implicated in a recent spate of attacks on women with headscarves, although charges had not yet been filed.

And finally there was the Virginia Defense League, which was urging their members to stockpile firearms to thwart the coming "Islamic invasion of America." They had proudly adopted fellow Virginian Patrick Henry's famous line "Give me liberty or give me death," and they were collecting information on the identity, assets, and habits of the "Islamic infiltrators who live amongst us." They published a list of Muslim-owned businesses, and warned their members not to shop there. But their intelligence was rather subpar—last year one of their members had received a ten-year sentence for attempting to set fire to a 7-Eleven owned by a couple of bewildered Sikhs.

As she looked at her watch and realized she was late for dinner at Vivienne's, Jeanne was struck by the absurdity of the situation. The culprits could either be in favor of radical Islam or against it. Algiers was apparently either too Islamic or not Islamic enough.

*   *   *   *

Fifteen minutes later, she was at her sister's enormous townhouse in Georgetown, suffering through Mitch's commentary on the news.

"Scott," the anchor boomed, "I understand there are new details emerging about the mysterious fire at Algiers on Saturday."

Mitch groaned. "Not this fag again. I'm surprised he doesn't wear a rainbow tie for all of his stories."

"Shhh!" Jeanne glared at him. Just one of Mitch's many flaws was his hyperactive homophobia. "I want to hear this."

"Although the fire department initially believed the fire may have been caused by an electrical short circuit, the confirmed cause is now arson. Copious quantities of accelerant were apparently used. The fire department has also confirmed that a body was found inside, and dental records indicate that it is the body of Yasmina Hariri, who has been listed as missing since Thursday. The body was apparently charred beyond recognition." Scott tried to appear somber for a moment, but he did a poor job disguising his glee at getting such a scoop. His hair was gelled into a stiff little peak, and he looked tanned and relaxed in his pink polo shirt and unbuttoned navy overcoat.

"You see, Jeanne," Mitch grumbled as he rifled through the sports section of *The Washington Post*, "he's not telling you anything you don't already know. Charred beyond recognition."

Vivienne patted him on the arm. "Please, dear. Try and be a little more sensitive. And stop using words like charred."

"I'm just being factual, dear."

"Yes, pumpkin. But factual and sensitive are not always the same thing." Vivienne clicked the remote control off. "Time for dinner!" she said brightly.

Jeanne felt a sense of relief as they trudged into the kitchen. Perhaps Mitch would focus on his food now rather than making snide comments.

The kitchen was an enormous and completely impractical space—an absolute nightmare for anyone who could ever, under any circumstances, be the slightest bit messy. Everything was always on display which, in Jeanne's estimation, showed a complete lack of understanding of the whole purpose of drawers and cabinets. The cabinets were glass-paneled, floor to ceiling, and filled with beautiful vases and china, expertly lit as though part of an exhibition at the Freer. The countertops were gleaming white marble, as if daring someone to actually use them and risk leaving a splotch, and there were cast iron pots and pans hanging from the ceiling as if a great Provençal chef were about to waltz in and whip up bouillabaisse. Jeanne doubted that Vivienne ever used these, since everything she served seemed to come in little containers from the ridiculously expensive Dean and DeLuca on M Street.

Sure enough, there were lots of little containers from Dean and DeLuca lined up on the kitchen island, which was as big as Jeanne's entire kitchen. Each one was labeled with its contents: chicken salad with pomegranate seeds, arugula, Camembert, and slivered almonds; ciabatta rolls; rum-cinnamon butternut squash. There was a large chocolate torte at the end of the buffet, its icing gleaming beneath the soft track lighting.

Jeanne licked her lips. Things were definitely looking up. She helped herself to a three-inch wedge, which landed on her plate with a satisfying thud, and followed Vivienne and Mitch into the dining room.

Unfortunately, dinner offered no respite from Mitch's diatribe.

"What I don't understand," he roared as he slurped his third martini, "is why she would wander into a burning room like that?"

"I told you. To save the costumes, including some that have been in her family for generations."

"Well she must be a real idiot."

"Yasmina was not an idiot." Jeanne could feel the color rising in her cheeks. "Perhaps overzealous."

"She would have to be an idiot, I tell you. My bread and butter may be drug possession charges, but a few of my clients' kids have been picked up for arson." He snorted. "Little pyros. One thing I know is that, if the fire started in the basement, and the smoke was as thick as you say, the flames would have been intense down there. I bet that even to get to the costumes, she would have had to leap through flames. Would she really have done that?"

"Maybe."

"I doubt it. I think she would have needed more of a motivation than that."

For once, Jeanne did not have a retort. Uncharacteristically, her brother-in-law actually had a good point. "Or," she said slowly, "maybe someone killed her."

Mitch shrugged. "Sounds plausible to me. She runs downstairs to get the costumes and then realizes there is no way this is going to work. The arsonist spots her, is afraid she'll get away and blow his cover, and so strangles her with a veil. Then he chucks her body into the fire."

Jeanne shivered. When he said it that way, it did sound plausible. "Wouldn't an autopsy reveal if she had been strangled?"

"Maybe, maybe not. How long did it take the firemen to put out the fire?"

"Three hours."

"In that case, probably not." He took a big gulp and his martini sloshed in his glass. "I had an arson case once that involved a corpse. My client got off because the coroner couldn't state the cause of death with absolute certainty. If exposed to heat of 5,000 degrees or so for over an hour, so much of the body is gone that you can't tell much of anything."

"Well it really doesn't matter now, does it?" Vivienne said. "The police will sort this out."

Jeanne nodded unconvincingly and pushed the pomegranate seeds around on her plate, lacking Vivienne's optimism. Based on her interview with Detective Walker, the police were focused solely on Ibrahim.

As far as Jeanne could tell, they didn't care about Yasmina.

Chapter Six

Jeanne always self-medicated after an evening with
Mitch; she took two aspirin, gobbled half a bag of Dove
dark chocolates, and then engaged in what she liked to
call "music therapy." The latter involved singing "You're
So Vain" at the top of her lungs, followed by a spirited
rendition of "That Don't Impress Me Much."

Usually, that was enough to lift her spirits and cure
her headache. Then she could fall peacefully asleep and
awake convinced it had all been a bad dream.

But today was different. She awoke feeling out of
sorts, her sugar high replaced by a nagging suspicion that
Mitch actually might have some idea what he was talking
about. Surely, Yasmina would have come to her senses
before the smoke overpowered her.

Unless something—or someone—prevented her
escape.

The thought nagged at her conscience all morning. It preoccupied her during her commute on the #32 bus, during the morning meeting with the paralegals, even during her quick trip to Starbucks. When her annoying office mate Kara slunk away to flirt with a junior partner in the break room, Jeanne took the opportunity to call Detective Walker.

To her surprise, Detective Walker did not embrace her theory. "Let me get this straight," the detective said. "You think your friend who—by your own admission— ran right into a blazing inferno, could not possibly have died of smoke inhalation. You think that, instead of melting into the anonymity of the fleeing crowd, the man who shot Ibrahim Abu Ali instead ran into the inferno, laid in wait for Yasmina, strangled her, and then escaped out the back door."

"Something like that," Jeanne said weakly. When it was repeated back to her like that, it did seem preposterous. But something told her that it wasn't.

"Look," Detective Walker said. "I know you cared about your friend, and I know you want justice done. Please trust that we are looking into every lead. But there is no evidence to indicate your friend was specifically targeted. Ibrahim Abu Ali, however, clearly was. And that's the focus of our investigation."

When she hung up, Jeanne felt even worse than before. She dug into her emergency chocolate supply, which was hidden underneath an old *New York Times* in her bottom drawer, interrupting her chocolate binge only for a brief phone chat with Sayed, Algiers's *tabla* player. But even with all of the chocolate coursing through her veins, she was in such a funk that by eleven o'clock she found herself doing the unthinkable. She called Mitch.

"Ah, Jeanne." His voice positively dripped with sarcasm. She could picture him in his huge corner office overlooking K Street, his Italian leather shoes propped up on his mahogany desk. "To what do I owe the pleasure of your call?"

"I was hoping you'd take a little field trip with me."

"Oh?"

"I've been thinking about what you said last night about Yasmina. How maybe she was strangled."

"And?"

"And I was hoping you would accompany me to Algiers. Well, what's left of Algiers. I talked to Sayed today, and apparently they've released the crime scene. I'd like to get your impression of it. Where the fire started, when—that sort of thing."

He snorted. "What's in it for me?"

It was a typical Mitch response, but one she had prepared for. She would start by low-balling him, then finally upping the ante. She would out-Mitch Mitch. "Free babysitting," she said innocently, "while you and Vivienne go to your conference in San Diego."

62

"Nice try, Jeanne. Viv already told me you were going to babysit."

"Think of it as an introduction to a potential client, then. After all, the staff members are prime suspects. They may be in need of a good defense attorney."

There was a moment of silence, and she could tell he was mulling it over. "It's going to be a very high profile case," she added. "Lots of great publicity."

He grunted. "What time do I need to be there?"

"This evening, nine o'clock," she said and hung up before he could change his mind.

Sayed met them in the parking lot. But it wasn't the Sayed that Jeanne knew, the Sayed whose huge meaty hands and fingers the size of breadsticks fluttered across the *tabla* with childlike excitement. That Sayed was playful, exuberant. This Sayed looked as though he were only capable of tapping out the slow, solemn rhythm of a funeral dirge. The harsh lighting cast long shadows across his sallow, sunken face and bloodshot eyes. Dressed in a long white *salwar cameez*, he shuffled about in a pair of old tennis shoes.

When he smiled at her, it looked as though it hurt. "Zahira," he whispered.

She kissed him on both cheeks. "It's good to see you, Sayed." She nodded in Mitch's direction. "This is my brother-in-law."

Mitch handed Sayed a card and launched into his standard sales pitch, which made it sound as though he could have gotten Himmler off the hook if only he'd been at Nuremberg. Nodding vacantly, Sayed held the card limply in his right hand. Jeanne doubted he heard a word.

"I hope this brings you some closure, Zahira." Sayed regarded her with sad brown eyes. "It was bad enough to lose Ibrahim. But Yasmina...." As his voice trailed off, he motioned for them to follow him around to the back of the building.

Jeanne caught her breath as she spied the faint outline of those angry red words. *Hagar was a whore.*

Sayed followed her gaze. "Yousef had it pressure-washed this morning."

With a final jangling of keys, the metal doors swung open and Sayed handed her his flashlight. As the beam swept across the room, she gasped. Like an illustration from *Dante's Inferno*, everything—walls, ceiling, floor—was an impenetrable shade of black. Twisted metal hung from the ceiling like distended limbs, pointing ominously to the soggy black heaps that spread over the floor like a slurry of coal dust. Jeanne felt slightly sick to her stomach. The furniture had crumbled to dust too, leaving only a few pieces of rusting metal. About the only things left standing were the wooden posts, now pockmarked with black charcoal blisters like an alligator skin dipped in India ink. When the beam swung to the left, she saw a pile of glass shards. The remains of the mirror. For a moment, she saw Yasmina's reflection, smiling as she pressed Jeanne's false eyelashes in place. Preparing for what turned out to be her last performance.

And finally the beam flitted over a small red flag placed on the floor.

"That's where,"—Sayed's voice broke and tears welled up in his eyes—"our Yasmina was found. Apparently they don't use chalk outlines anymore. Just something small, like that."

The body. Of course there had been a body. On an intellectual level, Jeanne knew this. Aisha had told her; tanned, gleeful Scott Daniels had announced it to the whole world. But she had not expected to be able to see, to touch, the exact place Yasmina had succumbed to the smoke. She did not want to. She wanted to think of her friend as missing, gone to a more peaceful place. This was a stark reminder that her last moments had been anything but peaceful. Jeanne's throat tensed as she pictured Yasmina gasping for breath, crawling along the floor, searching for the light and the fresh air. Jeanne could almost taste the smoke now. At what moment had Yasmina had the final horrible realization that there was no way out, that this was the very end?

"Please feel free to take a look around," Sayed murmured, averting his gaze. "I'll wait for you in the parking lot."

Jeanne handed Mitch the flashlight and followed wordlessly behind as he wandered through the basement. For once, she was glad to have him take charge.

He beckoned her into the next room, which had been used as a utility room, filled with rumbling dryers, a roaring furnace, and a cheerful mess of odd cleaning supplies. Now it was eerily silent. She remembered what Inspector Balistreri had said about accelerant, sending a shiver down her spine. It would have been so easy to hide accelerant here. Or just to use the ample supply that was already there.

"Check out this char pattern." Mitch swung the beam of light over a blackened wooden surface behind the furnace. "See how it forms a 'V' shape? The point of the 'V' is the origin of fire."

He followed the "V" to its base. There, along the baseboard, was a white, waxy substance, surrounded by a moat of ash.

The moat reminded Jeanne of the glorious day that she had spent at the beach with her sister's family. Mitch had downed a six-pack of Corona and then pretended to sleep beneath his big black shades while secretly ogling a pair of blonde teenaged twins. Leaving Vivienne alone to read, Jeanne had helped Everett build a sand castle with a turret and a moat.

Only Everett's chubby little fingers hadn't built this moat. It had been built by strong, practiced police hands. And the police weren't building moats as a setting for their fairy tales. They were collecting evidence.

Evidence that they had questioned her about.

"What is that?" Mitch asked.

"Candle wax," Jeanne whispered, her heart hammering loudly in her chest.

He bent down and rubbed his hand over it. "Damn straight." He turned to face her, his profile silhouetted against the light. "This wasn't an amateur," he said. "Whoever set this covered their tracks very, very well. A cheap drug store candle like this burns an inch every forty-five minutes or so. So the perp can light a candle, put a whole bunch of trash or other fuel at its base, and know that the fire will ignite when the wick reaches the fuel, which could be hours after he makes his escape."

He traced a path with the flashlight, across the utility room, back into the dressing room, and up the gaping chasm where the stairway had been. "It looks like this was the path of the fire," he said. "It started here and spread quickly."

Jeanne shuddered as she remembered how the stairs had creaked faintly beneath her. They had seemed so old, so solid. And now they were completely gone.

This wasn't an amateur. The perpetrator was smart, calculating. "So in other words," Jeanne said slowly, "it's very hard to tell when the arsonist set the fire."

"Right."

"Which makes anyone," she said softly, more to herself than to Mitch, "who had access to the area a suspect."

Chapter Seven

The next day, the women's restroom on the ninth floor at Higgins, Higgins, and Applebaum became ground zero for the investigation. Each hour, at seventeen minutes past, Jeanne met Lily in the handicapped stall to trade information and plot their next steps. The restroom was the perfect meeting place on a floor that was nearly all male; it was the one place they could be sure their bosses wouldn't disturb them.

"Women's troubles," Jeanne mumbled when her boss commented on her frequent bathroom visits. Like all red-blooded males, he trembled before the mysteries of womanhood and asked no further questions. Lily took a different tack. "You've been going quite a bit too," she remarked pointedly. "Has your prostate been swelling again? You should get that checked."

Jeanne felt a bit guilty about the time she spent researching Yasmina's past on company time. She rationed her searches to five minutes an hour, plus the three minutes each hour she spent huddling with Lily in the ladies' room. She even prayed about it, concluding that Jesus would be more likely to spend his time tracking down a menace to society than defending a multibillion dollar pharmaceutical company. She also rationalized that the eight minutes per hour she spent sleuthing was significantly less than the approximately fifteen minutes per hour that her office mate Kara spent ordering shoes online, or the approximately forty-five minutes per hour that Zach, her team lead, spent cooing sweet nothings into the phone, presumably to his girlfriend (or perhaps to his cat?).

Lily, of course, had no such compunctions. She spent all day researching Yousef and, by that afternoon, was convinced that he was behind the fire and Ibrahim's murder. "Don't you see?" she whispered, crouched on the toilet seat in her metallic blue combat boots. After their earlier near-miss, Lily always squatted on the seat as a precaution, so that no one would wonder why there were two pairs of feet in the stall. "There's an IRS lien on the property. So it's in his best interest to collect the fire insurance—I'm assuming they had some—and just walk away. He probably staged it as a hate crime to deflect suspicion."

Jeanne sighed. "But Yousef wouldn't collect all of the insurance, and he couldn't unilaterally decide to dispose of the business. What if one of Ibrahim's relatives inherits his half of the business?"

"I don't think he had much family, or at least not family he was close to." Lily reached into her dress and pulled a wad of newsprint out of her leopard print bra. "You want to know how I know? My horoscope," she announced, carefully unfolding it while Jeanne rolled her eyes. "It says, 'Keep your eyes open. All is not as it seems. Friends trump family.'"

Jeanne stifled a laugh. She knew Lily based her daily wardrobe selection on her horoscope, and she remembered how Lily had consulted her dead grandmother before moving to Turkey, but this really took the cake. "That's your horoscope from today, not Ibrahim's horoscope the day he died," she countered, trying to appeal to Lily's warped sense of logic. "Besides, he didn't have the opportunity. He was playing the *ney* the whole time, so he couldn't have shot Ibrahim."

"He must have had an accomplice."

Jeanne wasn't convinced. All day, her mind strayed to her conversation with Yasmina in the dressing room. Whom had she been talking to? Who was already there? And why did she seem preoccupied? What if it only seemed like Yasmina was collateral damage—what if she was in fact one of the targets, or even the primary target? Was it a hate crime, as the police seemed to think, or was Lily right about it being staged?

71

Reluctantly, she turned to Yasmina's Facebook page. She and Yasmina were Facebook friends, so it was not as though she were accessing something private. And yet she could not escape a certain voyeuristic feeling, an apprehension that perhaps she would find something that would shatter her image of Yasmina.

Most of what she found on Facebook was what she expected: photos of Yasmina's dance troupe, words of encouragement from family and friends before a big performance. In September, many of Yasmina's posts had been prayer requests for the *oud* player's wife, who had breast cancer. By November, Yasmina was reporting that his wife had successfully recovered from her mastectomy. Later, Yasmina started posting dozens of pictures of her brand-new nephew. "He's so cute!" she had written on December 15th. "I want to take him home with me, but my sister would never forgive me!"

Most of the comments were from people Jeanne knew, and many of the other posts appeared to be from family members. Jeanne wrote down only two names for further investigation: Rodrigo Robles and Maryam Massoud.

Rodrigo had written *"BELLA, BELLA, BELLA–Te quiero, mi amor"* beneath a dramatic black-and-white photo of Yasmina, which Jeanne recognized as the promotional photo for Yasmina's performance at the Kennedy Center. She had to agree with the sentiment: the light accentuated every rippling muscle in Yasmina's midsection as she gracefully arched her back. Yasmina was truly beautiful, and her expression was one that could only be described as smoldering. The "*te quiero*" suggested a rather serious love interest, and yet she could not recall Yasmina ever mentioning a beau. There were several other posts from Rodrigo, all between October and December.

Jeanne imagined Rodrigo to be a hunky Colombian underwear model, but was frustrated to find that his profile picture was an image of *Guernica*, Picasso's cubist homage to the victims of the Spanish Civil War.

Maryam had commented on almost all of Yasmina's posts. In several of them, she used an odd appellation: My Dear Mother Hen. Frowning, Jeanne enlarged Maryam's profile picture and studied it intently. The photo had been taken from a distance, so the facial features were indistinct. All she could tell was that the girl was slender, with dark curly hair. Clad in a white blouse and dark pants, she stood in front of a sign that read "George Mason University."

Next, Jeanne put Yasmina's name into Google. The first hundred and twenty hits were what she expected— mostly glowing reviews about Yasmina's dancing, advertisements for local Middle Eastern restaurants, and links to the webpage of her accounting firm, the Hariri Group. There was an article about her as a Rhodes Scholar finalist in her college magazine, and an article about her college thesis contrasting the treatment of women in Hinduism and Islam. Jeanne vaguely remembered hearing these highlights of her academic career. But number one hundred and twenty-one really caught her attention. Without taking her eyes off the screen, she dialed Lily's extension.

"Speak to me," Lily said. Her customary phone greeting was accompanied by a loud crack as her gum bubble burst.

"You're not going to believe this," Jeanne said. "But I found an old online holiday card. Yasmina was married."

"To whom?"

"Some doctor named Hamza."

The hospital cafeteria made every attempt to be cheery as it advertised its low-fat, low-sodium, low-sugar— and, Jeanne conjectured, low-taste—offerings. And yet nothing could dispel the gloom that pervaded every corner. Like smog trapped in a basin, it hovered over the steaming platters of rubbery lasagna and the weary diners speaking in hushed, forcibly optimistic tones. "The doctor says that her chances are better than most, because she's young and otherwise healthy," one sandy-haired young man said to an older woman, while pushing his collard greens around with a plastic fork.

"Maybe she'll be home by Valentine's Day," his companion murmured. "Wouldn't that be nice?"

The cafeteria smelled of bleach and lima beans. In the harsh fluorescent lighting, everyone's skin took on a ghastly gray pallor. The medical residents and interns hunched over their iridescent mystery meat and overcooked broccoli in their blue scrubs, staring vacantly at the wall. But no one looked worse than Dr. Hamza. "I've just worked a sixteen-hour shift," he croaked to Jeanne and Lily as they sat in the corner. "I'm losing my voice." His eyes were puffy and bloodshot and yet, Jeanne thought, quite kind. He had thick, wiry black hair, graying around the temples, and a bristly two-day beard.

As he spoke, Jeanne stared at his hands. Rough and calloused, with hairy backs and long, thick fingers, he wrung them together as he talked. When anxiety crept into his voice, the wringing accelerated in tempo. Were these the hands of a killer?

"You really think someone wanted Yasmina dead? If that's true," he said, sighing, "I'm afraid I don't have anything useful for you. Yasmina and I hadn't spoken since we got divorced five years ago. There was no need to. We never had any children, and we were too poor to have any assets to fight over. We had an amicable divorce...and one without any loose ends."

Lily tapped her fingernails, painted jet black in anticipation of Valentine's Day—"that vile holiday invented by Hallmark"—on the table. But Jeanne nodded sympathetically, trying to put him at ease. "But then why divorce," she asked, "if you got along so well?"

"Oh, I didn't mean to imply we got along well. We didn't. We fought constantly, over everything, large and small. But our divorce was amicable...or at least mutual. We both realized that we were good people, but not the right people for each other."

"What did you fight about?"

"Everything...kids, religion, politics..." he trailed off, his eyes misted over. For a minute, he seemed to forget all about Jeanne and Lily.

"You were saying?" Lily prodded him.

"Yasmina was a passionate woman. That's what attracted me to her in the first place. I was lonely, uptight, and depressed and when she came along, it was like someone opening the curtains and letting blinding light into a dank, dark room for the very first time. She could make a trip to the grocery store exhilarating. She'd pull up in her red convertible—which you could hear a mile away, since she had no muffler—and we'd race off at full speed, top down, the wind whipping through her hair, singing along to her ABBA CD at the top of our lungs. We'd freak out the other shoppers by speaking Arabic in loud, animated voices, making wild hand gestures. In reality, we'd be saying ridiculous things like 'This eggplant reminds me of my grandmother's head,' but people around us probably thought we were plotting to blow up buildings. We'd buy beautiful, fresh vegetables and exotic spices and come back to her place to prepare a feast."

Jeanne inhaled sharply. None other than Yasmina's ex-husband was validating her image of Yasmina as a woman who never did anything in an ordinary manner, not even grocery shopping. She felt as though she were talking to her own reflection in a mirror.

"Our relationship was like heroin," he said. "I've talked to a few addicts and they all say the same thing: heroin is really, really fun until it stops being fun. But I didn't realize I was addicted until we'd been married for about a year. She announced that she didn't want any children, which was quite a blow. I'd always wanted children, and I thought she did too. But suddenly she felt that having a baby would get in the way of her belly dancing career. Then I discovered that she hadn't paid our mortgage in several months. 'Oh, Ahmed,' she said, as though she didn't have the faintest idea why I was upset, 'It's no big deal. The bank won't come after us for months, and by that time we'll have received a few more paychecks.' We got a foreclosure letter a few weeks later."

He gripped the table, and for a moment, anger and indignation flashed across his face. "When I went to withdraw funds from our bank account to cover the funds owed for the mortgage, I discovered that we had eighty-seven dollars and sixteen cents."

"What happened to the rest of the money?"

Dr. Hamza grimaced. "The funds had been secreted to a dozen charities that assist women in the West Bank—micro-credit programs, funds to support women whose husbands have been jailed by the Israelis, shelters for abused women, you name it." His tone softened a bit. "It was strange. I was upset—and I knew our marriage had to end, before she ruined me financially and emotionally—but on some level I admired her. She really had a passion for Arab women's rights and she was willing to put her—our—money where her mouth was."

"Why was she so focused on the West Bank?" Jeanne asked. "Why not the Middle East in general? Why not Jordan?"

Dr. Hamza stared at her, puzzled. "Because she was from the West Bank. Because she'd seen the plight of women there first hand."

Frowning, Jeanne leaned forward. "She was from Jordan."

"Yes," Lily interjected. "She told everyone she was born in Jordan."

"Well then she lied to you," Dr. Hamza said. "She was born in the Balata refugee camp near Nablus, and she lived there until the middle of the first *intifada*, when her family fled to Jordan very briefly before coming to New York."

*   *   *   *

Lily and Dr. Hamza had done most of the rest of the talking. Jeanne had smiled dutifully as Dr. Hamza showed them pictures of his family: Samantha, his wife—"drama-free," Dr. Hamza had commented, laughing for the first time—and his two-year-old twins, Zoe and Sophia. She had jotted notes disinterestedly as he explained that he was working the night of the fire and hadn't heard about it until his wife saw the news the following day. He claimed not to recognize the name Ibrahim Abu Ali.

But beneath her tight-lipped façade, Jeanne's mind was reeling. At once convincing and unsettling, the portrait that he had drawn of his life with Yasmina raised some uncomfortable questions: Why had she lied about her country of origin? Why had Jeanne never gotten the slightest inkling of Yasmina's political proclivities? Had she been blinded to Yasmina's dark side, just like Dr. Hamza? And if so, did that have any bearing on her investigation into Ibrahim and Yasmina's deaths?

Now, as they marched up Wisconsin Avenue, Lily was no longer content to allow Jeanne to remain silent. "You're walking too fast," Lily huffed, shivering in her olive green trench coat and faux snakeskin boots. The four inches of bare skin beneath the hem of her coat and the top of her boots was raw and goose pimpled, and her

79

breath came out in short, staccato beats, crystallizing within seconds.

"You're wearing impractical high heeled boots."

"They're high fashion."

"In a club, maybe. In a murder investigation, they're a hindrance."

Lily grunted. "So do you think he's our man?"

"No."

"Why not?"

"Just a hunch," Jeanne said. "He seemed nice. He has no real motive...after all, if he wanted to harm her, he would have done so years ago when they divorced. He seems to have zero connection to Ibrahim. And he appears to have an alibi."

"Well unless we get access to the hospital's personnel records, we don't really know if he was working or not."

"True."

At the top of the hill, next to the Russian Embassy, they came to Jeanne's apartment building. Lily had once dubbed it "Dorothy's Yellow Brick Road torn up and re-assembled into a warehouse," but Jeanne had fallen in love with the view of National Cathedral from its rooftop terrace. On sunny afternoons, she would scoot a chair to the edge of the railing and gaze at the lofty spires. In spring, the grounds were a riot of delicate pink cherry blossoms and she imagined the scene as the inspiration for a wonderful Impressionist painting when, of course, she learned to paint like Monet. In October, the gargoyles peeked out from behind glorious fall foliage, and she imagined Bacchus himself cavorting across the rooftop in anticipation of the harvest. She enjoyed her birds-eye view of the sumptuous weddings and the state funerals.

They trudged up three flights of stairs—the elevator had been "awaiting repairs" for the past two weeks—and down the garishly wallpapered hallway. At the end of the hall, Jeanne saw a familiar figure lumbering towards number 309. "Head down," she whispered to Lily. "And walk slower." But it was too late.

"Twinkletoes!" he called out to them. "With the Asian Invasion!"

"Hey, Jerry," Jeanne mumbled.

Her friend was less accommodating. "My name is Lily," she said acidly. "And yes, I am Asian, like half of the people on the planet."

Jerry Petronelli was Jeanne's next-door neighbor, a hard-boiled former member of a Special Ops unit, and an Iraq War vet. More recently, he had worked for "The Agency," as he put it, which meant he was a spook. She considered him her nemesis, but he—for reasons she did not understand—seemed to regard her as some combination of a long-lost niece needing to be taken under his wing and a potential lover. Some days he offered her strange but avuncular advice, such as: "If someone decides to flash his hot dog at you in the Metro, kick him in the nuts and tell him you are dying of AIDS." On others, he offered creepy invitations for dinner. "I know a great little kebab place, Twinkletoes," he might say or, "You're looking stressed out. Let me make you some chicken soup and take you for a midnight ride on my Harley." He was bald and pot-bellied, with tattoos slithering up and down his beefy arms. His television blared late into the night—although he turned it down whenever Jeanne banged on the wall three times—and smoke curled from underneath his door at all hours of the day. "What? You haven't died from lung cancer yet?" Jeanne had said, only half-joking one day, as she stepped into the hallway, which reeked particularly badly from the smoke that day. "No, unfortunately not," he had replied, and Jeanne had felt a pang of remorse. "Well, good," she had said and hurried inside, only to find an expensive dog treat outside her door the next day. The biscuit was shaped like a cigarette—it must have been a special order—and attached to a hand-written note that said "For Scarlett."

Today, Jerry was proffering his chili. "It's my cousin Bob's recipe. Five-alarm chili. It really clears the sinuses."

"Uh, thanks for offering Jerry," Jeanne said as she furiously turned the key in the lock. "But we have leftovers."

The door swung open, and Jeanne and Lily found themselves safe within the confines of Jeanne's cramped efficiency. Scarlett hopped towards them, her bushy red tail wagging with glee. She bounced up, her one front paw scraping Jeanne's leg, and licked her across the face. "Hello Scarlett! I've missed you." Bending down, Jeanne scratched the back of Scarlett's neck, and then filled Scarlett's water bowl. Jeanne and Lily followed Scarlett as she hopped gingerly through the narrow galley kitchen, weaving through a forest of half-dead house plants.

Jeanne's futon lay behind a Japanese screen that she had picked up second-hand at a flea market, and a small living area lay behind this, by the bathroom. Lily set her coat on a pair of milk crates, which had been lashed together as a side table, and sank into Flaca. "I got the DVD back from the popos," she announced, sliding it out of her purse.

Jeanne rolled her eyes. Lily had evidently seen one too many Tyler Perry movies. Flicking the DVD player on, Jeanne settled into Flaca, pulling Scarlett onto her lap. They watched intently as Yasmina segued into her veil dance. "Do you recognize him?" Jeanne asked as Yasmina began to focus her attention on the portly Middle Eastern man in the white, button-down shirt and brown pants.

"No. I've never seen him before. And I'd never heard of him before they announced his name on the news. I didn't know there were any other owners besides Yousef."

They watched with rapt attention, but noticed nothing new. A few minutes later, as Yasmina began her sword dance, the camera appeared to shake. "I guess I didn't pay much attention to filming once I noticed the smoke," Lily observed ruefully.

As smoke began to fill the room, the image became grainy. And then the camera went black.

"Well, there's one thing this tells us," Jeanne said. "He was still alive and well about a minute before the fire alarm went off."

They were interrupted by a loud banging on the door. "Jerry, we already told you!" Jeanne yelled. "We don't need any chili."

There was a long silence and then a plaintive, small voice. "Jeanne, it's me, Vivienne. I'm leaving Mitch." And then the voice broke into a wail.

Chapter Eight

A quarter of an hour into Vivienne's rant, Jeanne had still not recovered. She hadn't said a single word in fact. She sat there mute, her mouth hanging wide opening, watching with a mixture of horror, fascination, and pity as her sister ripped the myth of her perfect marriage to shreds. "Wow, this is good," Vivienne said as she shoveled gobs of Cherry Garcia into her mouth. "So much better than celery sticks and carrots. The new me--the Mitch-free me—is going to get fat. It's liberating really. Have you noticed how the fat chicks always get compliments about their brains and personality? You can be skinny and your husband will still cheat on you— so why bother being skinny?"

"Is the bitch skinny?" Lily asked.

"Don't know, don't care. She's twenty-one and hasn't popped out a kid, so yeah, probably. She thinks Mitch is the cat's meow. But of course she would—she hasn't given birth to his child with no drugs, at his insistence, and then been mocked for having a baby belly two weeks later while on a raw foods diet." She snorted. "Which, by the way, is horrible. There's a reason our ancestors discovered fire."

Jeanne couldn't believe what she was seeing and hearing. She had always defined herself in opposition to Vivienne—she was everything Vivienne was not, even when that was decidedly negative—and now Vivienne was sounding a whole lot like her. Dressed in baggy sweats and old tennis shoes, with her mascara running down her tear-stained face, Vivienne even looked more like her. She had always dreamed of the day that Vivienne's perfect façade would be chipped away, but now that that day was here, she couldn't think of anything she wanted less.

Lily patted Vivienne's back. "What will you do now?"

"First, make up for lost time and eat all of the brownies, cookies, and ice cream I want. Second, throw all of his clothes on the lawn, especially his five hundred dollar Italian leather shoes. On a day it's raining. Third, take Everett out of baby yoga and baby Spanish and let him play more. The last thing the world needs is another over-managed, over-manufactured product of Mitch." She ticked off each item on her fingers.

Jeanne spoke for the first time. "And after that?"

Vivienne sighed. "I don't know."

"Want to help us solve a mystery?"

*   *   *   *

"Oooh, this is fun!" Vivienne squealed as they crossed the threshold of a fancy Dupont Circle art gallery. "I haven't shown this much cleavage since college. And I haven't been to anything this fantastically weird in a decade." She snatched a wine glass off of a passing tray and guzzled it.

"Remind me why we're here again," Lily whispered, sleek in her snakeskin pants and slinky black top.

Jeanne pretended to inspect a llama wearing a Che Guevara T-shirt with U.S. dollars pinned to its ears. "The Facebook post," she said in a low voice behind clenched teeth. "He's a possible love interest."

"The New/Old Latin America" was the newest installation art project of Rodrigo Robles who, while not a Columbian underwear model, had turned out to be a ruggedly handsome Argentine artist. Surrounded by a bevy of female admirers—whom Jeanne suspected might be more interested in him than his art—he stood by the entrance of the gallery, wine glass in hand. Tall and broad-shouldered, his salt-and-pepper hair fell to his shoulders in unruly curls, dramatically framing his rough-hewn features.

Vivienne licked her lips, which were slathered in an eye-popping crimson. "Mmmmm. A real gaucho."

Jeanne looked at her sister in amazement. What had happened to her respectable, mature older sister?

Suddenly she felt as if she were chaperoning a junior high school student at her first dance. "How much have you had to drink?" she asked suspiciously.

"Just two glasses...three...was it four? Who's counting when it's free?"

Jeanne raised an eyebrow but said nothing. She supposed she should cut her sister some slack under the circumstances.

The three women sauntered towards Rodrigo, stopping to admire the art every so often. Or at least pretending to admire the art. To Jeanne, the whole thing was not only bizarre, but pretentious—more chutzpah than talent. Lily, predictably, was more enthusiastic. "Kalashnikovs, stuffed llamas, and Antonio Banderas look-alikes wearing nothing but body paint," she murmured approvingly. "I might borrow a few of these ideas for my band's next stage set."

When they were about fifteen feet away, Vivienne suddenly shrieked, clutching her ample bosom. "Oh! My! Gawd! If it isn't Señor Robles in the flesh!"

Lily elbowed Jeanne in the ribs. "Where did she get that accent?"

"No idea."

"She sounds like she's going to sprout a hoop skirt at any moment. What's she going to do next? Offer him a sarsaparilla?"

The gaggle of admirers parted to make way for the spirited Southern belle in their midst. "Oh, I'm mighty

sorry if I gave you a start," she gushed as she took
Rodrigo's hands in her own. He looked both supremely
flattered and anxious, and Jeanne could tell he was
wracking his brain to try to remember where he might
have met her before. "I'm such an admirer of your work
and to see you here in person, surrounded by your
oeuvre, why it's just the bee's knees!" She pronounced
"oeuvre" as "oo—ev—RAY," and Jeanne had to turn away
to suppress a smile. That her sister, a native French
speaker, could purposefully mangle the language until it
sounded as though she were calling the pigs at a rodeo,
was a minor miracle. That she could butcher le français
without so much as cracking a smile, all the while
appearing to be supremely self-impressed with her
worldliness, was unbelievable. Jeanne had never had the
slightest inkling that Vivienne could act.

"I told my husband that I was going to pop up to
Washington D.C."—she drawled the "D" and the "C"
until they were at least four syllables each—"for the
weekend and see if I could commission some new art
before we host our little holiday party."

Jeanne and Lily watched in awe as she prattled on,
dropping some tantalizing little tidbits every few
minutes. With each hint of fabulous wealth and
questionable taste, Rodrigo's eyes grew bigger and bigger.
"Oh, I was thinking something like this," Vivienne
waved her arms expansively, "but Arabian themed. You
see," she said, grasping his wrist and pulling him closer

to her, "we often invite a few sheiks, and we want them to feel at home. My husband said, 'Sweetheart, there's loads of art right here in Houston,' but I knew that Washington D.C. was the place to come for international art. Plus, this weekend's the E.M. senior management retreat, and with my husband gone, I get so lonely!"

"E.M.?" Rodrigo inquired politely.

"Well aren't you as sweet as peas!" Vivienne laughed and tickled his nose. "Why, ExxonMobil of course!"

They both guffawed, and Vivienne's wine sloshed in her glass until she lost her balance, sending the wine splattering in all directions. "Oh, I'm so sorry!"

"Do not be preoccupied," he proclaimed chivalrously, in his sexy Argentine accent, as he bent towards her, handkerchief in hand, dabbing at her cleavage.

"Oh, no!" she wailed. "The wine spilled all over your shirt. And what if there are tiny little droplets on the art?"

He shrugged. "Then they will add a new and interesting dimension."

Jeanne was surprised how calm and collected he sounded at the possibility of an uncouth oil tycoon's wife soiling his art with cheap wine. She had thought all artists were dramatic, but apparently he was the exception. Either that, or Vivienne's cleavage had lulled him into a trance. If so, she hoped that they were long gone before the effect wore off.

"Honey, can I get some club soda?" Vivienne drawled at a passing caterer. "That should have been my talent at the Miss Texas pageant," she confided to Rodrigo in a stage whisper. "Removing stains with club soda. I'm such a klutz—I should carry it everywhere with me. Instead, I twirled a baton with flames shooting out of both sides."

"Did you win?"

"Oh, no, sweetie. I burned my left thumb. Like I said, I was a klutz."

"Can you sing?"

"I tried that. But I broke a window at church and almost decapitated the pastor's wife."

While Rodrigo's eyes grew bigger and bigger and the staff scurried around dabbing club soda on everything, Lily took the opportunity to lean in and unclip his phone from his belt.

Ten minutes later, the three ladies were skipping down Connecticut Avenue, linked arm in arm, with Rodrigo's phone number burning a hole in Vivienne's pocket.

"Viv! You were amazing!" Jeanne squeezed her sister's arm. "Where did you pick that up?"

"Mitch's dreadful cocktail parties. You wouldn't believe the amount of name-dropping that goes on. The accent, I have to admit, is a mix of *Steel Magnolias* and *Gone with the Wind*."

"It was so perfect how you lunged forward and hugged him just as I was putting his phone back," Lily gushed. "He was so distracted that he didn't feel a thing."

"Did you find anything useful?"

"Yasmina's in his contact list, but the last call was December 17th. And his calendar showed that he had an appointment at seven o'clock on the night of the fire so it would have been difficult—although perhaps not impossible—for him to be at Algiers by eight-fifteen."

"What kind of appointment?"

"Chest waxing," Lily said, and all three burst out laughing.

The next afternoon, Jeanne hovered by Lily's desk, trying to look purposeful, while Lily smoothed her long blue-black hair and re-positioned the phone against her ear. "Yes, this is Sarah Peters, Mr. Robles' personal assistant," Lily crooned into the receiver. "I'm so sorry to trouble you—really I'm so embarrassed—but I can't recall when his last chest waxing session was."

Greta, the nosy receptionist, had the gall to walk past just then and shot Lily a questioning look. "Sam Staunton," Lily mouthed. Sam was one of the old stiffs

with his name on the door, and Jeanne could tell Lily
had just given Greta the willies. Greta was no doubt
picturing old doddering Sam, with his glistening and
clean-shaven man boobs and pot-belly, prancing about
the deck of his yacht somewhere off the coast of
Antigua. Lily covered the receiver until Greta, who was
now looking a little green, trudged off to her cube.

"You see," Lily continued, "he insists upon having
his chest waxed every four weeks and I need to make
another appointment. But now I can't remember when
his last appointment was. I've been so distracted—what
with my mother undergoing chemotherapy and my sister
going through a terrible divorce. And my cat had a
tumor the size of a grapefruit. She looked like a feline
Quasimodo. Yes, I'll hold for a moment while you go
check. I really appreciate it."

Lily thumbed through *The Express* while she waited,
flipping to the horoscopes and celebrity news at the
back. Jeanne knew she was much more interested in the
latest installment of Charlie Sheen's "violent torpedo of
truth" than in the Eurozone crisis. After all, if she
needed to quickly be caught up with world affairs, she
could always ask Jeanne.

The voice came back on the line and Lily hit the
"speaker" button. "Ms. Peters?"

"Yes."

"His last appointment was Thursday, February 4th, at
7:00 p.m."

"And how long does the appointment normally last?"

"An hour and a half."

"Thank you very much. Let's schedule it for March 4th then." Lily hung up and shot Jeanne a look of defeat. "I guess his alibi checks out."

"I'm not surprised," Jeanne said, "but I do have some good news."

"Which is?"

"We're getting the rest of the day—maybe even the rest of the week—off." A smile spread across Jeanne's face. "According to the Weather Channel, Snowmaggedon should begin in a few hours."

Chapter Nine

There were few things that Jeanne loved more than a snow day. She loved charting a course down the middle of unplowed streets, the great white expanse glinting silver beneath the lamplights, her lone footprints stretching behind her as through she were Roald Amundsen trudging across Antarctica to the South Pole. If, of course, the Antarctic were lined with neat rows of two hundred-year-old townhouses, set together cheek-by-jowl, and populated by pundits and socialites. She liked to trudge past Jackie Kennedy's former home, a 1792 manse with an odd bust of George Washington peeking out from the living room windows, and then head north past Dumbarton Oaks and the old cemetery, lined with spooky crypts now blanketed in snow. Marveling at the lacy designs the snow-covered limbs cut across the gray, threatening sky, she would burst into the "Ave Maria," her voice swallowed up by the storm.

She did not understand how a few snowflakes could sow such terror—such panic!—among Washingtonians. At the first mention of "the white stuff," or more commonly, "a wintry mix," folks who could be blasé about a double homicide on their block, or losing a cool million in the stock market, would swoop into grocery stores, and buy loaves of bread and cartons of milk— never mind that their entire family is lactose-intolerant and hasn't drunk milk in a year—as if anticipating a sudden alien invasion. People with a mere thirty feet of sidewalk would race out to buy three hundred dollar snow blowers, and liberal types who vilified "crazy Red State survivalists" would suddenly snap up generators and talk gloomily about "hunkering down for the storm." An inch or two was good for a day off, and an event billed as "Snowmageddon" or "Storm of the Century"—despite occurring every few years—was good for several days, if not a whole week.

The hoopla all seemed silly to Jeanne, who had grown up in Maine's northern wilderness, one of only two areas in the country in which the census workers were reimbursed for the miles they logged snowmobiling or snowshoeing to each remote homestead.

Today, the snow was wet and heavy, and she heard a satisfying crunch with each footstep. When she arrived home at last, Scarlett greeted her at the door. "Yes, it's a snow day, Scarlett! Maybe even a snow week!" she exclaimed, and Scarlett's tail-wagging accelerated as if she understood. "That means more walks for you."

She made herself a cup of hot chocolate and settled into Flaca, with Scarlett sprawled across her lap. "This is the good life," she said as she stared at the snow swirling past her picture windows and slowly dialed her sister's number for a chat.

"Jeanne!" Her sister sounded much more chipper than she would have expected, what with her scumbag of a husband and all. "Can you believe how psycho people are going? It's crazy! But the snow is so beautiful! Everett and I have been making snow angels all afternoon. And we made an—wait, Everett wants to tell you himself."

"Hi, Everett," Jeanne said into the receiver.

There was a moment of silence, and then some weird rustling. Finally, she heard Everett's gurgling voice. "Ig-oo!" he shouted. "Ig-oo!"

She promised Everett that she would come and visit his igloo tomorrow and hung up. Not a moment later, she heard three thuds and felt the wall behind her reverberating. "How's your hottie of a sister, Twinkletoes?" a familiar voice roared.

"Just fine, Jerry," she yelled back, silently cursing the paper-thin walls.

"Can I come over?"

"No."

"Please? Jeanne, can I please come over? I really need to talk to someone."

It took her a moment to realize that he had actually called her Jeanne. Now that was an interesting development.

"Oh, all right. But you can't smoke. Promise?"

"Promise."

To her surprise, he was wearing a clean shirt and a nice pair of slacks when she opened the door. He didn't even reek of smoke.

"Thanks for letting me come over," he said, fumbling in his pocket for a dog treat. He shook Scarlett's one front paw and patted her on the head. "Good puppy."

"Would you like some hot chocolate?" Jeanne asked, flustered. She found it unnerving to see him act so...normal.

"That would be nice. Thanks."

She realized she had no idea what to say. She and Jerry had always exchanged barbs, plus occasional witty banter mixed in with neighborhood news. But now that seemed inappropriate. She tried to remember what polite strangers talked about. "It sure is snowing out there," she said, remembering how people in British comedies always talked about the weather. "We're supposed to get eighteen inches."

"Is that so?" She could tell that he had no idea what she had just said. He seemed fixated on her hands as they stirred the hot chocolate on the stovetop. Or maybe he was fixated on the hot chocolate itself. It was hard to say.

"You can sit down on the couch if you like. It's through there."

"I'd rather stay here if you don't mind."

"Suit yourself."

In silence, she finished preparing the hot chocolate, poured it into two mugs, and motioned for Jerry to follow her to Flaca. She sat on the side nearest the interior wall, angling her back to get a better view of the snow swirling outside, and he sat facing her, with his back to the window. Scarlett sprawled out between them.

Staring vacantly ahead, Jerry ran his fingers through Scarlett's fur. The clock over the bookshelf ticked loudly, and Jeanne was painfully aware of each silent minute passing. "Are you okay, Jerry?"

Startled, he looked up at her as if he had forgotten she was even there. "I can't stand the sight of snow," he murmured. "It reminds me of sand."

"Does it remind you of Iraq?"

He nodded and began petting Scarlett faster. "It's not my fault, I keep telling myself, it's not my fault."

"What's not your fault, Jerry?"

"She keeps talking to me in dreams," he insisted, ignoring the question. His voice was gravelly, his tone almost belligerent. "I see the black sedan speeding towards the checkpoint, emerging from the swirling sand

and the howling wind like a mirage, its occupants hanging out of the windows, shouting at me in their strange guttural dialect. The only words I understand are 'Allah.' 'Stop,' I shout, holding up my hands, but they do not see, or they do not want to see, and the car comes closer. I'm shaking with fear. Under normal rules of engagement, the next step would be to shoot for the tires. But these are not normal times—two of my buddies had been killed that week by occupants of vehicles that refused to stop. I think, this is it, it's do or die now, the fate of my platoon is in my hands. I grab my weapon, I raise the barrel. The gun glints in the sun. It's beautiful, really. So shiny. They are shouting, protesting, waving their hands, but I can hear nothing, only the wind. I pull the trigger and unload a clip. For a moment, all is still. The windshield cracks and the cries stop. I rush to the side and see the men slumped over in the front seat. In the back is a woman, clad in a black abaya, her legs wide apart. I stare in horror at her swollen belly and the pool of water beneath her legs."

Jeanne inhaled sharply. "She was in labor?"

Jerry scrunched up his face, his lips quivering. "Yes."

"And then what?"

"Suddenly I notice a slight movement in her throat. She is trying to speak to me. I lean closer, until we are pupil to pupil, the closest I have ever been to an Iraqi. She murmurs something and then she is silent, her eyes, green flecked with gold, staring up at me, glassy and

100

accusatory. My men rush forward, and I order the medic to perform an emergency C-section. He tells me that we're too late, but I urge him on, shouting all the while."

"Did it work?"

He shook his head, and as his big brown eyes welled up with tears, he pounded the wall with his first. "It hurts so bad, Jeanne."

She wanted to tell him that she understood, that she knew all about the vicious cycle of pain and guilt. But instead she crossed to the other side of the sofa, pulled him close, and cradled his smooth-shaven head against a crook in her arm. "You didn't know, Jerry. You did everything you could to save the baby."

He smelled of cologne, cigarettes, and Chinese take-out, and for the first time she saw his tattoos up close. Frightening yet beautiful, they were full of Biblical imagery and interspersed with Chinese characters and Arabic script. His chest cavity heaved violently, and she felt something metallic brush her wrist. Hung from a chain around his neck, it was a dog tag bearing the name of a fallen comrade.

Silently, she forgave his smoking, his penchant for weird nicknames, his television blaring into the night. Neither of them spoke until the sobs at last began to quiet.

"Jerry," Jeanne finally whispered, "my arm is falling asleep."

"Well, of course it is, Twinkletoes. You've got your obese, uncouth, boorish neighbor lying on it. Poor kid."

Jeanne smiled. "Are you up for a game of Scrabble?"

"I'm gonna crush you like a bug."

Two Scrabble games, three games of Chinese Checkers, four episodes of *Law and Order*, and three cans of soup later, in the wee hours of the morning, the snow finally stopped. "I guess I'll be going back home," Jerry mumbled as he lifted his head from the coffee table, the "Q" Scrabble tile sticking to his cheek. "Thanks for the hospitality, Twinkletoes. I'll try not to have a meltdown too often."

"Any time, Jerry."

Chapter Ten

When Jeanne awoke the next morning, she found herself staring straight into Scarlett's eager face. "Yech!" she grumbled as Scarlett panted directly into her nostrils. "We need to brush your teeth. And really, Scar, you've got to stop staring at me while I sleep. It's kind of unnerving."

Scarlett's ears perked up and she hopped up on her three legs, her leash and Red Riding Hood Cape in her mouth. The cape had been a present from Lily, who insisted that capes were much more in vogue than coats, not to mention easier to wrangle a dog into. "Oh, I know, Scarlett!" Jeanne exclaimed, exasperated. "You're telling me that you are all ready to go."

She changed into her green and gold William and Mary hoodie, jeans, and an old pair of hiking boots, attempted to run a comb through her matted hair, and wolfed down a bowl of Cheerios. Scarlett eagerly followed her around the apartment, occasionally running to the door and whimpering before realizing it was yet another false alarm. "I'm almost ready, Scar," Jeanne reassured her as she fished out of the closet an old gray and blue ski jacket, a stocking cap knitted with little prancing antler-sporting pigs ("they're reindeer," her aunt had trilled upon presenting her with her first attempt at knitting), and some old grease-stained work gloves. She knew Lily would not approve of this ensemble, but it was all she had to work with and besides, she was unlikely to run into anyone, since everyone born south of New England was scared out of their wits by snow.

She unlocked the door and Scarlett raced down the hallway as fast as her three legs would take her, dragging Jeanne behind her.

"Mommy, I hear a herd of reindeer coming," she heard a toddler exclaim from inside apartment 301.

"No, honey, it's just that poor three-legged puppy," was the response.

They raced down the steps, out the front door, and through several blocks of deep, fluffy snow until they arrived—Scarlett panting with excitement, Jeanne panting from exhaustion—at the dog park. To her surprise, they were not alone.

In the corner, by the bare lilac bushes, a ginger-haired labradoodle was fetching a red ball for his owner, a slight young man with shaggy blond hair. He hunched over, shivering in a pink parka with a fur-trimmed hood and black driving gloves. What a shame. She had finally run into a man who liked dogs and snow, and he was obviously gay.

"Well, hello there," the man shouted, waving at her. His voice was surprisingly masculine, deep and resonant with a thick, gravelly brogue.

"Hello," she called out, unhooking Scarlett's leash and setting her loose. Scarlett and the labradoodle sniffed each other's butts, as was customary, and began chasing each other's tails.

As Jeanne plodded through the snowdrifts, he came into sharper view. He had thick copper-colored stubble, wire-rimmed glasses, and eyes that reminded her of the Atlantic on a cloudy day: a deep gray-blue that hinted at something mysterious and turbulent beneath the smooth glassy surface. But his eyes were not threatening; on the contrary, they crinkled at the edges in evident mirth.

"I see you have the same fashion sense I do!"

"Perhaps even slightly better," Jeanne retorted. "This cap, I'll have you know, is very high end. Hand-knit, in fact."

"But not Fair Isle, I imagine. By your mum, I would guess."

"My aunt, actually. Who happens to be an award-winning knitter of Christmas pigs. Which are extraordinarily popular in the U.S., which you wouldn't know because you are, judging from the charming

MAUREEN KLOVERS

accent, foreign. Irish, perhaps?" She was quite proud of herself for slyly working a question about his nationality into the conversation. It was a bit absurd, she realized, to strike up such a saucy repartee in the park with a perfect stranger, but it was also quite entertaining and she couldn't see what the harm was. What could he do: strangle her with a leash?

"Scottish, actually."

"And your lovely parka? Is it a gift from your boyfriend? The fur is quite becoming on you."

"My aunt's, actually. I don't have any proper winter clothing. I never expected the weather to get this cold."

"I'm Jeanne," she said, extending her left hand. She normally shook with her right, but the left glove had fewer grease stains than the right.

He grasped her hand and shook it firmly. "Fergus McCarrick. Pleased to make your acquaintance. And this—"

Jeanne did not have a chance to hear the rest. Suddenly, she was knocked off her feet, propelled forward through the snowbank. Out of the corner of her eye, she saw a blur of reddish fur, a tangle of leashes, and a quivering rabbit struggling frantically to escape the dogs' clutches.

"No!" she shouted, as Scarlett and the other dog dragged her through the snow. "Scarlett! Stop!"

Fergus ran along beside her. "Magnus! Let the poor rabbit alone! Sit! Stay!"

106

She lunged forward, reaching for Scarlett's collar. But as she grabbed ahold, she felt something tighten around her ankles. Her knees buckled, sending her tumbling into the snow, until she landed with a loud, surprisingly hard thud. She felt a stabbing pain in her left knee and her entire leg began to throb.

"Jeanne? Are you all right?" He turned to face her as he yanked Scarlett and Magnus back by their collars and the rabbit limped away.

"Ow! No. I mean, yes, eventually I will be. I got caught in a leash. But I think I hit something."

"I'll help you up." He slung a pink parka-clad arm underneath her and she felt his rough cheek brush against hers.

Woozy, she stumbled to her feet and then winced as she saw that the snow around her had turned pink. "It looks like a strawberry Sno-Cone."

"A what?"

"Never mind."

"If you don't like blood, don't look," he said as he bent down and lifted up her pants leg. "The wound's pretty nasty. I think you hit a tree root."

"It's my fault," Fergus sighed. "I should have kept a closer eye on Magnus the Great. He's always looking to impress the ladies with his hunting prowess." He looked down at her knee again. "I don't normally take home women that I've just met, but in this case I'm going to have to make an exception. My aunt lives right around the corner. I can take you there, clean you up, put on a bandage, and have you back at home in front of the telly by tea time."

She knew she should protest. After all, everyone knew that you should never go to a stranger's house. But her knee was throbbing, she was covered in snow, and she felt sure that, even in her weakened condition, she could wrestle a gun out of his matchstick-thin arms and get off the first shot.

"Oh, all right," she murmured. "Now, Scarlett, behave."

Fergus and his aunt lived in a beige brick townhouse that sat high above the street, up a steep flight of concrete stairs. A cheery Christmas wreath adorned the canary yellow door.

"Aunt Margaret!" Fergus boomed as they crossed the threshold into a dark, hazy interior that smelled of sickness and old age poorly masked by lavender potpourri. Lively blue and white flowered wallpaper belied the gloom, while old black and white photographs of unsmiling, corseted relatives stared out from every nook and cranny. The décor reminded Jeanne of grade school field trips to see how people lived "back then." She almost expected a historical interpreter to come out any minute and begin her spiel about twice-yearly baths and medical treatments involving leeches.

Scarlett for once held back, unsure of her surroundings, while Magnus the Great strutted back and forth. He was clearly king of the castle.

"She's a little deaf," he said to Jeanne and then called out in a still louder voice, "Aunt Margaret, we have visitors!"

"I'm in the family room, dear," a small, quavering voice said, and they made their way to the back of the house.

On a small orange flowered couch—which, to Jeanne's pleasant surprise, looked a lot like Flaca—Aunt Margaret sat transfixed by *Jeopardy*. Magnus the Great bounced over to her and she pushed her walker away, scratching him behind the ears. Scarlett cowered by Jeanne.

"That young man is doing so well," she remarked without looking up. Jeanne squinted at the television to see whom she was referring to, but the youngest person she saw was a gray-haired man in his sixties.

Fergus cleared his throat. "Aunt Margaret, we have visitors."

She craned her neck towards them and reached for her small, square-framed glasses, which hung around her neck. Pushing them up her nose with a gnarled, vein-twisted finger, she raised her wispy eyebrows as Fergus, Jeanne, and Scarlett at last came into focus. "Why,

Fergus," she said in a hoarse, quavering voice, "I didn't know you knew any girls!"

"We just met in the dog park."

"You met in Noah's Ark?"

"The DOG"—he pointed at Magnus the Great—"PARK. She cut herself so we are just going to go into the bathroom and clean her up."

Aunt Margaret looked confused for a moment, but was soon distracted by a Daily Double. Fergus and Jeanne took the opportunity to extricate themselves from the family room, with Scarlett hopping after them.

Fergus opened the second door on the left hand side of the corridor and gently seated Jeanne on the toilet seat, which was covered in what appeared to be pink shag carpeting. "I see Aunt Margaret likes pink," Jeanne remarked, trying not to laugh, as she took in the pink and baby blue floor tiles, pink sink, and pink shower curtain embroidered with yellow daisies. A stack of *Reader's Digests* were tucked under the sink, and four canine portraits, each one hung in a fancy gold frame as though they were protecting a Van Gogh, lined the walls. "Magnus and his predecessors?" Jeanne guessed.

"You're bloody good," he laughed as he eased her pants leg above the wound. He retrieved a bottle of rubbing alcohol from the medicine cabinet, unscrewed the lid, and doused a cotton ball in the liquid. "Sorry, love, this is going to hurt a wee bit."

"So how long are you—OWWWW!" The stinging pain jolted through her as she clenched the edge of the sink.

"I warned you."

She took a deep breath and the pain began to subside. "How long are you staying with Aunt Margaret?"

"I don't know. She had a stroke back in October. Someone needed to come stay with her—her husband died years ago and they never had any children—and I thought it would be a great opportunity to come see America."

"And you could just leave your job like that?"

"I haven't left my job at all. I'm a cyber-security consultant, and I can do my job anywhere I can get online."

Jeanne's eyes lit up. "Really? So you are a hacker?"

"No." He placed a piece of gauze on her knee. "Here. Hold this while I wrap the bandage."

"But you know how to hack into computer systems."

"Of course," Fergus said. "I need to know what our opponents' next move is going to be."

"Well then I have a proposition for you." She took a deep breath. "I need you to hack into a few—okay, maybe several—computer systems to help me solve one—possibly two—murders."

He laughed. "Well that sounds both intriguing and dangerous."

"No, I'm serious." She held his gaze for a moment, and watched as his lips drew together in a thin straight line.

"You really do mean it."

"The body of a very close friend of mine was found in the charred ruins of a nightclub. I think she was murdered before her body caught on fire."

In silence, he wrapped the bandage around her knee, and secured it with a little metal clip. When he looked back up at her, his eyes had turned steel gray. "Isn't that a matter for the police?"

Jeanne shook her head. "They don't believe me. They think I can't accept that my friend died in the fire."

"When I was seven," he said, "a lass from my neighborhood went missing. Her neighbor swore she'd overheard a violent argument between the woman and her husband, but the police didn't consider him a suspect. He was well liked by his employer, went to church every Sunday, you know the type. And the neighbor who supposedly overheard them was a drunk and rumored to be a prostitute."

"Was it him?"

Fergus nodded slowly. "But they didn't figure it out until ten years later, when he killed his new girlfriend." His voice cracked. "Who happened to be my friend's sister."

"I'm really sorry."

"I'll help you as much as I can." Fergus suddenly smiled, and his countenance was suddenly transformed from sad to resolute. "On one condition."

"Which is?"

"You'll be my date to the Celtic jam session at Nanny O'Brien's next Monday."

"But that's Valentine's Day!" she protested.

"Is it?" he asked innocently. "I guess we don't pay much attention in Scotland. Do you have a hot date or something?"

"Well no..."

"So you'll come?"

She had never been asked out in a bathroom before, certainly not one with a pink shag toilet cover and a photo gallery of pooches. She had also never been asked out by a man who she had a sinking feeling she could defeat in an arm-wrestling match. Of course, the truth was she was rarely asked out by anyone, so there wasn't much of a pattern to analyze. Still, there was something endearing about him, and he was rather cute in a ninety-eight pound weakling sort of way. "Okay," she said.

"Bloody good. So when do I get the scoop on my new and dangerous assignment?"

"After an igloo unveiling ceremony. Which, by the way, we are already ten minutes late for."

Chapter Eleven

For the first time ever, Jeanne and Scarlett were able to walk right down the middle of Wisconsin Avenue. Normally, it was choked with buses, cars, and the odd suicidal cyclist, but now it was deserted, their footsteps the only signs of life. The snowplow had come through once, turning the surface beneath them into six inches of hard-packed snow which crunched pleasantly beneath their feet. "I love snow," Jeanne enthused as she stuck out her tongue to catch a falling snowflake. "Does it snow much in Scotland?"

"Well, unfortunately, not in Glasgow, where I live." Jeanne noticed that he pronounced it "Glasge."

"But in the highlands," he said, "it can snow quite a bit. The snow can last until August on Ben Nevis or in the Creag Meagaidh hills."

Jeanne loved the way he said "Creag Meagaidh." She loved his accent, period. It reminded her of someone gargling, and yet she found it somehow quite pleasant.

"And you?" he asked. "Are you from around here?"

She shook her head. "Northern Maine, a few miles from the Canadian border."

"I wager you grew up skiing then."

"No," Jeanne said, "unless you count slip-sliding around the hill in my grandmother's back yard on some old fence boards. We didn't have any money for proper skis."

"And I thought all Americans were rich," he joked.

"Only in the movies."

"Aye. I learned that almost as soon as I got here." He turned up his collar against the wind. "The number of people sleeping rough is staggering."

They trudged past the National Cathedral, its snow-sheathed spires gleaming, and the stone buildings that comprised the exclusive, all-boys St. Albans school. With their pointed archways and mullioned windows, Jeanne thought that they wouldn't have looked out of place at Oxford or Cambridge. Fergus must have been thinking the same thing because he muttered, "That must be where the minted lads go."

They crossed forlorn little Bryce Park, which was really little more than a glorified traffic circle, and suddenly came to a halt in front of Temple Micah.

Hitler Should Have Finished the Job. That was the chilling message covering its brick façade.

As she whipped out her phone to call Detective Walker, she couldn't help but notice that it bore a resemblance to an angry red script Jeanne had seen once before.

"Is the queen doing the honors this afternoon?" Fergus inquired as they bounded up the steps to Vivienne's imposing red brick mansion. On the tree-lined and very exclusive P Street, it exuded stodgy, old-money Georgetown charm and was so old that the base of its staircase contained two cast iron doors for delivering coal.

"No, only my sister and nephew."

"It looks quite dear."

"Wait until you see the inside."

Vivienne came to the door, with Everett balanced on her hip, and greeted Jeanne warmly. "And who's your friend?" she asked, giving Fergus the once-over.

"Fergus McCarrick," he said, extending a hand. "Pleased to meet you. Jeanne and I met in the dog park this morning."

"What an unusual way to meet. Well, I'm Vivienne, Jeanne's younger—"

"Older," Jeanne corrected her.

"Sister. It's nice to meet you, Fergus."

Jeanne, Fergus, Magnus the Great, and Scarlett
followed Vivienne and Everett through the living room,
which was adorned with mahogany antiques, crystal
chandeliers, nineteenth century paintings, and velvet-
upholstered chairs that looked as though they could only
be occupied by someone with a smoking jacket, and out
a set of French doors, into a little walled garden at the
back of the house. In the warmer months, it was
romantic and sophisticated, shaded by a weeping willow
and a grape arbor, home to a small waterfall that
emptied into a pond of Japanese coi. But now the willow
tree was bare, the fountain had been turned off, the coi
were swimming in the warm waters of Everett's
enormous aquarium, and the garden was dominated by a
gigantic mound of snow.

"My ig-oo," Everett said proudly, taking Jeanne by
the hand and demonstrating how she had to crouch into
near-fetal position to fit through the small opening.

"The igloo's bloody brilliant," Jeanne could hear
Fergus remarking to Vivienne outside. "I think your
bairn's going to be quite an architect."

They spent the next hour indulging Everett's whims,
pretending to roast reindeer over a fire and even
fashioning a family of inhabitants for the igloo,
including a snow dog modeled on Scarlett. "Tree legs,"
Everett insisted when Fergus tried to add a fourth.

MAUREEN KLOVERS

Jeanne tried to avoid eye contact with Vivienne, who mouthed the words "I like him" or "He's cute," every time Fergus was distracted by Everett.

"You look like you have some sort of gum-flapping disorder," Jeanne groused, standing next to Vivienne as she pretended to feed the snow dog raspberries, which Everett insisted was the snow dog's favorite food. "Besides, this is purely professional. Fergus is a cyber-security consultant and he's going to help us blow this case wide open."

"Couldn't you mix business and pleasure for once?"

"He's not my type, Viv. I would win if we arm-wrestled."

"I'm not so sure about that. Besides, he has a sexy foreign accent. Doesn't that compensate?"

Jeanne harrumphed and picked up the snow dog's snow turd.

An hour later, Vivienne put Everett down for a nap and the three adults gathered around the kitchen table to discuss the case. Scarlett dozed at Jeanne's feet, while Magnus the Great lay in the corner.

"Here is what we know," Jeanne said as she squirted lemon into her tea. "Algiers's fire alarm went off at approximately eight-fifteen. The camera footage that my friend Lily shot indicates that Ibrahim was alive until at least eight-fourteen, and that he received the single gunshot wound that killed him before eight-sixteen or eight-seventeen, when I found him slumped over in his chair."

"Our working theory," Vivienne interjected, "is that the fire alarm was a clever means of diverting attention from the shooting and possibly a way of covering up the sound of the gunshot."

"The media reports seem to suggest that the police are investigating the incident as a hate crime. The words 'Hagar was a Whore' were spray-painted across the back wall. There are a few possible local culprits—Crusaders Against Sharia, the Virginia Defense League, and Islam Al-Ulaama. And some of these have been pretty active lately." Jeanne swallowed hard. "Today actually," she said, stealing a glance at a glum-looking Fergus. "I didn't want to say anything in front of Everett, Viv, but there's some awful graffiti on the façade of Temple Micah. Fergus and I walked past it on our way here."

"What did it say?" Vivienne asked.

Jeanne looked down at the table. "Hitler should have finished the job."

Vivienne gasped. "That's terrible."

"You're telling me," Fergus said, shaking his head. "This kind of thing happens fairly frequently in Glasgow. My church has had hateful graffiti scrawled on it three or four times. But I didn't expect this kind of thing to happen here."

"So who could have done this?"

"Detective Walker's looking into it, but my money's on Islam Al-Ulaama. Crusaders Against Sharia and the Virginia Defense League aren't particularly anti-Semitic." Jeanne took a sip of tea. "Its leader, Sheikh Al-Ulaama, is particularly fond of issuing fatwas. He wants to convert us all to Islam by force and remove all the 'infidels' from the Holy Land."

Fergus frowned. "Isn't that the nutter who threatened Miss Malaysia?"

"Well, technically," Jeanne corrected him, "he threatened the pageant organizers. He just called her an Islamic harlot."

"Well if I were she," Fergus said, "I would find that threatening enough." He brought his fingers to his temples and massaged them slowly. "So, how's this for a working theory of the crime? Sheikh Al-Ulaama sends his henchmen to Algiers. One sits in the audience, with a gun hidden in his coat, and the other goes around to the back, covers the wall in graffiti, enters through the back door, and starts the fire."

Jeanne shook her head. "The only time the back door was open was when I exited the dressing room to give Yasmina some privacy."

Fergus looked confused. "Why were you in the dressing room?"

"I was getting ready to perform."

Fergus choked and spit out his tea. "I thought you were a barrister, not a belly dancer."

"I'm just an amateur belly dancer. I'm a contract attorney by day. Just like Yasmina was an accountant. Belly dancing doesn't pay much, even if you're great like Yasmina."

"Or you."

Jeanne blushed. "I'm not that good."

"You must be if you perform professionally."

"She's very, very good," Vivienne said in her sultriest voice as Jeanne glared at her, feeling the color rising in her cheeks. Why did Vivienne all of the sudden feel the need to play matchmaker? But Vivienne paid her no attention, adding with a wicked smile, "You should see her perform some time."

Fergus had turned red. "I'd love to see you dance," he said softly.

"Well, I doubt you'll get the chance," Jeanne said briskly, "now that Algiers is no more." She cleared her throat, as if to indicate the end of conversation on that topic. "As I was saying, I propped the door open for a couple of minutes and went out to stand by the dumpsters. But I am positive that I closed the door after me. And the minute you close that door, it locks behind you."

"So he used a crowbar."

"There were no signs of forced entry." Jeanne sighed. "No, he had to have come through the front, like everyone else."

"Okay," Vivienne said. "So two of the sheikh's followers entered through the front with everyone else and—" She frowned. "Mitch was frisked when we entered. It seemed like most of the men were."

Jeanne shrugged. "Maybe the bouncers were in on it. Maybe they were sleeper cells, doing their job for years, just waiting for this mission."

"You always did have a vivid imagination," Vivienne said dryly. "Here's a more likely scenario: they knew and trusted the guys. Maybe they were regulars, even friends."

"Or," Fergus said slowly, "they were frisked and nothing was found. Someone could have hidden the gun in the club for them to retrieve." He leaned forward. "Imagine this. Henchman number one hides out in the bathroom near the stairs, waiting for the perfect opportunity to slip downstairs and start the fire. Henchman number two positions himself with a direct line of sight to Ibrahim, who is after all the owner of this 'Islamic whorehouse.' When the lights are dimmed and the audience's attention is focused on Yasmina's performance, henchman number one sneaks down the stairs and lights the fire. Right when the fire alarm goes off, henchman number two pulls the trigger, instantly killing Ibrahim. He escapes out the front with the rest of the crowd. Meanwhile henchman number one is about to escape out the back when he spots Yasmina coming down the stairs and thinks he has yet another opportunity to show Allah how devout he is. After all, for a Muslim fundamentalist, what's better than killing an Islamic harlot?"

Jeanne found it uncanny how similar his theory was to Mitch's. She could tell it sounded plausible to Vivienne, too, because they all sat there in an uncomfortable silence for several moments.

"But what if," Jeanne conjectured, "Yasmina was actually one of the targets?"

Fergus frowned. "That doesn't make any sense. She wasn't killed until she was in the basement, and they couldn't have known she would flee in the direction of the fire."

"Maybe. But if they knew her personally, they would know how almost manically dedicated she was to belly dance. They might have suspected she would try to rescue the costumes."

"That's an awfully big risk to take."

"Or," Jeanne said, a lump in her throat, "they could have been aiming at her. She was right near Ibrahim the whole time, lavishing attention on him. Sometimes he was only a few inches away from her."

"So you think the gunman meant to shoot her, shot Ibrahim instead, and then his partner got a second crack at her when she went back into the basement?"

"Could be."

"I don't know. It sounds far-fetched to me."

Instead of offering her opinion on Jeanne's theory, Vivienne got up and rummaged around her cabinet until she found a box of animal crackers. "All this deep thinking is giving me the munchies," she said as she stuffed a couple in her mouth. Jeanne had never seen her sister eat in so unladylike a manner; usually, she nibbled on fruit or celery sticks. "Want some?" Vivienne asked, with her mouth half full, as she thrust a big heaping handful onto each of their saucers. "They're delicious. Ever since Mitch left, I realize how good food tastes."

"I take it Mitch is your wanker of an ex," Fergus said, biting into an elephant.

Vivienne nodded vigorously. "A total asshole."

"Sorry," Fergus said as if he were somehow responsible for the misbehavior of his entire sex. He reached deep into the box and pulled out a rhinoceros. "Well, in addition to our barmy sheikh, who else would want to kill Ibrahim, Yasmina, or both of them?"

"She was married to a Dr. Hamza," Jeanne said. "My friend Lily and I talked to him, and Lily thought he might be involved, but I really didn't get that sense. They seemed to have an amicable enough divorce several years ago, and he's happily remarried."

"He could have been putting on an act. Maybe the bloke's seething with jealousy inside."

124

"Maybe. More recently, she had a relationship with a hunky Argentine artist named Rodrigo"—she shot a glance at Vivienne, who blushed—"but his alibi checked out."

"Unfortunately," Jeanne continued, "we don't know much about Ibrahim. Lily thinks that Yousef, Algiers's managing partner, had a motive, but I doubt it. Ibrahim's will hasn't been made public yet, but I doubt Yousef would have inherited his share."

"Did Yousef have the opportunity to kill Ibrahim that night?"

"No." Jeanne shook her head. "At least not directly. He was not only the managing partner, but also one of musicians. He was playing the entire time Yasmina and I danced."

"But he could have hired an arsonist and a hit man," Vivienne pointed out.

Fergus raised an eyebrow. "Or someone with special ops training. There isn't a shortage of those blokes around here."

"Hired hit men aren't free," Jeanne mused. "He would have had to transfer funds somehow." She glanced at Fergus. "Could you hack into Yousef's bank account and see if there are any large transfers in or out?"

Fergus took a sip of tea. "Where does he bank?"

Jeanne sighed. "I don't know. He only pays in cash. And there aren't any banks near the club. There's not much of anything near the club, really."

"How well do you know Yousef?"

"Not that well."

"Well enough that he'd open an email from you?"

She nodded. "Sure."

"Then you've got to send him an email that contains a link to a website that I set up. Something he'd actually open. Maybe an article about this sheikh that could be responsible for the attack. Maybe something about rebuilding after a fire or a grant program to help struggling businesses after a disaster."

"And then?"

"And then, with any luck, he opens it." Fergus smiled. "And I get access to his computer. If he's like most people, he'll log onto an online banking site within a few days. Plus I'll have access to his files, his email. Everything."

Jeanne could hardly believe her ears. "It's that easy?"

Fergus shrugged modestly. "I didn't say it was easy, but it's doable. Anything else?"

"Yes," Jeanne said in a small voice, hoping she wasn't pushing her luck. "I'm going to need Yasmina's phone records too. She was a Verizon customer."

"Did she pay her phone bill online?"

Jeanne thought back to the months she spent on Yasmina's couch. Jasmina seemed to pay all of her bills online, with one eye on her laptop and the other on the belly dance videos on her TV. "I think so."

"Do you know her email user name and password?"

Jeanne winced. "I might have accidentally snuck a peek when she was logging in."

Fergus smiled. "Accidentally, huh? Well write it down and let me get started."

Chapter Twelve

Four days later, three hours into another *Law and Order* marathon with Jerry, Jeanne's phone rang. As she rummaged through her purse to retrieve it, she prayed that it was not Lily. Jeanne could not imagine how her friend would react if she knew that Jeanne was not only talking to Jerry, but actually allowing him into her apartment, even sharing her precious supplies of New York Super Fudge Chunk with him.

To her relief, it was Fergus. "I've got some information for you, love."

She crossed her fingers. "Phone records?"

"I've got Yasmina's phone records and Yousef's bank account statements."

"Fergus, you're the best!" she squealed, which caused Jerry to look up sharply from the murder and mayhem unfolding on the screen. In a slightly more restrained voice, she said, "Meet me at The Tombs in thirty minutes."

Named after an obscure reference in a T.S. Eliot poem, The Tombs was a student dive bar tucked into the bowels of an old townhouse a block from Georgetown University. Despite its name, there was nothing particularly sinister about the place, apart from its location across the street from the *Exorcist* stairs. It was a cozy realm of dark polished wood, shiny red booths, exposed brick walls, and kitschy, black-and-white photos from the twenties.

Fergus and Jeanne slid into a booth near the fireplace, and a young, baby-faced waiter brought them ice water. "Are you folks ready to order?"

Fergus looked up from his menu. "Have you got any haggis?"

"Um...no." The waiter flipped his notebook hesitantly and shifted his weight back and forth. "I'm not sure what that—no, we don't have it." Then, almost as an afterthought, he added, "Sorry, sir."

"Bangers and neeps then?"

"We don't have that either. Perhaps I could interest you in a burger? Or maybe fish and chips? That's British, right?"

"Stovied tatties? Forfar bridies? Hotch-potch?"

Jeanne gave him a swift kick under the table.

"Ooooh! These American lasses have a lot of spirit, don't they?" he croaked to the waiter, who stared at him. "And phenomenal aim. I think my voice just permanently went up a full octave. Maybe just a pint of Guinness, then."

"I'll have a cup of hot tea," Jeanne added, smiling sweetly and handing their menus to the waiter before turning to Fergus with eyes full of wrath.

"I'm just pulling the piss out of him a bit," he explained with a shrug while sinking deeper into the smooth, shiny booth. "You Americans are so serious."

She laughed in spite of herself. "Now tell me what you found out."

"First off," he said, "I hacked into Yousef's bank account. His credit union's IT security is bloody pathetic."

Jeanne looked at him hopefully.

"Sorry, love. No unusual transfers in or out."

The waiter brought their drinks, and Jeanne waited until he left to continue. "And Yasmina's phone calls?"

Fergus pulled a ragged-edged piece of notebook paper from his pocket and unfolded it. "Fifteen calls to Maryam Massoud. Any idea who she is?"

"Not really. They're Facebook friends, and she commented quite a lot on Yasmina's page recently, but Yasmina never mentioned her to me. In Maryam's picture she looks young and pretty, probably Muslim, but that's about all I can tell you."

"Rodrigo Robles, fourteen calls in early and mid-December, and then nothing." He shot her an inquiring glance. "Is that the wacky artist?"

She nodded, and Fergus cleared his throat and continued reading. "Tons of calls—an average of one a day—to Sara Hariri, Aisha Hariri, and Fatima Hariri. Houston area code."

"Sara and Aisha are her sisters. I'm guessing Fatima is her mom."

"A couple of calls a week to Destiny Abrams, Rachel Tanley, Annie Matthews, Tania Stephenson—"

"All belly dancers."

"Three calls to Harding Funeral home, and four more to a Mr. Thomas Harding."

Jeanne frowned. "That's odd. I've never heard of him, and he's not her Facebook friend."

"Maybe Mr. Harding was a secret lover?"

"At this point, nothing would surprise me. I thought she was Jordanian and had never been married." Jeanne sighed. "He definitely sounds like someone worth checking out."

The rest of the names were people that Yasmina had only spoken to once or twice that month, and Jeanne doubted they were of interest.

Out of the corner of her eye, she spied a dark-haired woman. Her long black hair brushed the table as she leaned forward, cradling her phone to her ear, oblivious to her three clearly intoxicated friends. She was turned away from them, and there was something almost furtive about her mannerisms. Whom was she talking to? An ex-boyfriend her friends disapproved of? A friend in trouble?

She reminded Jeanne of Yasmina. And there was something about her position right now that brought back a vivid memory of their last conversation.

"Earth to Jeanne."

She looked up to see Fergus regarding her with amusement.

"I overheard her talking to someone," Jeanne said, "when I walked in the dressing room before our performance. Whom did she call?"

"Populo's Pizza. She called there once before, on the second."

Jeanne smiled smugly. "Well I can tell you one thing. She wasn't ordering a pizza."

"How do you know that?"

"She was a celiac."

"A cel-ee-what?"

"Celiac. She was horribly allergic to gluten. And Populo's is a straight-up traditional pizza joint. No gluten-free crusts."

"And the next step is?"

"For Vivienne to flirt with some clueless pizza boys."

Chapter Thirteen

While Vivienne was making the pepperoni sizzle at Populo's, Lily and Jeanne were preparing for Jeanne's date with Fergus. "What do you think, Everett?" Lily cooed as Jeanne modeled a white cashmere turtleneck sweater and a brown pencil skirt.

"Ug-gy!" Everett clapped his hands and grinned, revealing two front teeth.

"He's right," Lily said. "You look like a sixty-year-old librarian."

Jeanne was not surprised. Most days, she felt like a prim and proper sexagenarian, boring and colorless, especially next to wild child Lily and glamorous Vivienne. She took some comfort in the fact that she did not have cats. At least she would not end up a crazy cat lady.

She plopped onto Flaca. "I'm not sure we should be taking fashion advice from a two-year-old," Jeanne sighed.

"Hey, he's the only male we've got to ask. Here,"—she tossed Jeanne a green wrap blouse—"Try this instead."

Jeanne disappeared behind the Japanese screen. When she emerged, Lily nodded her approval. "What do you think, Everett?"

"Prett-y!"

"But green is Everett's favorite color," Jeanne protested. "It doesn't mean anything. And besides, it's too tight." She stood in front of the mirror and pulled at the bust. Her breasts looked like two perfectly symmetrical green mountains jutting out of a vast mossy plain that rolled slightly at the bottom. She patted her stomach. How perfect—the mountains had foothills.

"The tighter, the better," Lily said. "I only wish I had your boobs. But I think you need some more pizzazz." She unbuckled her wide brown leather belt, whipped out a Swiss army knife, poked two more holes in it, and slung it around Jeanne's waist. Unclasping her turquoise necklace, she fastened it around Jeanne's neck. "*Voilá! C'est magnifique.*"

The phone rang as Lily was putting the finishing touches on Jeanne's make-up.

"Hello?"

"Jeanne, it's me, Viv."

"Hang on a sec. I'm going to put you on speaker. Lily's here."

"Viv, you cougar!" Lily boomed. "What did you find out?"

"Not much," Vivienne sighed. "No one recognized Yasmina or Ibrahim."

"Are you sure?"

"Look, I pulled out all of the stops. I told them Ibrahim was my no-good cheating ex who cheated on me with Yasmina and that I would be very grateful for any ammunition they could give me for my custody case."

"Did you emphasize the 'very grateful' part?"

"Yes, Lily, I—is Everett listening?"

"Yes."

"Well then use your imagination. But trust me, I was convincing. The kid even offered to commit perjury for me, but he said he honestly didn't know anything so I would have to coach him."

"Bummer."

"Is Everett behaving himself?"

"He's been good as gold." Jeanne looked over at Everett's chocolate-stained mouth and decided that her sister didn't need to know that a little bribery was involved.

"Okay. I'll be there in thirty minutes to pick him up."

"Okay. Lily will be here with him because—"

Bzzzz. Bzzzz.

"Oh, that's Fergus. I've got to go."

"Good luck!" Vivienne shouted giddily into the phone.

"Vivienne, don't get too excited." Jeanne tried to sound calm and detached, channeling Ben Stein as he called out "Buehler" for the umpteenth time as she slid an arm into her leather jacket. "It's a little professional quid pro quo. I go to his little concert and he throws in some hacking for free."

Now it was Vivienne's turn to harrumph.

Jeanne raced down to the first floor, Lily and Vivienne's laughter echoing in her ears. This is not a date, she silently repeated to herself, merely a favor for a friend. A ninety-eight pound weakling of a friend with a visa that expires a few months. She bared her teeth at the mirror above the mailboxes and was relieved to discover that the angry woman staring back at her didn't have any telltale super fudge chunks lurking in her incisors. She smoothed her hair behind her ears and turned sideways to admire her silhouette. Lily was a genius when it came to accentuating one's assets.

And then she was supremely irritated. She couldn't remember the last time she gave herself the once-over before going out with Lily.

"A woman needs a man like a fish needs a bicycle," she muttered, parroting the old Gloria Steinem line. Scowling, she stomped out the door.

She was halfway down the concrete stairs leading to the street when she heard a low, long whistle behind her, followed by a familiar brogue. "You look beautiful."

She spun around to find Fergus, perched on the ledge to the left of the door, a battered violin case beside him. Glinting beneath the streetlights, his eyes flitted appreciatively over her, lingering for a moment on her chest. His gaze was searing, and Jeanne's mouth suddenly felt very dry. She prayed for Jerry to come barreling down the stairs, ranting about the latest developments on Fox News, or for old Mrs. Berenstein to appear, grumbling darkly about Russian spies poisoning her Siamese cat Tolstoy. It was one thing to be appreciated and noticed in costume. That was a performance. But it was quite another to receive this kind of attention while merely playing herself. She was not sure that it suited her.

And then, it was as if a law of physics took over and the heat transfer reversed itself. First, Fergus's neck began to redden. Then, it began to spread upwards, wiping the mirth and wonder from his face and replacing it with a look of apprehension, maybe even terror. He gulped and stuffed a hand in one pocket, jangling his keys. "It's not that bad, I hope. Spending the evening with me, that is. Even if the company's lame, the music will be good."

He glanced up at her, then away. He wore that wounded puppy look, the one Scarlett gave her when Jeanne stepped on her paw by accident. It must be her scowl; she was sure she looked really pissed off. She made a conscious effort to relax her face muscles and assume a look of beatific neutrality. "I'm sure both the music and the company will be lovely."

Heaving the violin case over his shoulder, he skipped down the stairs towards her. "You sound like my mum," he said, "when she is invited to a cream tea."

They both laughed and Jeanne slugged him on the arm. "Come on, Mozart. We are going to be late."

Nothing more was said of Jeanne's transformation from frumpy sleuth to comely patron of the arts as they strolled past the floodlit National Cathedral and through the tony Cleveland Park neighborhood. By the time they arrived at Nanny O'Brien's, Jeanne's heart rate was almost back to normal.

"Guinness?"

Jeanne nodded and Fergus slapped the bartender on the back. "Two pints of Guinness, Sean."

Sean nodded in Jeanne's direction. "Who's your new lady friend?"

Jeanne bristled. The way he said "new" made it sound as though she were not the first. Or perhaps even second or third. "Jeanne Pelletier," she snapped. "And I am not his lady friend. I am his friend. His associate in fact."

"We're working on a murder investigation together," Fergus added.

Sean's green eyes crinkled around the edges and a hint of a smile played on his lips. Arching a shaggy eyebrow, he set two frothing glasses down on the bar. "You're a real Sherlock Holmes, are you?"

"She's Sherlock," Fergus corrected him, shaking his head. "I'm just Watson." He winked and put an arm around Jeanne's waist. "And she's right. She's no lady."

Sean laughed. "Fergus, I think you've met your match."

"I hope she's met hers."

"Why'd you tell him that?" Jeanne hissed in his ear as he steered her towards the back room.

"To support your claim that we are associates, not lovers. That's what you wanted, right?"

She felt his fingers press into her back. He dodged to avoid a gaggle of giggling blondes, and his cheek brushed against hers. It was clean-shaven for a change and she caught a whiff of something. Was he actually wearing cologne?

"Of course," she said quickly. "But I don't want him blabbing and having the police think I'm too interested in the case. My last interview with them didn't go so well."

"Relax, love. Bartenders are like priests. Sworn to secrecy."

He gave her a little push and she took a seat in the corner. Fergus joined the other musicians at the table.

As they tuned their instruments, Jeanne savored the sensation of being in one of the few places in D.C. that had not succumbed to the onslaught of yuppification. The floor was cheap linoleum, the ceiling was painted black, and the pock-marked logs wedged into the half-timbered walls appeared to have been harvested from a rotting barn, not a fair trade eco-forestry project in Borneo. Light fell in dim little pools like the flickering flames from a peat fire. A crinkled sign was taped to the ladies' room door: 'Doorknob Broken—Use at Your Own Risk.' The sign looked as though it had been there for years.

She felt much more at home here than in other bars. The beautiful people bars, she called them. They were the kind of place where people like Vivienne and Mitch met, throbbing with great expectations, a current of insecurity flowing beneath the rivers of alcohol. The drinks were overpriced and overhyped, the cleavage abundant, the conversations inane. As far as Jeanne could tell, most people shouted a few words about their excruciatingly boring (but well-paying) jobs and then proceeded to talk about how drunk they were. It was almost a competition—they compared notes about who was a bigger lush as if they were discussing their annual raises. She found it all quite dull. But, then again, no one ever seemed to find her sober conversations about Tuvan throat singing or Jane Goodall's work very scintillating. Small talk was not her strong suit. Overgrown frat boys did perk up at her mention of belly dancing, but that was about it.

She took another sip of Guinness. She loved its earthy, malty flavor and deep chocolate brown color. But she never allowed herself more than two, and then only on a full stomach. Most of the time she nursed just one for hours. Jeanne had never been drunk or even tipsy. She never allowed herself to lose control.

The opening chords of a reel jolted her out of her reverie. She watched with rapt attention as Fergus fiddled at a furious pace, keeping time to the music. A balding heavyset man on his left strummed the banjo, while a petite brunette played the flute. No one had sheet music, and they rarely even looked at each other. Somehow they instinctually all felt the same beat.

The next piece was slower and more somber, the plucky little banjo cast aside in favor of the mournful bagpipes. Fergus laid his fiddle in its case and picked up the *bodhran*. Jeanne watched as he rubbed his left hand along the inner surface, the fingers of his right hand strafing the outside. There were subtle shifts in sound depending on the relative positions of his right and left hands, and whether he used his palm, his finger, or each of his fingers in quick succession. It reminded Jeanne of

Yousef playing the *tabla*, and that reminded her of Yasmina.

Not tonight, she told herself. Tonight I will not think about Yasmina.

"Fergus, that was wonderful!" Jeanne stood in her tiny galley kitchen, stirring the hot chocolate, relieved she was able to actually say so with sincerity and enthusiasm. She was worried that he might deliver a plodding, leaden performance after which she would struggle to come up with something positive to say.

"I'm glad you enjoyed it." He paced across her floor, seemingly unsure what to do or say. For a moment, it occurred to Jeanne that he might be as nervous as she was. But then she remembered Sean's words: *Who's your new lady friend?* He's a playboy, she reminded herself. He'd probably be shocked to know that he's the only male that's been in my apartment outside of Jerry, Everett, and the plumber.

He reached down to pet Scarlett, who licked him across the face. He laughed and sat on the edge of Flaca, drumming his fingers, as if he might need to spring up any moment. "Nice couch."

"Shitty couch, you mean. Everyone hates it. Lily says it smells like a Bolivian dog named Flaca. Vivienne said it makes her feel like throwing up."

142

"I like it. It reminds me of home."

"Do your parents have a Bolivian dog named Flaca?"

"Nay. Just a sheepdog named Seamus."

She poured the hot chocolate into two mugs, handed him one, and set the other on the coffee table. "Well your parents must have impeccable taste in couches."

"The best."

She unzipped her boots and kicked them off. There was a run in her nylons, her big toe was sticking out, and even by the dim light of her Ikea lamp—with two of the three bulbs burned out—she spotted a forest of wiry black hairs. Cursing under her breath, she wondered if she should put her boots back on, but then she reasoned that would only call more attention to her legs. She could almost hear her mother's voice telling her to be more like Vivienne; at that exact instant, she wished she were. Vivienne would shave even if she were wearing a burqa.

"Are you okay?" he asked, and she realized she was standing on one foot, staring at her boots.

"Terrific," she trilled and then realized she sounded a tad too enthusiastic. "Just fine."

Taking a seat on the other end of Flaca, she tucked her hairy legs underneath her. Jerry's TV rumbled through the wall, but for once it was not loud enough to drown out the ticking of the clock. She counted forty-seven seconds of silence. What did one talk about on a non-date date? She tried to think of what Vivienne would say. "You're very talented," she finally said, channeling her sister. Vivienne had always dated the football captain, the basketball star, the class president. And as far as she could tell, Vivienne's dating technique mostly involved batting her eyelashes and telling her date how great he was. There was also a hair-pat involved. It was very slow, so as to accentuate her soft, shiny, long hair.

He snorted, gesturing to the diplomas on the wall. "You're talented. Georgetown Law. Phi Beta Kappa. I bet you were humanitarian of the year and head cheerleader too."

"Oh, no, that was Vivienne."

"She is very pretty," he conceded, "if you are into that whole leggy supermodel thing." He picked up a framed photo from the bookcase next to Flaca. The photo was of a toddler in brown corduroy overalls with a yellow daisy emblazoned on the front. Wisps of white-blond hair were kept in place with little pink barrettes, and she regarded the camera with a broad toothy smile. "Is this her?"

Her heart skipped a beat. Why hadn't she buried the photo at the bottom of the drawer? She should have known he would ask about it. He was so perceptive—too perceptive. She chalked it up to his artistic temperament, or maybe being European. And, at that moment, it was not a virtue.

She swallowed hard and stared at a spot on the wall behind him, trying to keep her voice as even as possible. "No, that's my other sister, Annie."

"Does she live around here?"

Jeanne shook her head, racking her brain for some new topic of conversation. The crisis in Syria? The national debt? Out of the corner of her eye, she saw him watching her intently, and she knew he wouldn't be so easily distracted. She contemplated telling him some outrageous lie—that Annie was a circus trainer in Australia, a yak herder in Mongolia, or a midwife in Haiti—but she could not bring herself to lie about Annie. But neither could she bring herself to speak the truth out loud, especially to a man she had met in a dog park less than a week ago.

The phone rang. Under normal circumstances, Jeanne would have let it ring, but now she sprang up and leapt over the coffee table, digging through her purse with great alacrity as through she were expecting a call from the president. "Excuse me, Fergus. Hello?"

"Good evening, ma'am. This is the operator. Will you accept a collect call from the Willamette Women's Correctional Institution?"

She cursed under her breath. How could she have been so careless? She had let down her guard, forgotten to check caller ID. She was usually vigilant about checking it, especially on Sunday nights. For some reason, that's when most of the calls came.

"Ma'am?" The voice on the other end was hard-edged and impatient.

"Yes. I mean, yes, I can hear you, that is. But I can't," she said, and then added more firmly, "I won't." Her hand shook as she snapped her phone shut.

"Someone soliciting something?"

"Binoculars." Jeanne was perpetually amazed how much easier it was for her to tell outrageous lies than to make pleasant small talk. "A Future Ornithologists of America chapter from Mississippi."

"Really? I bought some from them last week." He laughed. "You don't need to tell me who called, Jeanne. It's none of my business. We don't know each other that well. Yet."

The word "yet" hung in the air, heavy with possibility.

She had never met anyone who saw through her so easily, which was both intriguing and unsettling. He was witty and smart and kind, but he was also a playboy with a few months left on his visa. And most importantly, he was just too damn normal. "I'm exhausted," she said, feigning a yawn. "I ought to go to sleep."

"I like you, Jeanne. A lot."

"I like you too, Fergus." She swallowed and looked him straight in the eye, trying to look as firm and resolute as possible. "As a friend."

He leaned in and kissed her on the cheek. "I'm very persistent, Jeanne. And for the record, I prefer brainy, belly dancing barristers to leggy supermodel types." And without another word, he headed out the door.

Chapter Fourteen

Jeanne's morning routine normally consisted of twenty minutes of ignoring her alarm clock, five minutes of rooting around for the cleanest dirty clothes she had, and twenty minutes of beating her hair into submission. Then she was off for a quick walk with Scarlett, followed by scarfing down two chocolate-drenched biscotti while watching *The Today Show*. She knew she should eat better, but she reasoned that her mental health was just as important as her physical health. And there was no denying that chocolate made her feel good.

Over the past two weeks, she had added a new element to her morning routine: checking the Arlington County Clerk of Court's website to see if Ibrahim's will had been posted.

Today, she typed in the address absentmindedly as Al Roker delivered the weather report, who was warning of yet another "wintry mix" that was going to descend on the East Coast.

Crossing her fingers as she scrolled down the page, she hoped the forecast was a good omen. She scrolled past the names of dozens of deceased Arlingtonians, their Anglo names and tony addresses suggesting that they lived to advanced age, puttering about in their little gardens, taking the Metro to the Kennedy Center for an occasional night of opera.

Ibrahim Abu Ali. It was printed in little blue letters, like every other name, which sanitized it somehow, making it seem as though his death was neither unusual nor violent. Bureaucracy had a way of doing that.

Holding her breath, she clicked on his name. She scrolled through, now heedless to the storm warnings that flashed across her television. There could have been a hurricane raging outside and she wouldn't have noticed. All of her energy, all of her attention, was focused on one thing: identifying his heirs.

Except that there were not heirs. Not in the plural, at least. There was just one heir, and it was a name she had seen before: Maryam Massoud.

According to his will, she was the daughter of his deceased sister Fatima. He apparently had no other family, no friends, no interest in donating anything to charity.

Jeanne had no doubt that she was the same Maryam Massoud who had called Yasmina "Mother Hen." The same Maryam Massoud that Yasmina had called fifteen times.

There was one other name that caught her attention, and she wasted no time in dialing his number.

"Good morning," the perky voice on the other end intoned. She almost sounded like a robot. "This is Peters, Peters, and Cohen. How may I direct your call?"

"Blake Jensen, please."

"May I ask who is calling?"

"Jeanne Pelletier. I'm an old friend of his from law school."

She was treated to three minutes of jazzy hold music before a familiar bass with a Southern twang boomed across the line. Blake was the son of a sheriff from the swamps of East Texas, and he never let you forget it. She moved the phone a foot from her ear.

"Jeannie! It's so good to hear from the woman whose notes got me through law school. How the hell are you doing?"

She sighed. "I've been better. I'm still toiling in the bowels of Higgins, Higgins, and Applebaum—"

"Bastards. If they had any sense, they'd make you permanent. Hell, if we were hiring, I'd hire you. Always hire someone smarter than you. That's what my grand pappy always said."

"—and I'm working freelance on a murder investigation."

He let out a low, slow whistle. "Well that there's a humdinger of a project." He lowered his voice, and she moved the phone back against her ear. "Any particular murder?"

"Your client, Ibrahim Abu Ali."

"I was afraid you was gonna say that. You know I can't tell you anything."

Jeanne was not normally in the business of calling in favors. She typically dispensed them freely, just grateful to be of service. But today she was making an exception. "Don't be silly," she said breezily. "You can and you will. I got you through law school. Now all I want to know is whether his business partner Yousef or any other person had a life insurance policy on Ibrahim, and whether Yousef and Ibrahim ever executed a buy-sell agreement in the event of either of their deaths. I will never attribute anything you say to you, and if the police ever ask why we talked, you can honestly say that I called to inquire how much it would be for you to draft a will for me."

"So ask me," he said.

"Ask you what?"

"How much it would be to draft a will."

She decided to play along. "How much would it be for you to draft a will for me?"

"With the family and friends discount and the cute dog discount—you've still got Scarlett, right?"

"Right."

"Well with the family and friends discount, plus the cute dog discount, applied to Peters, Peters, and Cohen's extortionist rates—which of course the associates only see a fraction of—it'll come to about a thousand for a standard will, including setting up a trust for Scarlett."

"I'll have to think about that," Jeanne said, even though she knew very well that she wouldn't. She had nothing to bequeath to anyone, she didn't plan on dying any time soon, and in any case, if she wanted a will, she would draft it herself.

"Well we certainly hope you consider Peters, Peters, and Cohen for your legal needs." He cleared his throat. "Now, regarding your question, Yousef and Ibrahim both had taken out life insurance policies against each other, and there was a buy-sell agreement in place that required the surviving partner to purchase the decedent's interest in the business from the decedent's heirs."

"So in other words," Jeanne said, "Yousef is going to receive a large insurance payment, which he will use to purchase Ibrahim's share in the business from Maryam Massoud. So because of Ibrahim's death, Yousef will end up controlling one hundred percent of the business and Maryam will wind up with a pile of money."

He laughed, but it was a mirthless, anxious laugh. She could tell that his suspicions mirrored her own. "Well, Jeannie, there was a reason I chose you as a study partner. You sure are a smart cookie."

*   *   *   *

There were always several people on the #92 bus—the bus Jeanne took to the studio—who talked to themselves. They debated whether the president wanted to see them later that day, whether the devil was telling them to do this or that, or whether the CIA really had implanted a chip in their butt. The ones who thought the CIA controlled them were the most tragically interesting. They were dreadfully afraid of the two red eyes glowering from the top of the Washington Monument (which some, perhaps more sane, individuals believed were innocuous warning lights for aircraft); it was a sign that someone was always watching.

The #32 bus was totally different: a sea of familiar faces that looked blankly past Jeanne on her commute each day. It was as if they had never seen her before, and maybe they hadn't. They were wrapped up in their own world. Mostly a virtual world, full of tweets and IMs and little buzzing contraptions, it came with its own, unique soundtrack. Everyone had an earbud cord dangling from one ear, a cell phone glued to the other.

Sometimes Jeanne wondered if the second crowd really was saner. They looked so cold, so lonely, wrapped up in their identical black trench coats, heads down, deaf to the world.

These were the thoughts that often preoccupied Jeanne on her morning commute. But today was different. She skipped to the bus stop, her scarf flying behind her, swinging her briefcase like some kind of deranged Mary Poppins figure. She boomed a cheerful "good morning" to the driver, squeezed her way to the back of the bus, and clung to the little plastic hanger strap.

Her lips curled into a smug little smile. She had proof that both Maryam and Yousef had strong financial motives, and she couldn't wait to tell Lily.

When they arrived thirty minutes later at Farragut Square, she hopped off the bus, ran up to her office, flung off her coat, and hurried to meet Lily in the seventh floor bathroom. But to her chagrin, Jeanne could barely get a word in edgewise; Lily was intent on interrogating her about Fergus. As if there had been no murder, no fire. As if Yasmina were not dead. As if Jeanne's love life were the most important thing on the planet.

"How was your date?" Lily asked breathlessly.

"With Fergus?"

"No, with Charles Manson. Of course with Fergus."

"His band was very good."

"You know that's not what I mean."

"The Guinness was excellent too."

"Jeanne!"

"Lily, there's nothing to tell. Seriously, nothing happened. It wasn't bad, and it wasn't great. Just a little music, a little conversation. Very platonic." She looked Lily straight in the eye, hoping she was convincing.

"Are you going to see him again?"

"Well it depends on your definition of 'see.' I don't plan on going on another date. But, of course, we'll continue to work together on this case." Jeanne tried to look and sound as business-like as possible. Even though she considered Lily to be her best friend, there were some things that she couldn't share with Lily. And those things included the reasons she was reluctant to get involved with Fergus.

Lily shot her a skeptical look, but Jeanne ignored it. "Enough about Fergus. Ibrahim's will was posted online today."

She could tell she had finally gotten Lily's attention. "And the heir is...?"

"Maryam."

Lily smiled. "It sounds like we are going to have to pay her a visit."

Chapter Fifteen

That Saturday, Jeanne and Lily cruised through Old Town Fairfax in Lily's enormous Crown Vic. "We're in luck!" Jeanne exulted as they flew past the old courthouse, its cannons gleaming in the sunlight. "Maryam has got to be one of the most prolific tweeters ever. Five minutes ago: 'Studying for calc exam in Fenwick. Ugh.' Two minutes ago: 'Got a latte to keep me awake.'"

"So we're looking for a Middle Eastern woman with a calculus book and a latte. That should narrow it down."

They wound their way past the endless lawns and parking lots that sprawled on either side of Patriot Circle before pulling into a tight parking spot near George Mason University's auditorium.

The day was crisp and clear, the piles of snow blindingly white in the bright afternoon sunshine. A pedestrian path led them into the heart of campus, which Jeanne doubted would ever win any awards. Modern and utilitarian, lined with boxy brown buildings whose flat rooflines cut angry horizontal slashes against the clear blue sky, it had sprung from the uninspired imagination of engineers and transportation planners focused solely on moving commuter students as efficiently as possible from car to class to car once more. There was not a picturesque cobblestone or gargoyle in sight, not a speck of ivy hinting at hallowed halls of learning, not a single moss-covered gravestone or secluded garden.

Fenwick Library was a tall, brown brick building fronted by a flat expanse of lawn. The study lounge was tucked away on the second floor, overflowing with grungy nineteen-year-olds, empty coffee cups, and stacks of musty old books, the soundtrack a constant click-clacking of laptops and the occasional quickly-hushed whisper.

As Jeanne scanned the room, she was struck by the diversity of the student body: tall, slender Ethiopians; stocky and mustachioed Latino men; calculator-wielding Southeast Asians. There was a bewildering assortment of headgear: baseball hats, stocking caps, Sikh turbans, yarmulkes, and a surprising number of Islamic headscarves, some snug and black, others casually slung over the shoulders, tufts of dark hair peeking out from beneath rich, multi-hued silks.

"Check out the fashionista at five o'clock," Lily whispered to Jeanne. "And check out the bling. She's engaged to some big shot."

Lily motioned towards a pretty young woman sprawled out on an old gray couch, clad in knee-high brown suede boots, cream tights, and a belted taupe sweater dress. She had the same dark curly hair and slim build as the woman in Maryam Massoud's profile. Absentmindedly brushing a mass of glossy dark chestnut brown curls off her neck to reveal enormous gold hoop earrings, the woman was engrossed in her textbook. A Starbucks cup lay on the table next to her, and a knock-off Coach purse lay beside her, a plain black headscarf tied around the strap. A diamond ring on her left hand glinted in the late afternoon sunlight that filtered through the curtains.

Tiptoeing up behind her, Jeanne and Lily peered over her shoulder at a page filled with derivatives. When the young woman turned her head to the side, Jeanne froze. She would have recognized those long eyelashes, aquiline nose, and pouty lips anywhere. "That's the young woman from the funeral," she mouthed to Lily.

They watched as Maryam began texting furiously on her phone, then shoved her books into a navy blue backpack, put on a bright red wool coat, and slung the backpack and purse over her shoulder. Jeanne motioned for Lily to follow her.

They kept a respectful distance as Maryam skipped down the stairwell. For someone so sophisticated and mature-looking, she had a rather girlish spring in her step.

It did not take long for Jeanne and Lily to discover the source of this giddiness. A few hundred feet from the entrance, Maryam hurled herself into the outstretched arms of a tall, broad-shouldered young man with curly golden brown hair. He wore blue jeans and a black leather jacket. Throwing his arms around her waist, he hoisted her into the air and gave her a twirl. Jeanne and Lily could hear a couple of shrieks and belly laughs, but the words themselves were indistinct. And then the twirling morphed into an eye-popping display of public affection.

"How nauseating," Lily said. "There is so much tongue action going on there one of them is liable to pry a molar loose."

"She's going to need to re-apply her lipstick."

"I wouldn't say she looks like a grieving family member, would you?"

Jeanne shook her head.

Ten minutes later, the greedy lip-sucking had devolved into more demure Eskimo kisses. "Time to make our move," Jeanne murmured.

Maryam and her paramour were oblivious to Jeanne and Lily's approach and looked up, startled, as Lily called Maryam's name.

"I'm sorry...do we know each other?" She turned to face them, with furrowed brow, and Jeanne couldn't help but gape at her long fake eyelashes, heavily rouged cheeks, inky black eyeliner, and startling plum eyelids. Maryam was breathtakingly beautiful, but not in a natural way: more like a beauty queen or reality TV star. Jeanne glanced down at her cast-off headscarf. She was definitely rebelling. But against whom?

"I'm Lily Garcia, and this is my friend Jeanne Pelletier. We're friends of Yasmina's from belly dance."

Jeanne watched Maryam closely. At Lily's mention of Yasmina, she blinked and tensed her jaw. There was a long, awkward silence, during which Maryam stared stonily ahead.

"We understand you're a friend of hers too," Jeanne continued. "We saw your posts on her Facebook page."

"She was a friend of my sister's," Maryam said quickly, squeezing her companion's hand. "Although we were in touch recently."

"Oh. Does your sister live in the area too?"

"She died of appendicitis when I was six. I don't remember her all that well."

"What's this about?" her companion demanded, his liquid brown eyes flashing. With his long curly lashes and elegant, slightly curved nose, he was almost too pretty to be a boy. "What happened to Maryam's uncle and Yasmina was tragic. But we're leaving it in the hands of the police. We've told them everything we know and now it's up to them to solve this."

Jeanne pursed her lips, racking her brain for a lie that would both seem truthful and induce them to divulge information. He had a good point. Why should they tell her anything? They were persons of interest in a murder investigation. And she knew she wouldn't have volunteered anything to some nosy young attorney.

"We were hoping," Jeanne finally said, "that you might have some items for our memorial to Yasmina at the studio. You know—photos, stories, that sort of thing."

Maryam's face softened and she released her grip on her fiancé's hand. "I'm afraid I don't really have anything. We only reconnected a few months ago."

"I see. We understand, of course. We were just hoping you could help. Well, thank you, for your time, Maryam and...?"

"Ari." He shook Jeanne's hand firmly. "Ari Fleishman."

"Ari. And congratulations on your engagement. That certainly is quite a rock."

A shy smile spread across Maryam's face as she and Ari strolled away from them, hand in hand.

When they were out of earshot, Jeanne turned to Lily. "Are you thinking what I'm thinking?"

"Star-crossed lovers?"

"Her family is clearly conservative, I am guessing, based on the headscarf she keeps at the ready. She's marrying a guy named Ari—"

"The name does sound Jewish," Lily said.

"—which her uncle couldn't have been too happy about. Except I am guessing," Jeanne said, "that he didn't know. I don't recall seeing that rock on her finger at the funeral."

"So either she wasn't engaged then, or she only wears her engagement ring on selective occasions."

"Exactly," Jeanne said. "And based on the fact that her moniker for Yasmina was 'Mother Hen,' I am guessing that Yasmina, if she knew about it, was not too pleased. Maryam may have suspected that Yasmina would tell Ibrahim, giving Maryam—"

"Or Ari."

"—a reason to want both Ibrahim and Yasmina out of the way."

They started down the path back to the parking lot. "Well if we're right," Lily mused, "they sure one-upped Romeo and Juliet. Why commit suicide when you can just kill your uncle, inherit all of his money, and live happily ever after?"

*   *   *   *

Jeanne's inner civil libertarian was horrified to
discover that there were dozens of websites from which
you could gather personal information on just about
anyone. But her inner sleuth was morbidly fascinated.

She didn't know whether to laugh or cry as she
perused the testimonials on each site. "I found out my
boyfriend of two years was a registered sex offender!"
Rebecca R. informed the users of one particularly
sensational site. "Thanks to your website, I tracked down
my baby's daddy and am finally collecting child
support," advertised another.

She laughed out loud as she was asked to specify
whether she was using the site for "dating" or for
"reconnecting with an old friend" during the registration
process. She presumed that they were not implying that
their users actually seek out criminals for dates.

"What's so funny?" Kara demanded from the other
side of the wall.

"A Texas Supreme Court case," Jeanne replied as she
entered her credit card number. She decided to pay
$23.99 for the monthly "heavy user" fee, which would
entitle her to unlimited background checks. She smiled
as she imagined what she might dig up on annoying
Kara. "You know how they cling to their guns and
religion," she said by way of a cryptic explanation,
knowing full well that Kara was a huge—one might say
rabid—Obama fan.

She typed in Maryam's name first. There was nothing out of the ordinary in her profile. She had no gun license, no criminal record. She'd never been married or divorced. About the only interesting thing about her was that Ibrahim Abu Ali was her only listed relative over the age of twenty-five, which implied that her parents were either abroad or dead.

But Ari Fleischman's profile was another matter. She remembered his face as it had been two days ago at George Mason—delicate, almost beautiful—and tried to reconcile this image with the hollow eyes that stared out at her from the screen. In this photo, his eyes were glassy, and his full lips were drawn into a thin, sneering line. His hair appeared two or three shades darker, dirty and matted against his forehead. He had the look of a hardened criminal, and maybe a junkie to boot.

According to the white lettering beneath the mug shot, it had been taken three years ago, shortly after his eighteenth birthday. He'd been booked in Fairfax County.

She scrolled quickly to the charges and then dialed Lily's extension.

"Speak to me."

"Possession with intent to distribute," Jeanne read off the screen. "Heroin."

Chapter Sixteen

Fergus and Jeanne reconnoitered at The Tombs at ten o'clock that evening so that Jeanne could give him the scoop. Even though she had so much to tell him, she found herself strangely tongue-tied at first. Every time she looked into his eyes, his words echoed in her head. *I prefer brainy, belly dancing barristers to leggy supermodel types.*

The silence between them was oppressive, and she got the sense that he had decided to let her be the one to break it. She felt as though he were challenging her, hoping to trap her into revealing her true feelings. But she was too smart for that.

She busied herself with surveying their convivial surroundings. Georgetown undergraduates bellied up to the bar, flirting shamelessly, and bearded, bespectacled professors huddled in the corner booths, deep in intense conversations. The enormous brick fireplace roared and crackled, the flames a mesmerizing kaleidoscope of fiery orange, golden yellow, and the occasional wisp of electric blue. Her left side was hot to the touch. But most of all she felt Fergus's intense blue-gray eyes boring into her.

"Scoping out your snogging options?" he inquired. Jeanne thought she detected the slightest bit of irritation creeping into his voice.

The question startled her. "Of course not."

"You asked me here."

"Right," Jeanne said. "To fill you in on the case." She cleared her throat. "It turns out the mysterious Maryam Massoud is Ibrahim's sole heir. She gets his interest in the business, which Yousef will buy out with the life insurance policy he has on Ibrahim."

"So Maryam had a motive to kill Ibrahim." He took a sip of Guinness. "Did she have any reason to kill Yasmina?"

"Lily and I paid Maryam a visit. She claims not to have been especially close to Yasmina—she says Yasmina was a friend of her sister, who died of appendicitis when she was young."

"But of course she's lying. Yasmina made fifteen calls to her in the last two months."

"She did say they'd reconnected recently," Jeanne mused. "But fifteen calls sounds excessive."

"What was her expression like when you mentioned Yasmina?"

"Tense. But then everybody who knew Yasmina is probably on edge."

He swilled his beer in his glass. "Do you think she's hiding something?"

"I don't know," Jeanne said with a shrug. "I do know, however, that she's newly engaged to a guy named Ari Fleishman, whom we had the pleasure of meeting." She decided to spare Fergus the details of their nauseating public display of affection.

"What's Ari like?"

"Cute," Jeanne said. "Adorable, really. Also possibly Jewish, which her family may not have been too crazy about. And, according to NailHisAss.com, a felon. Convicted of heroin possession with intent to distribute."

"How big of a drug dealer was he?"

"Not that big. He got off pretty easy, so I'll bet he was just a junkie who supported his habit by selling to friends."

Fergus let us a long, long whistle. "Well, he certainly stands to benefit from Ibrahim's death if he marries Maryam. You think he's the triggerman?"

"Maybe. Or maybe Ari hired a hit man. Can you look into it?"

"Aye." He peered over his glass at her. "So you don't think it's a hate crime anymore?"

"I don't know. Maybe Maryam and Ari saw all of the news stories about Sheikh Al-Ulaama and decided that a hate crime would be a convenient cover. But Lily and I are going to keep pursuing the hate crime angle."

"And how are you going to do that?"

"There's a demonstration tomorrow," she said. "And I have a feeling Sheikh Al-Ulaama might show up as a counter-protester."

At nine-seventeen the next morning, Jeanne ducked inside the ninth floor restroom of Higgins, Higgins, and Applebaum, a brown Whole Foods bag tucked under her arm. She was never particularly pleased by the sight of her reflection, but this morning it was downright horrifying, her mousy brown hair standing on end in an unruly ball of frizz. No matter how many times she smoothed her hair behind her ears, clamping a barrette firmly in place, it kept popping back up.

She dug a tube of lip gloss out of her frayed purse and casually dropped it on the floor, then bent down to reconnoiter. There was a pair of sensible brown pumps in the first stall. In the handicapped stall, she spied a pair of red suede ankle boots studded with what looked like tiny thumb tacks.

Swinging open the door to the latter, she slipped inside, placed the Whole Foods bag on the floor, and raised her hand in a silencing gesture. Lily hopped up on the toilet and waited for the sound of toilet flushing, followed by the slamming of the heavy oak door, before impatiently asking, "What's in the bag?"

"Your costume."

"My costume?" Lily sputtered. "For what?"

"The Crusaders Against Sharia demonstration." Jeanne checked her watch. "Which starts in ten minutes."

Smiling, she added, "And trust me, you're going to want to put it on at the Starbucks across the street."

As they sauntered past the Treasury Department, trying to look as nonchalant as possible, Lily adjusted her blond wig. She wore several layers of old bulky sweaters and beige elastic waist pants. "I look like a beluga whale with a bouffant hair-do," she muttered.

"Perfect," Jeanne quipped. "No one from Higgins, Higgins, and Applebaum will recognize you during the perp walk."

"How come I get to be the dowdy middle-aged journalist from Oklahoma named,"—she fished a laminated press badge out of her pocket— "Bertha Wu, and you get to be a nubile young intern named Charlotte?"

"There's nothing wrong with the name Bertha. I had a third-grade teacher named Bertha."

"Was she as big as a house?"

"Yes, but—"

"I rest my case." Lily peered over the edge of her cat glasses at Jeanne. "You know, with the red hair and the tight skirt, you look a little like Vivienne."

Jeanne laughed. "That's the first time anyone's ever said that."

Their pace slowed as they approached the White House. The usual denizens were there, of course. From his perch on a sun-drenched park bench, the disheveled homeless man, naked save for a loincloth, was holding court for a group of bemused tourists. The wizened old woman continued her lonely vigil, mumbling dark prognostications of nuclear holocaust beneath photos of the victims of Hiroshima and Nagasaki; she had been there as long as Jeanne could remember.

But today they were joined by several dozen Crusaders Against Sharia. They were an odd mix: bare-faced housewives with short, no-nonsense hair, children balanced on their hips; flaccid middle-aged men stuffed into matching white T-shirts emblazoned with red Jerusalem crosses; and a few broad-shouldered young men sporting crew cuts. All eyes were focused on their leader, an imposing man who struck Jeanne as both ridiculous and frightening. He strutted about in full Crusader regalia, chain mail and helmet glinting in the sun, his tunic flapping in the breeze. In a deep, rumbling baritone, he ticked off all of the terrible things that would come to pass if Congress did not pass a law forbidding any federal court from considering sharia.

"Imagine," he thundered, "being told you can't eat hot dogs on the Fourth of July. Imagine our women forced to stay at home. Imagine us unable to teach our children about Jesus. Imagine an America where we all live in caves, where we live in fear instead of in the love of Jesus Christ."

His acolytes nodded vigorously, their eyes brimming with rage. His voice cracking with emotion, he put his megaphone down for a moment and nodded sagely in the direction of his followers. "Yes, my friends, believe it." His cadence was slow and measured, and his voice dropped to an anguished stage whisper. "That will be the end result if we are not vigilant. Baltimore will be the next Beirut, Boston the next Baghdad. Our churches will be destroyed and turned into mosques. That's why we need to follow the example set by our brethren in Louisiana, Tennessee, and Arizona and urge Congress to pass a federal law banning federal judges from applying sharia law in U.S. courts."

The crowd cheered and, from the back of the crowd, a tremulous soprano voice burst into "America the Beautiful," and the rest of group soon joined in. "O beautiful, for spacious skies, for amber waves of grain...."

Lily nudged Jeanne. "I'm freezing. Let's start the interviews."

They scanned the crowd for prospects and decided on a pair of sandy-haired men near the back. "Howdy, boys!" Lily spoke from deep within her chest, as though she were a lifelong smoker in an emphysema ward. She flashed her press badge. "Bertha Wu, Oklahoma City Bee Gazette. This here's my useless assistant Lottie who got hired because her tush looks better than mine in a mini-skirt." She slapped Jeanne's rear.

"Ow!"

"She does fetch coffee, though. Anyway, boys, I've got a couple of questions for you, if you don't mind."

The shorter one looked at his companion, who nodded his assent. "Shoot."

"What was your reaction to the news that a federal judge overturned Oklahoma's law forbidding state judges from applying sharia in court decisions?"

"A travesty. A real violation of states' rights."

"I bet the judge is a closet Muslim," his companion interjected. "Like Obama. They are taking over, and most people don't even realize it. People need to wake up."

"Do members of Crusaders Against Sharia advocate violence to reverse this take-over?"

"Not exactly. No, ma'am. But we do advocate self-defense if necessary. And at some point, if there is a civil war—a new war for independence, if you will—we need to be ready."

"Do you think any members of Crusaders Against Sharia might be responsible for the burning of Algiers nightclub in Northeast D.C.?"

"No, ma'am," the taller one said evenly. "We aren't against belly dancing. We aren't against entertainment. We're against the forces of radical Islam that are threatening America." He went on, patiently explaining their philosophy, while Lily took copious notes, but Jeanne was distracted by a group of bearded men in long black robes, one of whom was missing an arm. "The one-armed sheikh," Jeanne muttered.

"What was that?"

"Just going to Starbucks for coffee."

"Make mine a double caramel macchiato, sweetie," Lily said, but Jeanne was already out of earshot.

"Charlotte Stanton, Oklahoma City Bee Gazette." She met the sheikh's dour expression with a smile. "I have a few questions for you, if you don't mind."

"I do mind. And if you have any questions, you can consult our website."

He had a long, scraggly beard and piercing dark eyes, and his thin lips were twisted into a sneer. A shiver ran up Jeanne's spine in spite of the heat. He reminded her of Stan Nickles, her kindergarten tormentor, who was strangling kittens for sport by the second grade and was now in a state penitentiary. It was never a good sign when someone reminded her of Stan.

173

"I have consulted your website, actually." She tried to stand up straighter and to stare confidently into those unnerving, hollow, black eyes. "And I don't see any statement about the recent mysterious fire and murder at Algiers nightclub in Northeast D.C. Police have classified it as a hate crime, and our readers are interested to know if Islam Al-Ulaama might be behind this attack, or if you condone this attack."

"Algiers was an immoral, un-Islamic institution. The women there were immodest. I'm not sorry about the attack, but neither I nor my followers had anything to do with it. It was all thanks to Allah. That's all I have to say. And now, if you will excuse me, it is time to pray."

He turned on his heel and padded off down the brick path, his robes swirling about his ankles. Jeanne wondered exactly what he would pray about and whether God found it irritating to listen to him five times a day.

Crossing the square, Jeanne loitered in front of the home of Stephen Decatur, a naval hero from the War of 1812. Trying to look like a tourist, she read the historical plaque slowly, keeping one eye on Lily, who she could barely see on the other side of Lafayette Square, still immersed in conversation with the Crusaders Against Sharia. While she waited for "Bertha" to finish her interview, Jeanne decided to give Fergus a call.

On the fourth ring, he picked up. "Hello." His brogue was even thicker than usual, and he sounded distracted.

"Did you find out anything?"

"Sorry. No transfers from Maryam's or Ari's accounts."

She could hear voices in the background and an occasional beep. "Fergus, what's wrong? Where are you?"

"Georgetown University Hospital. My aunt's had a heart attack." His voice was tremulous, and for a moment, Jeanne was afraid he might start crying.

Jeanne longed to say something comforting, but the only words that came to mind were platitudes. "I'm sure she'll be fine," just didn't seem to cut it. What if she wasn't? She was, after all, a rather frail woman in her seventies who had already had a stroke.

"Jeanne, I'd really feel better if you were here."

"I'm on my way."

Chapter Seventeen

Jeanne made it to the hospital in record time. She darted across four lanes of traffic on H Street, stuffed a twenty dollar bill in the hand of a woman in a fur coat whose taxi she commandeered, and offered the driver a fifty dollar tip if he could get her to the hospital in ten minutes. While she texted Lily, she kept one eye peeled for cops. Jeanne had promised to pay any speeding tickets he racked up, but she really didn't want to take any chances.

When Jeanne arrived in the ER waiting room, Fergus was pacing back and forth. Her heart nearly broke when they locked eyes across the room. He was normally so ebullient and witty; a smile was never far from his lips. But today his eyes were a pale, mirthless blue, and his lips were set in a thin, determined line.

In a moment, he crossed the room and hugged her so hard that she felt as though he were squeezing all of the oxygen out of her. "I gave her aspirin," he whispered into her shoulder. She felt his hot breath in her ear, and his stubble brushed her chin. "I gave her two aspirin. It's all I knew to do."

"You did the right thing, Fergus." Patting his back, she tried to gently pry his head from her shoulder. "You did everything you could, and I'm sure the doctors are doing everything they can."

"Are they?" She took a seat in the corner, and he plopped down next to her. "How do I know? I'm not a doctor."

"What's the last thing they told you?"

"She's in surgery. They're doing a coronary artery bypass something. They gave her some blood thinners too."

"Okay," Jeanne said, trying to sound encouraging. "That sounds good." Not knowing what else to do, she fiddled with her smart phone, navigating to the Mayo Clinic's website. "That is good," she said again, this time with far more authority. "According to the Mayo Clinic, standard treatment is to give a patient aspirin, blood thinners, and oxygen—did they give her oxygen?"

He nodded.

"Coronary artery bypass grafting is also a popular technique, according to Mayo Clinic." She scrolled further down the page and read, "During CABG, a surgeon removes a healthy artery or vein from the patient's body. The artery or vein is then connected, or grafted, to the blocked coronary artery—"

She suddenly realized that Fergus was not listening. He had nudged his way into the hollow between her shoulder and her neck, and she reluctantly reached out and put her arm around him. His eyelids were starting to droop.

"Fergus, when's the last time you slept?"

"What?" One eyelid opened.

"When's the last time you slept?"

"Thursday night," he mumbled. "I just need to take a little nap." His words came out slower and slower, and his eyes closed again. "Please stay, Jeanne. Wake me if the doctor comes."

She gently repositioned his head into a more comfortable position, and watched his chest rise and fall. She was starting to feel sleepy herself, when suddenly he awoke for a moment, reached into his pocket, and thrust a few crumpled pieces of paper into her lap. "Here," he said. "Ibrahim's emails. Something to read while I nap."

Jeanne was incredulous. "How did you—?"

"His password was 'Algiers.'"

And then he was out like a light.

She smoothed each piece of paper out, and held it out in front of her with her right arm. Her left was pinned under Fergus. Under the harsh fluorescent light, with the folks from the Wendy Williams Show yapping in the background, she read them silently. There were indeed a couple of hateful emails, although under normal circumstances they wouldn't be considered threats, per se. But in light of what had happened, they certainly sounded incredibly sinister. And the wording echoed some of Islam Al-Ulaama's overheated rhetoric. "Repent, brother, you are a traitor to Islam. Do not profit from the flesh of Islamic whores," read one. They were all pretty much variations on the same theme. But she noticed that not one made reference to Hagar.

The most surprising email was the only one that Fergus had printed out that was actually sent by Ibrahim. She eyes skipped right down to the body of the email and read, "This is your last chance to pay up before I resort to more drastic measures."

When her eyes flew back up to the address line, she gasped.

The recipient was none other than Thomas Harding.

To both Jeanne and Fergus's relief, the doctors said that Aunt Margaret could come home on Sunday. Jeanne offered to come over and help Fergus cook and clean on Saturday, but he declined all offers of help. "What do you think?" he said. "Because I'm a bloke, you think I can't clean? And my cooking's bloody brilliant. You'd think you'd died and gone to heaven if you tasted one of my scones."

"Well, if you feed Aunt Margaret scones," Jeanne retorted, secretly relieved that Fergus's old bravado was back, "she might die and go to heaven. I don't think buttery scones are what the doctor ordered for someone with a coronary blockage."

So while Fergus spent Saturday morning cleaning and making tasteless, low-fat food, Jeanne and Lily met at Kramer Books, fortifying themselves with eggs benedict, mimosas, and Goober Pie.

"So let me get this straight," Lily said as she licked a smear of gooey chocolate off her fork. "According to your boyfriend—"

"According to Fergus, who is not my boyfriend."

"—Yasmina had a guy named Thomas Harding on her speed dial, and Thomas Harding owed money to Ibrahim."

"Right."

"How much money?" Lily asked.

"I don't know. But enough to imply that nasty things would happen if he didn't pay up."

"And where are we going to ambush this guy?"

"A funeral home."

Lily cocked her head and gave Jeanne a quizzical look.

"I'm serious," Jeanne said, skimming the plate with her knife to scrape up the last of the peanut butter. "He happens to be a funeral home director. Besides, it's perfect. We can pose as potential clients who want to learn more about his services."

When they had gotten every last bit of chocolate and peanut butter off the plate, they paid the bill and headed up Connecticut Avenue. As they approached the funeral home, an SUV pulled out, and Lily began maneuvering into the spot. She had perfected the art of the 20-point turn, which was an absolute necessity when reconciling D.C.'s tight parking spots with her Crown Vic. "This is right near Yasmina's house," Lily observed.

"It's not too far from the Friendship Heights studio, either."

"Conveniently located for an affair."

"*If* they had an affair," Jeanne reminded her.

Lily rolled her eyes.

Harding Funeral Home was a brisk five minute walk away. "I wish we'd worn black," Jeanne muttered as they approached, glancing at Lily's fluorescent orange skinny jeans as a steady stream of black-clad mourners trickled out the front door.

Inside, the mood was somber. In one of the rooms, an ashen-faced, middle-aged man knelt in front of the coffin, his hands clasped in prayer, and then planted a kiss on the deceased's smooth, waxen forehead. Jeanne felt a wave of nausea and busied herself studying the flower arrangements. The man closed the casket, and the pallbearers, strapping young men in their twenties, took their places and carried the casket towards the rear exit.

Lily nudged Jeanne and nodded in the direction of a small, officious man who seemed to be directing the proceedings. Jeanne recognized the wizened visage, the beady little eyes, and the thin fish lips from the photo on the website, but she was startled by his diminutive size. She hadn't expected him to be particularly tall. But in the flesh, Thomas Harding was positively puny, no more than five-foot-four, with a shrunken chest cavity, drooping shoulders, and spindly little arms. He had also aged considerably since the photo had been taken. Jeanne estimated that he was at least fifty, and possibly as old as sixty.

The two friends retreated into a dark corner as Thomas and the pallbearers filed past, oblivious to their presence, and carried the casket out into the parking lot. Car doors slammed and engines started. A few moments later, Thomas Harding's frail frame heaved the door open and slipped back inside. He was startled to come face to face with Jeanne and Lily.

"Oh! I didn't expect to see anyone here," he exclaimed, placing a hand over his chest. Jeanne wondered if he had a heart condition and hoped he wouldn't expire before they could ascertain his relationship with Yasmina. "I'm sorry, girls," he said, regaining his composure, "but the Murphy funeral just ended." He squinted at Lily's orange jeans. "Or perhaps you are here to discuss funeral arrangements for a loved one."

"A close friend of ours did pass away recently," Lily said. "But the funeral was held in Houston, where her family is from."

"Closed casket," Jeanne interjected. "She died in a terrible fire."

His wiry body tensed and he blinked several times behind his thick, clunky glasses. He clenched his jaw. "Oh?"

"Yasmina Hariri," Lily said. "I believe you know her."

"Only vaguely," he said quickly. "I've bumped into her at Starbucks a few times. Her office is near here, I believe. And maybe we ran into each other at the florist or the grocery store. I think she once asked me how much a standard funeral should cost. I think she had an aunt that died. No, it was a great-aunt. Yes, that's definitely it. A great-aunt died and the family was concerned they were being bilked. We talked by the deli section of the Safeway—they have such great cold cuts there. Nice lady. Too bad what happened to her."

Jeanne exchanged a glanced with Lily. What a terrible liar. She was sure it wouldn't be too hard to extract information from such a twitchy, over-talkative moron.

"Relax," Lily said, sticking to their script. She cracked her gum loudly. "We weren't sent by your wife or her attorney to check up on you."

He mopped his forehead with a handkerchief. "Oh."
He lowered his voice. "Perhaps we could continue this in
a room down the hall. For a more private discussion."

He led them down a dark corridor to a door marked
"Employees Only." For a moment, Jeanne dreaded what
they would find inside. Was this where he embalmed the
bodies? She had never been comfortable with death. The
fear of her own mortality had kept her up at night as a
child; she had been afraid to shut her eyes, terrified she
would be sent straight to hell. And, worst of all, death
reminded her of Annie.

When he opened the door, Jeanne was relieved to
see that the room was nothing more than an office.
Chock-full of file cabinets, it smelled faintly of
chemicals. The desk in the center of the room was
draped with crude finger-paintings of blue stick figures
dancing beneath stars and rainbows. "Did your children
make these?" she asked, feigning interest. She traced her
finger over the rainbow, while staring intently at the
family photo propped up behind it.

"Yes. Kayla's ten and Maggie's eight."

"They're such beautiful girls," Jeanne said, picking
up the photo. She zeroed in on the woman standing
behind them. Were it not for her expression, she would
have been attractive. Long platinum locks framed her
heart-shaped face, setting off her clear blue eyes and
long, aquiline nose. But the gaze was icy, and the lips
were set in a sneer.

"My wife and I are very fortunate," he said quickly, snatching the photo from her grasp and setting it face down. "But you aren't here to talk about them."

"We know you and Yasmina were an item," Jeanne began, noting with a twinge of sadness that his frozen countenance confirmed the truth of her accusation. Her idol was an adulterer after all. "She told us all about it."

"She did? You must be mistaken. I—"

"She told us what an amazing lover you were," Jeanne persisted. "She said you were so sensitive and understanding. So focused on her pleasure."

"She said she never knew she was multi-orgasmic until she met you," Lily gushed, and Jeanne poked her from behind. Flattery was one thing, but Lily was wading into dangerous territory, inventing details that were far too specific, not to mention incredibly unlikely. Jeanne had a sudden mental image of Thomas Harding naked, and she shuddered. She could not imagine what Yasmina would see in an unattractive middle-aged man with a bland personality who was married to boot. She doubted Yasmina had enjoyed a single orgasm, much less several per night.

There was a glimmer of pride in his eyes, tempered by confusion. Even he seemed to find it unlikely that Yasmina would describe his prowess in those terms. He cleared his throat. "I don't quite understand why you are here. There's nothing I can do to undo this horrible tragedy."

"We're cleaning out Yasmina's apartment at her family's request," Jeanne explained. "Since she was always talking about you, and how much your relationship meant to her, we thought there might be some mementos—some items of sentimental value—that you might want." Jeanne smiled at him and tried to ooze warmth and beneficence.

"I see." He mopped his forehead again, but his shoulders relaxed. He studied the two women intently, and Jeanne could tell he was trying to discern whether it was a trap.

Lily smiled sweetly. "That's it. That's all we want to know. We're contacting everyone close to her to see if there's any small thing they would like."

"Photos," he said, looking at the floor. "If there are any photos of us, I would like them. A coral necklace. It's not worth anything, but it's from a day trip to Rehoboth."

"That should be no problem," Lily said. "Anything else?"

He pulled a key chain out of his pocket and pointed to the fourth key. Long and copper-colored, it had a green plastic coating over the bulbous end. "And a key just like this one."

Lily raised an eyebrow.

"I'm married," he said sheepishly. "And I work long hours, with only a few breaks in the day. The funeral home's not a glamorous place to meet..."

Jeanne finished his sentence. "But it's convenient."

"Did you at least get to see her last performance?" Lily asked.

He shook his head sadly. "Zarei funeral."

Jeanne nodded sympathetically. "Well with so many funerals going on here, I take it you didn't get to her funeral in Houston."

"No." His voice was very quiet, and she noticed that he gripped the edge of his desk. "Besides, that would be a little hard to explain to my wife. Or her family."

"And what about Mr. Abu Ali's funeral?" Jeanne asked gently. She tried to sound as though she were just mentioning this in passing, but she stared right at him to gauge his reaction. "I thought you might have known him, since he ran in the same social circle as Yasmina."

Mr. Harding looked down, but she caught a fleeting glimpsed of his furrowed brow and pursed lips. When he looked back up, his face was perfectly blank. "No," he said. He shrugged casually. "Never heard of him. Yasmina and I didn't talk much about the club, you know."

"Well, thank you for your time," Lily said sweetly, bringing their interview to a close.

Jeanne shook his hand and tried not to cringe as his sweaty, clammy palm grasped hers. "Thank you, Mr. Harding. We'll send you the necklace," she lied, "and the key."

Chapter Eighteen

Jeanne took off running the minute she rounded the corner and was out of Thomas Harding's sight.

"What's the rush?" Lily groused. "You know I can't run in these shoes."

"She's in the video."

"Who's in what video?"

"Mrs. Harding. Our dear old philanderer's wife was at Algiers the night of the fire. I remember seeing that bottle-blond hair and those icy blue eyes in the video."

Lily broke into a run, struggling to keep up, as they sprinted past Starbucks. "Think about it," Jeanne said as she weaved to avoid a redhead with a baby carriage. "She's got a great motive. If Ibrahim dies, her husband's debts go up in smoke—literally. If Yasmina dies, she gets rid of her husband's mistress at the same time."

"That certainly gives a new meaning to 'kill two birds with one stone.'" Lily gasped for breath. "But why not just shoot Yasmina? Why set fire to the club and risk having Yasmina escape?"

"To make Yasmina's death look accidental. To make it look like the work of some deranged hate group."

"What about Yousef?"

"What about Yousef? We've got nothing on him, other than a possible financial motive. But he clearly didn't have the opportunity to shoot Ibrahim since he was playing the *ney* the whole time. We speculated he might have had an accomplice, but we can't find any evidence he paid anybody. Based on the database searches I did this week, nobody in his immediate family has a handgun—a legal handgun, anyway—nor do we have evidence that any of them have any kind of military training."

"Well then what about Maryam and Ari? They have a great motive."

"Sure, but they didn't have the opportunity, as far as we know." Jeanne was panting now. "Maybe they lucked out. Mrs. Harding offed Ibrahim and Yasmina, and Maryam and Ari get the money and rid themselves of a meddlesome uber-conservative relative. They probably can't believe their dumb luck."

Lily's Crown Vic came into view.

"Why are we running anyway?" Lily shouted.

"According to his calendar, Harding's got two more funerals today, and then he's picking his wife up at six o'clock at the Ballston Mall. That gives us four hours to find her and talk to her alone."

"Well count me out. I've got a date with my hot Moroccan neighbor."

"But I need you." Jeanne could hear a hint of desperation creeping into her voice, which annoyed her, but she wasn't sure she could confront Mrs. Harding on her own.

"I'm sure Fergus would be more than happy to accompany you," Lily said.

"He's cleaning today."

"I'm sure he can take an hour out of his day for a trip to the mall. He could be quite an asset, you know. Maybe he'll bring out the cougar in her. Maybe,"—Lily licked her lips and shot Jeanne a meaningful glance— "she's dying to unburden herself to some attractive young boy toy."

An hour later, Jeanne and Fergus were searching the Ballston Mall for any signs of Mrs. Harding. A steady stream of teenagers preened and giggled their way up the escalators, bouncing back and forth between the food court and the movie theater. A few serious movies were playing, but as far as Jeanne and Fergus could tell, everyone was going to see flicks with names like *Really Bad Date Movie Seven* and *Attack of the Werewolf Zombies:*

Cancun. Fergus shook his head. "They're not exactly budding cineastes, are they?"

"Well perhaps Mrs. Harding isn't either." The corners of her mouth turned up as she pictured the funeral director's flinty-eyed wife craning her neck to see over a couple of horny teenagers. She scanned the list of movies. "Perhaps she's seeing *Dusk on the Danube.*" She pointed at a movie poster that seemed designed to appeal to women of a certain age, with a beautiful actress who was a bit older, luminous beneath the smoldering gaze of an olive-skinned man who looked vaguely like Omar Sharif. A wide, silvery river cut a swathe through a gently rolling lush landscape. Presumably, that was supposed to be the Danube. "I probably would too if I were married to an unattractive, mousy, two-timing funeral home director like Mr. Harding."

"Well in that case," Fergus said, "you should marry me. The men in my family age very well, we can be assertive—but not too assertive of course—and we don't smell of those nasty embalming chemicals."

They arrived at the front of the line, sparing Jeanne the need to respond.

"Yes, ma'am?" The clerk spoke in an even, almost robotic voice, and blinked several times. Jeanne was slightly horrified to learn that she was now so old that clerks felt compelled to address her as "ma'am."

"I was wondering if you've spotted my mother. She's not answering her cell phone—I'm sure she shut it off so as not to disturb others—but I really need to get a hold of her. You see"—she lowered her voice—"we've just had a death in the family." Jeanne hung her head and hoped she looked sufficiently grief-stricken.

Amazingly, the clerk's expression did not change in the slightest. "What does your mother look like?"

"Blond hair, blue eyes. In her late forties."

"Other than the five blue-haired old ladies watching *Dusk on the Danube*," the clerk replied with a smirk, "everyone here is too young to see an R-rated movie."

They thanked her and headed back out into the mall. The rest of the shopping center was eerily empty, as though an atomic bomb had gone off and killed everyone old enough to drive. The Macy's furniture salesman looked up at them hopefully as they ambled past. "I've got great deals on sofas today," he said. "And waterbeds are twenty percent off."

There was more action on the first floor, which had several bars. Waitresses bustled around Union Jack's and Bailey's, bringing buckets of unidentified fried objects to heavyset, glassy-eyed patrons who rained invective on the hockey players whizzing across the screen. "Play, you namby-pamby nitwit!" one particularly boisterous patron shouted, the veins bulging in his neck, as if he were ready to take to the ice and show #22 how it was done. Jeanne doubted he could even skate, much less take a shot on goal. "Whadaya afraid of? Losing a tooth?"

They were about to give up when Jeanne saw a familiar blonde emerging from the ladies' room. Clutching a Victoria's Secret bag, Mrs. Harding teetered towards the bar on six-inch spike heels, a telltale leopard print strap peeking out of her low-cut white blouse. There was nothing subtle about her look: fire engine red lipstick, black fishnet stockings, dark eyeliner smudged about the edges as if to imply she had rolled out of someone's bed—and wanted to roll into someone else's.

She was not going for the classy look, or even the look of a prim and proper librarian about to unleash her wild side. Her wild side had already been released. She was just looking for some sloppy drunk boor to notice.

Jeanne felt as though she could see the hairs on Fergus's neck stand straight up. She didn't have to nudge him or point her out. Men—even sensitive men like Fergus—had not evolved that much since bringing home the bacon meant bringing home the woolly mammoth. There was prey to be caught.

Lily was right. Mrs. Harding would probably tell a man just about anything, as long as he gave her the one thing she wanted: revenge.

Jeanne thumped Fergus on the back. "Go get her, tiger."

*　　　*　　　*　　　*

To Jeanne's surprise, Fergus had a lot more game than she had thought. He eschewed the lame one-liners and instead gave Mrs. Harding what Jeanne liked to call the Tom Cruise Treatment. The key to the Tom Cruise Treatment was to focus one's gaze, with blazing intensity, on the other person, in a way that suggested that she was the most fascinating, entrancing, intoxicating person you had ever met in your life, but in a way that did not, in any way, seem creepy. The recipient of this laser-like stare feels not only supremely flattered, but also swoons with the romantic notion that this intensity is indicative of your reckless, passionate, swash-buckling personality. Jeanne supposed it gave some women the illusion that they could date a "bad boy" who, despite maintaining an aura of danger, never actually does anything bad. She had coined the term before Tom Cruise had started jumping on couches and denouncing supermodels with post-partum depression. Because that *was* creepy.

From what Jeanne could see and hear from her perch at the end of the bar, Fergus did it exceptionally well. His blue eyes blazed with anger as Mrs. Harding described her "sham marriage" to "a vile little man who smells like death." His fingers lightly brushed her hand, sometimes reaching out to squeeze her hand, to reassure her that yes, her husband really was a wanker.

"How could his mistress stand that smell?" Her voice was whiny, petulant. It was a rhetorical question, but there was also genuine bewilderment at its core. "I can't

stand that smell. I won't let Thomas come near me
before he showers."

"Maybe she's in the funerary industry as well,"
Fergus offered helpfully, then added for good measure,
"the slut."

She shook her head. "A dancer. Can you believe it?
Of all the tawdry clichés. I would have at least thought
Thomas would have the decency to cheat on me with
someone with a real job. A doctor or a lawyer. Maybe a
professor." She pursed her lips. "I guess it's true what
they say. Never marry a man dumber than you. They feel
inferior. They need to cheat with someone of their own
intelligence level, less even, just to feel important."

Fergus shrugged. "Some blokes, maybe. I like smart
women myself."

Mrs. Harding laughed and smoothed her hair. "Well
then, honey, you're in luck tonight. I've got a bachelor's
from Stanford and an MBA from Harvard."

Fergus leaned towards her. "Did you see her? The
slut, that is?"

"I saw her, all right," she shot back indignantly.
"Wiggling her big breasts, shaking her hips. What a
hussy. Beautiful, for sure, but a hussy." She took a sip of
her margarita. "Honestly, I have no idea what she saw in
him. She could have gotten someone younger, smarter,
and better looking."

Jeanne smiled. If only Mrs. Harding knew about
Rodrigo.

"You could ask her," Fergus said. "You know, confront her. Maybe you could talk her out of seeing him."

"Talk her out of seeing him?" She choked back a laugh, spraying her drink on the bar. Fergus didn't even flinch. "Why would I want to do that? Honey, I want my freedom. That's why I was there. To get a picture of her, gather some intel, and hand it over to my attorney." She pounded a fist on the bar. "Finally! I was going to have proof to nail his ass to the wall. Adultery! Believe me, I would have done it years ago if I could have. But he would have sued me for alimony. The money's all mine, you see. I make the big bucks, and I have the huge inheritance."

"What about the funeral home? Doesn't that make money?"

"Barely. My father bought it for him, mostly to give him something to do. He can have it." She swilled her drink. "Once he pays his gambling debts, he'll even lose that." She arched an eyebrow at him. "That's right, you heard me. On top of being a philanderer, he's got a gambling problem. Owes some Arab guy twenty grand. He thinks I don't know. I thought of paying it—it's pocket change compared to my trust fund—but then I thought, why not let him sweat a bit?"

Jeanne's face fell. If Mrs. Harding didn't mind his cheating and had more than enough money to pay his gambling debts, she had no motive. It was back to

Yousef and Maryam and Ari and the hate groups, all of
whom she was beginning to suspect were dead ends.

"So you didn't talk to her at all that night?" Fergus
probed.

"No. I thought about it, but fate intervened. She was
a dancer at Algiers. You know, the one that's been on
the news lately? She died in the fire." She grimaced.
"Poor thing. To think her last lover was my lousy excuse
of a husband."

Fergus finished his drink and slipped a five dollar
bill under his glass. "Diane, it's been a real pleasure
talking with you, but I'm afraid I've got to get home."

Mrs. Harding bit her lip, clearly disappointed.
"Running home to the missus, are you?"

"Worse than that, I'm afraid. I'm helping an
unrequited love with her little research project. There is
no missus, no girlfriend. I'm holding out for this one,
who doesn't seem to want to give me the time of day.
But as my mum would say, never underestimate the
determination of a bloke spurned."

"Well if you ask me," Mrs. Harding said tartly, "I
don't think she deserves you."

"That's the problem. She does. She's wicked smart,
brilliantly witty, insatiably curious—which I adore in a
lass—and an incredibly loyal friend." Out of the corner of
her eye, Jeanne could see him glance in her direction,
but she kept her eyes steadfastly glued to the TV. Jeanne
didn't want to give him the impression she was

interested in his bizarre psychoanalysis of her. "And for some strange reason, she thinks she's boring," he said. "She thinks her crazy friend is more adventurous and her sister is sexier."

Jeanne nodded. The last part, at least, was true. But was he agreeing that Lily was more exciting and Vivienne sexier, or not? She wanted to look in his direction, to see his exact expression, his hand gestures.

"Well is she boring?" Mrs. Harding asked.

"Not by half! With her, you never know what she's going to think of next. Which I like," he said, stooping to plant a chaste kiss on Mrs. Harding's cheek. "It keeps me on my toes. There's never a dull moment."

"Well if you get tired of things being exciting outside the bedroom and boring in the bedroom, give me a call."

"I most certainly will."

To her irritation, Jeanne found herself hoping he was joking.

Chapter Nineteen

Everywhere Jeanne looked, there were black smudges taunting her. Some were rough approximations of crosses, others mere thumbprints. They were the mark of Cain, a public act of atonement for very private sins, a rare and almost subversive acknowledgement of man's fleeting existence.

She hated Ash Wednesday. It was the only time of year she hailed a cab, so anxious was she to avoid eye contact with the passengers on the #37 bus. Then she would trudge into work, eyes downcast, and try to avoid getting up from her desk all day. If she had to use the restroom, she would walk around the long way, past the vending machines and the break room; there were just two lawyers' offices that she had to pass, and they were both Jewish. Around five o'clock, she would start feeling queasy. Her palms would begin to sweat, sticking to the files. With each passing minute, she knew she was closer to having to make a decision. And then at six-thirty, she would have a rush of courage and decide yes, this is the year I will finally go and get this over with.

Today was no different. She found herself in front of Burberry's at 6:53, eyeing St. Matthew's Cathedral through a thin film of tears. The cathedral looked so imposing, so solid and resolute. God is eternal, its façade reminded passersby, but you are not. Throngs of worshippers sped past her, crossed the street, and marched up the steps. They looked solemn, but not worried. No one seemed to think they had any sins that couldn't be forgiven.

She wished she had that same confidence. Two years ago she had finally mustered the courage to go inside, and she had even joined the line for ashes. She had watched as the priest pressed a pale, fleshy thumb into a mound of ashes. White-haired and stooping with age, his hands had shaken as he held his thumb aloft, poised above her forehead, smeared with coarse black soot. He had pronounced the words that Jeanne had long feared with a thick Eastern European accent: "Repent and sin no more." His thumb had moved closer and she had felt as though she were falling down, far down, into the black hole that was her soul. She needed much more than a thumb's worth of ashes. She could bathe in a vat full of ashes, and that would still not be enough. And somehow, she had known that he knew.

She had opened her mouth to scream, but no words came out. But he had caught the sheer terror in her eyes, and they had stared at each other for a moment, his hand trembling above her. She had known that if he touched her, it would be irreversible. She would have to repent. And repentance meant acknowledging her guilt. Repentance would mean letting go of all of her rationalizations, the comforting things people had said over the years. And worst of all, it meant forgiving the person she held most responsible. It meant that she, in turn, would have to forgive. And that was the one thing she could not do; it would be the biggest betrayal of all.

She had taken off running just as the priest's thumb grazed her hair, stumbling past businesswomen in power suits, baby-faced interns, and bureaucrats swathed in drab gray, all of whom look untroubled by their status as sinners.

Through a torrent of tears, she had run down M Street, across the bridge, and up, up through Georgetown, all the way to Glover Park. No one had asked her if she was okay, or if she needed help. That's how D.C. was—people minded their own business.

At home, she had showered, over and over again, until she was at least satisfied that no trace of ash remained. She had taken the picture of Annie from the bookshelf, slid it under her pillow, and cried herself to sleep.

No, Jeanne decided, this was not the year either.

*   *   *   *

Later that evening, Scarlett and Jeanne took the long way to the park, along tiny side streets, avoiding all of the churches. While Scarlett limped along, half-heartedly chasing any rabbits or squirrels they encountered, Fergus's words echoed through Jeanne's head. *Never underestimate the determination of a bloke spurned.* She wondered how determined he really was. Part of her wanted to find out, but she knew it was futile. She would push him away, like everyone else. There was no sense in torturing him in the meantime. Were it not for the fact that she needed him to apprehend Yasmina's killer, she would cut off contact altogether. But even as she thought this, she realized she was lying to herself.

Her thoughts drifted to Mrs. Harding. Now there was a woman with a horrible love life. Trapped in a marriage with a two-timing miserable excuse for a man, she was desperate to get out, but too proud—or too greedy—to split her fortune with him in a no-fault divorce. Was she greedy enough to kill Ibrahim to save twenty thousand dollars and vengeful enough to kill Yasmina out of spite? As tidy of an explanation as this would be, Jeanne was doubtful. After all, if Mrs. Harding were willing to kill, the most likely victim would be Mr. Harding himself.

Mr. Harding's motive to kill Ibrahim was quite strong, especially if he feared for his life if he didn't pay up. But he had no reason to kill Yasmina, unless she was threatening to tell his wife. And if he didn't even have money to pay his gambling debt, Jeanne could hardly see how he could pay a hit man.

Maryam and Ari had strong personal and financial motives, and her conversation with the sheikh had done nothing to allay her suspicion of him and his acolytes. If only she could place them at the scene of the crime....

In sight of the dog park, Scarlett bounded forward, her tail wagging furiously. She strained at the leash, panting loudly. Freedom was within reach; the hated leash would soon be removed. "Slow down, Scar," Jeanne pleaded in vain.

They hurtled over uneven ground towards the play area. Encircled by a fence, the playground was filled with little children in designer clothes. Most were chaperoned by their nannies, an eclectic international cast of characters: gold-toothed, ebony-skinned women draped in kente cloth; gorgeous young women straight from the beaches of Rio; long-legged, wide-eyed blondes from Russia and the Ukraine. The mothers—forty-something career women clad in Ann Taylor pantsuits and expensive but tasteful jewelry—were easy to spot. They hovered over their children, eager to please, waiting for a sign, any sign, that they were the center of their children's universe. For them, childrearing was a vocation, a sacred calling, yet one more arena in life in which they wished to excel; for the nannies, it was a job.

Jeanne zeroed in on the pairs of sisters. In a matter of seconds she could determine which one was pretty

and popular, and which one was the other child. She
knew from experience that the other child could have a
variety of monikers. Sometimes they were the "creative
child" or the "smart child" or even the "unusual child."

Jeanne hadn't even been upgraded to the "smart
child." Since pretty was not in the cards, smart or
creative were what she strived for, but even these labels
proved elusive. Reliable was the best she could do.

"Zahira!"

Looking up, she was surprised to come face to face
with Aisha. The last time they had seen each other,
Aisha had been draped in black, her visage wrinkled and
somber. Today, in a long green coat and bright pink
headscarf, strolling hand in hand with two dark-eyed
toddlers, she looked much younger and more carefree.

"Aisha! I didn't realize you lived around her."

"I don't. But my grandchildren do."

She introduced her grandchildren, who fell in love
with Scarlett. Scarlett obliged by rolling over onto her
tummy and wagging her tail while they rubbed her thick
fur. If they stopped, even for a moment, she reached up
and tapped them with a paw.

"Any more news from the police?"

Aisha shook her head. "They don't tell us much."
She glanced over at her grandchildren. "When I see
them, I feel very happy. I feel that the future will be
good. But then I think about what happened...and I
worry. I worry that Yousef and I could be next." She

sighed. "I've been praying a lot. Trying to understand why Allah willed this to happen. The Prophet, may he rest in peace, said, 'Show mercy to those on earth, and He Who is in heaven will show mercy unto you,' but when the killer is finally identified, I don't know how easy it will be for me to show mercy."

All this talk of mercy was beginning to irk Jeanne. First the Catholics, then the Muslims. Why was everyone obsessed with forgiveness? She decided to change the subject. "Will you be able to rebuild the club?"

"We've already started!" Aisha exclaimed, clapping her hands. Two dimples appeared on her broad cheeks, and a gold crown glinted beneath the lamplight. "Yasmina, may she rest in peace, suggested that we review our fire insurance coverage a couple of months before the tragedy occurred. So we will recover everything! She was such a wonderful person. Like a daughter to me."

Jeanne stared at Aisha. Her knees felt weak, and she grasped at a park bench for support. Had Yasmina known that someone was planning to burn the club down? And if so, had she aided and abetted this person? Or merely said nothing, for fear of her life? Did the plotter suspect that she knew and kill her to keep her from going to the police?

All kinds of scenarios raced through Jeanne's head. Yasmina could have overheard Mr. Harding plotting the attack; Maryam could have confided that she saw no way out other than killing her uncle.

Aisha was looking at her expectantly, and Jeanne realized she should say something. "What a wonderful person," she repeated hollowly, but for the first time, she was not sure she meant it.

Chapter Twenty

Twenty minutes later, as Jeanne and Scarlett were hurrying past the Russian Embassy, Fergus called.

"How's Aunt Margaret?" she asked.

"Feisty as ever. Which is a sure sign she's feeling much better." He lowered his voice. "With the help of a friend, I did a little digging through Ibrahim's finances."

Her eyes narrowed as she crested the hill and her yellow apartment building came into view. "A friend?"

"My flatmate from uni, actually. He works in the MI-6 division that investigates money laundering. They follow the money trail for criminal and terrorist organizations, that sort of thing."

Jeanne stopped dead in her tracks. "And?"

"And let's just say Ibrahim is not who you think he is. He's got some bank accounts that suggest he's a perfectly normal guy...and then he's got some other accounts." There was a long silence. "Can we meet?"

She decided not to tell him about her conversation with Aisha until she could make sense of it. So all she said was, "My place, in an hour. I'll ask Lily to come."

By ten o'clock, they were hunched over Jeanne's coffee table, huddled around a piping hot veggie pizza from The 2 Amy's. Jeanne and Lily thumbed through Fergus's thick stacks of print-outs in numb disbelief.

"Nine thousand a month transferred from Malta," Lily croaked, massaging her temples. Jeanne had never seen her this rattled, not even when Gloria, her pet pit viper, had gone missing during a Halloween party. She was so distracted that, as far as Jeanne could tell, she wasn't even scoping Fergus out. Which was quite unexpected, given Lily's intense interest last week.

Fergus handed her another sheet of paper. "Which was transferred from an account in the Cayman Islands."

"Which was transferred from Cyprus, which was transferred from Lebanon."

"What's the name on the Lebanese account?"

"Jaysh el-Shahid."

"What does this mean?" Lily asked in a small voice. "What have we gotten ourselves into?"

Jeanne chewed her lip. She knew exactly what— whom—they needed, but she knew Lily wouldn't like the idea. "We need Jerry," she finally said.

"You can't be serious."

"Of course I'm serious. He worked for the CIA for years. He's a Middle East expert."

"Yeah, and he is a dirty old man who is probably trolling the Internet for a mail-order Russian bride as we speak."

"First of all, he's not that old. He's forty-seven. Second of all, I caught him trolling for Moldovan brides, not Russians. Third of all, he's more lonely than dirty."

Lily arched her eyebrows. "I didn't know you and Jerry were suddenly B.F.F."

"We're not." She tried to suppress the hint of defensiveness she heard creeping into her voice. "But let's just say the man has issues, like we all do, and he's working through them. And in any case, we need him. He's the only person who can make sense of these messages and tell us if they are legit."

"But can we trust him?" Fergus interrupted. "How do you know he won't call the police—"

"—or the spooks?" Lily broke in.

"We can trust him," Jeanne said, "and you will both welcome him to this investigative team. In fact, I'll go get him now."

She left an astonished Lily and puzzled Fergus huddled around the coffee table and padded off down the hallway. "Jerry?" she called out, banging the knocker. She could hear an infomercial for kitchen gadgets blaring through the door. "Jerry, are you home?"

After the third knock, she heard a muffled grunt, followed by slow, heavy footsteps shuffling towards her. "Twinkletoes?" a deep baritone boomed.

"Yes, Jerry, it's me, Jeanne. I need your help."

She heard the sound of the dead bolt being undone, and the chain being slid across. The door opened a crack and a single bulging brown eyeball peered out at her from behind a burgeoning cloud of smoke. The smoke tickled her throat and she fell into a coughing fit.

"Sorry, Twinkletoes," Jerry said sheepishly, opening the door wider. "I wasn't expecting company."

Behind him was a gloomy black interior lit only by the glow of the television. They stood there in silence for a moment, as Jeanne fought to breathe, and Jerry at last flicked a light on. His complexion was sallow in the harsh fluorescent light, and it appeared as though he had not showered or shaved in days. His eyes were bloodshot and he clutched the kitchen counter for support.

"On, no," Jeanne groaned. "You've been drinking again."

"And smoking," Jerry offered lamely, attempting a smile. She could tell he was embarrassed. "I've been hanging out with Jim Beam and the Marlboro Man."

"How would you like to hang out with some people who actually talk?" Jeanne asked. "My friends Fergus and Lily are visiting, and we need your Middle East expertise." He gave her a blank look, so she added, "Lily's the one you call Asian Invasion."

He nodded, but she noticed a look of wounded pride in his eyes. "I'm not in the best way for company right now."

"I'll wait, Jerry," she said. "Why don't you take a nice hot shower, shave, and put on some clean clothes? Then I'll Febreeze you and make you some nice hot coffee to help you sober up."

"Thanks, Jeanne," he said before shuffling off to the bathroom.

An hour later, Jerry was on his second cup of coffee and looking halfway presentable as he pored over the chain of bank transfers. "Jaysh el-Shahid," he muttered, shaking his head. "Now that's a blast from my past. I spent several months researching them. The name means 'The Martyr's Army.' They claim to be a charitable organization, providing health care to those who were wounded in Lebanon's long civil war. But as best as I could tell, they were really a front for Hezbollah. The State Department classified them as a terrorist organization, which was very controversial. Believe it or not, there were a lot of American donors."

Jeanne noticed how authoritative he sounded when analyzing the print-outs, and yet there was still a sad and vulnerable air about him; he avoided looking Lily and Fergus in the eyes and his hands trembled whenever they asked him a direct question. He was more relaxed when Jeanne asked him questions, and soon the three fell into an unspoken accord that only Jeanne would ask him direct questions. "Did the donors know what the funds were actually being used for?" Jeanne asked.

"Hard to tell. Some probably did, some didn't."

Jeanne snuck a look at Lily, whose brow was furrowed. She looked mightily confused. Current events were not her friend's strong suit. Lily thought the colonists actually sipped tea and munched scones at the Boston Tea Party, and expressed surprise that anything historic had happened in Colonial Williamsburg. As far as she was concerned, it was an important site indeed, but only because of the outlet malls.

Jeanne took a deep breath and bit into a slice of pizza. This was a twist she had not anticipated. "So Ibrahim may have been on Hezbollah's payroll."

"Or some allied organization."

"Which would be?"

"Most likely Hamas, the extremist Palestinian faction that controls the Gaza Strip. They're practically joined at the hip. Hezbollah, with Syria's and Iran's support, harasses Israel from the north. Hamas harasses Israel from the south, smuggling in arms from Egypt and lobbing rockets into Israel."

Fergus leaned across the table, credit card statements in hand. "And Ibrahim's shady activities aren't limited to the mysterious bank transfers. According to his credit card statements, he's also been to some pretty dodgy places in the past year—Beirut in May, Cairo in June, Karachi in September."

"So he's a terrorist," Lily said flatly.

Jerry nodded. "It would appear so."

Chapter Twenty-One

That night, Jeanne could not sleep. Fergus's sleuthing had expanded the list of potential assassins exponentially. Yousef, Maryam, and Ari still had financial motives, and the sheikh was still on her list of suspects. But now there was a whole new angle to consider. Ibrahim could have double-crossed his fellow terrorists, or squealed to the authorities, or maybe just botched a job. Or maybe he was the victim of an overzealous young Islamic radical eager to purge Hamas of its more secular members.

Her fleeting impression of him had been of a lascivious, self-absorbed sybarite. She hadn't pegged him as a terrorist, and she couldn't imagine how members of Hamas could stomach consorting with a man who made his living by exhibiting the flesh of "immodest" women, some of whom were even Muslim. But perhaps, she reasoned, it was some sort of deep cover, or possibly gross hypocrisy explained away as some sort of cover.

After all, the 9/11 hijackers had turned out to be enthusiastic patrons of porn.

When Yasmina had suggested to Aisha that they increase the fire insurance, had she known about the plot to destroy Algiers? Did she know that the plot also involved killing Ibrahim? And if so, was she involved?

It pained Jeanne to even consider the possibility that Yasmina could have terrorist connections. But she hadn't wanted to believe that she would seduce a married man, and yet the proof was incontrovertible. The truth was that she hadn't known Yasmina at all.

Her head throbbed and she felt a pang of envy as she looked over at Scarlett, who was curled up beside her, her one eye shut tight, her jaw clenched as she whimpered and shook with excitement. "It must be a good dream, Scarlett," she whispered. "I bet you're finally going to catch that bunny this time."

In search of inspiration, she went to the kitchen and rummaged around in the freezer. Far at the back, behind the frozen peas and wild Maine blueberries, she found a half-empty carton of New York Super Fudge Chunk.

She sat cross-legged on her futon, wearing an old pair of pink bedroom slippers and the leopard-print Snuggie that Aunt Mildred had given her for Christmas, along with the ringing endorsement that "it was a great gift for a single young woman without a man friend to cuddle up to!" As she bit into a chewy walnut, she realized that something was still bothering her, and she knew only one person could shed light on the matter. She fumbled in the dark for her cell phone and scrolled to the "H's."

"Dr. Hamza?"

"Yes?"

"This is Jeanne Pelletier, Yasmina's friend. We met last month."

"Who?" His voice was groggy and garbled. "Oh—Jeanne, that Jeanne. I thought you were a—what time is it?"

"Way too late. Are you on duty?"

"No," he said, and she could hear irritation creeping into his voice once more. "I'm at home, in bed, next to my peacefully slumbering wife for a change."

"Oh, I'm so sorry to disturb you," she said quickly. "I was hoping you might be working and I could pop down to G.W. to see you."

"What for?"

"Did Yasmina have a close friend who died of appendicitis?"

There was a long pause, and Jeanne held her breath. It would have been better to ask in person, but he sounded so annoyed she feared she might never have the chance.

He cleared his throat. "The Exorcist steps are around the corner from my house. Since you're up, you may as well meet me there in thirty minutes."

And without waiting for an answer, he hung up.

*   *   *   *

It was two-thirty a.m. when Jeanne slipped out of her apartment and began the long trek down Wisconsin Avenue. The air was humid and relatively warm, and for the first time she noticed that a few of the hardiest trees were beginning to bud in the late February thaw. Normally, she would have felt elated at the first sign of spring, but now she could feel nothing but apprehension. She felt disconnected from the merry college students straggling out of the bars following last call. Their cares all seemed so pedestrian—whether they would get carded, whether they would have a hang-over tomorrow, whether the cute guy from the School of Foreign Service would end up calling. Even the cops, idling on the corner, coffee in hand, one eye on the tipsy college students (and generally more on those tipsy college students who were both scantily clad and possessing two X chromosomes, she observed), one eye on their buddy in the next car, seemed frivolous to her. Sure, they might give out a citation for public drunkenness or a DUI, but were they arranging furtive meetings at horror movie locales to discuss long-held secrets about events that happened half a world away and that may have led to murder?

She passed the Whole Foods, the bagel shop, the Turkish restaurant, and the Georgetown Library, scene of a mysterious fire several years ago that had destroyed priceless historical documents. Next came a row of ludicrously expensive boutiques—an exquisite patisserie, an Argentine gelateria, shops for fabulously rich doyennes of a certain age, with their tasteful silk scarves and long, slimming skirts, and antique stores brimming with ancient Chinese vases and colonial silver. On P Street, where the old trolley tracks peeked through the cobblestones, she turned right into the eerie silence of the neighborhood. Casting a nervous glance behind her, she reached into her pocket and felt around for her mace. In the heat of the moment, it had seemed a good idea to arrange a spontaneous rendezvous in Georgetown, but now the deserted streets reminded her that Georgetown had one of the highest crime rates in the District. She remembered reading a news article long ago about how none other than Madeleine Albright—the four-foot-ten former Secretary of State—had been mugged in Georgetown in broad daylight. Madeline had foiled her attackers by curling up into fetal position, with her purse tucked underneath her, and wailing like a car alarm until the bewildered thugs fled. Jeanne resolved to do the same if challenged.

As she rounded the corner and passed Holy Trinity Church, a cream-colored edifice that had once been J.F.K.'s home parish, it occurred to her that the greatest threat of all could be Dr. Hamza himself. She had never pegged him for a killer, but Lily had not been entirely convinced of his innocence.

She inhaled sharply as she spied a dark figure huddled under the streetlight on the next block, across the street from The Tombs and beside the Exorcist stairs. She had never seen *The Exorcist*—she hated all horror movies and, in fact, had been unable to take a shower with the shower curtain closed for a full two months after seeing *Candy Man*, her first and only horror film—but, like everyone else, she knew exactly where this landmark was. It was really just an ordinary flight of narrow stone stairs, but their vertiginous descent and extraordinary length ("better than fifteen minutes of Stairmaster," according to Lily), coupled with their association with the film, gave them an air of malevolence.

He looked up as she passed The Tombs, and she waved. He grimaced in acknowledgement but did not return the wave.

"Hello," she said, attempting a smile.

"You're late." He wore a trench coat over a pair of flannel, plaid pajamas, and his hairy feet were stuffed into some old brown leather slippers. He didn't appear to be in the mood for pleasantries.

"I'm sorry. I live in Glover Park."

He grunted. "You asked me if she had a friend who died of appendicitis. Whom did you hear that from?"

"Maryam Massoud."

His eyes glimmered beneath the lamplight, and she could tell she had touched a nerve. "Yasmina's friend's sister."

"Yes."

219

"I don't know if Maryam believes that or not," he said, sighing and rubbing his temples. "But that's not true. At least, according to Yasmina. Whenever we fought about money, and I tried to get her to cut back on the charitable donations, she always brought the conversation back to Nejla Massoud. 'Do you want to condemn other women to Nejla's fate?' she would scream, tears running down her face. 'Is having a nice car more important than your conscience?' It was hard to argue with that."

"How did she die?"

"How do you think?" he snorted. "She was from one of these conservative West Bank families. Everything was about honor, the Koran, the hadiths. The women were veiled—never mind that the Prophet never required women to cover their face. The Prophet's wives were veiled, and that was good enough for them. Their women were their chattel. Prized chattel, of course, but still chattel." He paused for a moment and his eyes locked with Jeanne's. "Don't think, though, that only women suffer from this fundamentalist version of Islam. Men suffer just as much. It's such a burden, always having to protect your sister's and mother's and daughter's honor. It exhausting, never knowing where the next threat will come from."

Jeanne could barely breathe. At last she mustered the courage to ask, "So Nejla did something to dishonor her family?"

"She was seen in the village with a young man. I'm sure it was innocent—I doubt they even kissed. But that was enough to seal her fate."

He shifted uneasily. "They beheaded her." He spit out each word as though he were expunging something repulsive. With each consonant, his Adam's apple jerked violently upwards. "They probably didn't even use as much care as they did slaughtering their sheep."

It sounded so inadequate, but all Jeanne could muster was, "I'm so sorry to hear that."

Dr. Hamza regarded her with his deep, searching brown eyes, and his gaze was kind once more, albeit tinged with sadness. "You mustn't think that all Muslims are like this," he said. "I myself have found Islam a great source of strength and comfort from time to time. It has its wonderful points: emphasis on giving to the poor, rejection of usury, the unity of all Muslims. I love the sense of peace and mystery in the mosque, I love the quiet dignity of Muslim burials, how all of us, from the richest to the poorest, are buried in a simple wooden box. But there are tribal traditions that have become embedded in Islam, that have perverted it. And they are hard to change. Yasmina, though, couldn't be content with that state of affairs."

Jeanne pondered this for a moment and then, before she could stop herself, she blurted out, "Maryam's engaged. To a Jew."

Dr. Hamza's eyebrows shot straight up. "Her uncle wouldn't have tolerated that. If he knew."

Part of her wanted to squelch her doubts and walk away, forget about their entire conversation, and wake up tomorrow next to Scarlett, remembering it all as a distant nightmare. But another part of her, something that stirred deep within her soul, would not rest until she knew the truth. She stepped towards him and lowered her voice. "If Yasmina knew about Maryam's engagement, do you think she might have intervened?"

Their eyes locked and they stood there for a moment, enveloped in the streetlight, neither of them breathing. His lips puckered, then relaxed, then tensed once more. The frown lines in his forehead grew deeper. In the distance, a glass bottle shattered and a drunken college student shrieked, "Oh, Charlie, you're so bad!" A stray cat meandered past and meowed.

At long last, Dr. Hamza whispered, "I hope not." He clasped Jeanne's hand in his, and she felt the rough calluses press into her palm. A wiry black hair tickled her wrist, and somehow she felt that he was saying good-bye. "Good luck, Jeanne, and be careful." And then, without looking back, he strode across the street and turned the corner.

Chapter Twenty-Two

Hunched over, leaning against the lamp post, Jeanne felt as though she might be having her first real panic attack. She gasped for breath, and it came in short, stilted puffs that cascaded over one another, each one beginning before the previous one ended, and yet brought her no relief. It's all in my mind, she scolded herself, my muddled, muddled mind. And yet the panic only grew worse every time she tried to push her worrisome thoughts away.

Somewhere, on the edges of her conscience, in that gray area where facts subside and hunches predominate, Jeanne had long suspected that everything might not be as tidy as it seemed. But as long as she never had to voice her doubts aloud, she could pretend they did not exist. And she had never had to. Vivienne, Fergus, and Lily didn't share her doubts, or if they did, they had never said so.

But now, she had to at least entertain the previously unthinkable. Images flit through her mind as she raced through Georgetown's still, quiet streets: the pallid little man at the funeral parlor who claimed to be Yasmina's lover, the rock on Maryam's finger, Dr. Hamza's sad, searching brown eyes. At every turn, Yasmina had surprised her. She was more passionate, more magnanimous, more manipulative, and more complicated than Jeanne had ever dreamed. She was a true performer, a master of illusion, loved by many and understood by none.

Jeanne broke into a run. The pavement sped by, eerily white in the moonlight. To Jeanne, the sidewalk squares looked like so many gravestones, stacked up neatly in a row. She got into a rhythm, her feet beating a path in time to the mantra that raced through her head, *I look like death, but I am not.* She didn't know where the words came from, but at that moment they seemed appropriate.

The Russian Embassy came into view, and finally her apartment building. At last, her feet were bounding up the familiar linoleum stairs and down the long corridor. Scarlett opened her one good eye as Jeanne came through the door, and raised one pointy ear.

"Go back to sleep, Scar," she whispered. "It's just me."

She opened her laptop and took a deep breath. Now was the moment of truth.

Her fingers flew over the keys. There were two obituaries in the *Washington Post* on February 3rd that listed Harding Funeral Home as assuming funeral arrangements, and three on the 4th. As she skimmed each entry, most were what she expected: a society matron who died at the ripe old age of 98, a lobbyist whose family requested donations to the American Cancer Society in lieu of flowers. They never listed the cause of death, but it was pretty easy to guess based on the donation request.

She caught her breath as her eyes glanced over the fifth one:

Nasrin Zarei, 36, of McLean, Virginia, died February 3, 2012. Survived by her beloved husband Mark, daughter Ellen, and father Reza, in addition to numerous aunts, uncles, and cousins. Family requests that donations be sent to the Fairfax County Fire Department or the D.C. Baha'i Center in lieu of flowers. Closed casket viewing will be held February 4, 2012, at Harding Funeral Home, 4000 N. Connecticut Avenue, from 1 to 3 p.m., with burial to follow.

For a moment, she struggled to remember why the name sounded so familiar. But then she remembered Mr. Harding's sad response when she had asked if he had attended Yasmina's last performance. *Zarei funeral,* he had said.

Her fingers shaking, she entered "Nasrin Zarei" into her search engine. The first hit was a *Washington Post* article about the fire in which she and three other family members died. But further down the page, she was surprised to see a link to Bright Smiles Dentistry. When she clicked on it, Nasrin Zarei's blindingly white smile glared at her, accompanied by a glowing testimonial.

When she googled "Bright Smiles Dentistry," the result was just as she had feared: it was one of the Hariri Group's clients, along with five other dentists.

Without taking her eyes off the screen, she reached behind her and knocked three times on the wall. Long, short, long.

"Is it too loud, Twinkletoes?"

"I need to come over, Jerry. Yasmina is alive."

Jerry hunched over an old coffee mug and stared into it as though hoping to find the truth in its inky depths. Chipped along the handle, it said, "Kiss Me—I'm Italian." He took a long drag on his cigarette, and then pushed his hand behind him so that the smoke would waft towards the window. "Explain this to me again," he said slowly.

"My guess is that she realized several months ago that Ibrahim was her old friend Nejla's uncle, but that he didn't recognize her."

"Makes sense," Jerry muttered. "She was just a teen. She's probably changed a lot more than he has."

"She reconnects with Nejla's sister Maryam and finds out about Maryam's liaison with Ari. She realizes that Maryam is in danger, and decides to take matters into her own hands."

"Why not contact the police?"

"As far as we know, he hasn't committed any crimes in this country. Maybe she thinks no one will believe her if she tells them that he killed his niece back in the West Bank. After all, the police there will say that there is no record of any such thing happening. And his own family will deny it—they will say she died of appendicitis." Jeanne took a gulp and spit it out. "Jerry, this tastes like sludge."

"It's Turkish coffee," he said sheepishly. "It's the one thing I loved about Iraq." He took another long drag of his cigarette and then snuffed it out on an old, grimy ashtray. "Well if that's true, I can see why she faked her own death. But how? That's not something an amateur can pull off."

"She's a genius," Jeanne said. "And a master manipulator and an opportunist. She's got the advantage of working closely with dentists. And not just any dentists. Dentists close to her and the Harding Funeral Home."

"Interesting."

"She knows," Jeanne continued, "that she can switch her dental records for any of her clients' patients' at any time. She just needs to wait for a body."

"You think she arranged for Nasrin to die in a fire?"

"Of course not. But she looked around for a funeral home in the same neighborhood as her dental clinic. It was a good bet that many of her clients' patients would have their wakes there if they kicked the bucket. She starts having an affair with the funeral director—exactly the kind of guy who would be unbelievably flattered by her attentions. He's never had anyone half as good-looking give him the time of day, and now Yasmina's throwing herself at him. He becomes obsessed. He wants to meet her at all hours of the day and night. Since he's married, they can't have trysts at his home, so they meet at the funeral home. He gives her a key. She waits months until a woman roughly her age—who happens to be one of her clients' patients—dies in a fire and has a wake scheduled. And since the woman died in a fire, she knows the funeral will be closed casket and that the autopsy will show death from smoke inhalation. She lets herself into the funeral home in the middle of the night, steals the body, and replaces the body with something that weighs about the same. She switches her dental records with Nasrin's."

Jerry considered this for a moment. "But here's the problem," he said slowly. "The autopsy would have revealed embalming fluid, and they would have realized that something wasn't right."

Jeanne frowned. "What if the body wasn't embalmed?"

228

Jerry leaned forward. "Read me the obit again."

"Nasrin Zarei, 36, of McLean, Virginia, died February 3rd, 2012. Survived by her beloved husband Mark, daughter Ellen, and father Reza, in addition to numerous aunts, uncles, and cousins. Family requests that donations be sent to the Fairfax County Fire Department or the D.C. Baha'i Center—"

"Well that explains it," Jerry interrupted her. "She's Baha'i. They don't embalm the dead."

Jeanne shot him a quizzical look. She was amazed by all the random tidbits of information that floated around in Jerry's head.

He shrugged. "I had a Baha'i girlfriend once. When her uncle died, we had a whole morbid discussion about funerary rites."

"Okay," Jeanne said. "So she doesn't just pick any fire victim. She picks a fire victim she knows won't be embalmed. She steals the body. Before I arrive at Algiers, she lugs the body into the dressing room and puts it in a closet."

"Wouldn't you have smelled something odd?"

She had to admit that he had a good point. "Maybe she kept it frozen. Or maybe she moved the body after I started my performance." She thought back to the night of the fire. "Maybe she kept it in the dumpster. No one would have found it odd for that to stink."

Jerry picked up the story now. "Then, while you are performing, she stages it as a hate crime. She spray paints

'Hagar was a whore' on the exterior wall, arranges the body on the floor, douses everything in accelerant, and sets the fire."

"After the fire alarm goes off, she makes sure that she is seen going back down the stairs towards the fire. Then, under the cover of smoke, she sneaks out the back door, runs down the alley, and is in a cab or on the Metro—"

"Or in a get-away car driven by someone else—"

"While the rest of us stand there, dazed and confused, waiting for the fire department."

Jerry whistled. "You sure have quite an imagination, Twinkletoes."

"Always have, always will. But in this case, it's serving a good purpose. Trust me, Jerry, if you'd met that sniveling idiot of a funeral director, you'd know that Yasmina had an ulterior motive for having an affair with him."

"Money? Stability? Maybe he's a great cook?"

Jeanne shook her head and Jerry sighed. "I'd like to think us sniveling idiots of the world have something to offer the beautiful women of the world."

"You're not a sniveling idiot, Jerry. But this guy was. It's just too perfect of a coincidence that this woman died the day before the fire. And that she died in a fire, so an autopsy would show smoke inhalation as the cause of death. And that her wake was at the funeral home run by the guy Yasmina was having an affair with. And that she was a patient of Yasmina's client. Plus, I don't think that it is a coincidence that Yasmina suggested to Aisha that they increase their fire insurance a few months before. She knew that she was going to set the club on fire, but she didn't want them to suffer just because of Ibrahim's sin."

Jerry shifted uncomfortably in his chair. "But she didn't shoot Ibrahim. I don't care how many veils she had—I don't think she could have concealed a weapon and shot him with hundreds of people staring right at her."

Jeanne set Lily's videotape on the table and tapped it lightly. "That's right. She had an accomplice."

"A Hamas militant?"

"That's my bet."

He stirred his coffee thoughtfully. "How would she have met such a guy?"

"No idea. But her ex-husband said that she agitated for Palestinian rights. She could have met someone in those circles."

"You think he's on this tape?"

"I sure do."

  *   *   *   *

They sat by the flickering blue light of Jerry's television. A 1970's set from a pawn shop in Baltimore, it sported big clunky knobs, bent antennas, and a mass of protruding red and yellow wires.

Jeanne's hands picked absentmindedly at the cigarette burns in his tangerine loveseat, her feet resting against a stack of old pizza boxes. Her elbow was wedged uncomfortably between piles of tattered paperbacks, which rose from the couch like so many leaning towers of Pisa. Today, however, she was oblivious to the décor, engrossed in the grainy images that flitted across the screen. "Notice how she's making prolonged eye contact with someone off screen," she murmured.

"I thought you said he was on the tape, Twinkletoes. Off screen is not the same as on camera."

"Be patient, Jerry."

"Is the guy she's dancing around Ibrahim?"

Jeanne nodded. She regarded Ibrahim with new revulsion, knowing what she knew now, and she shuddered as she watched his eyebrows wiggling up and down like two hairy caterpillars. What she had formerly seen as mildly disgusting, she now saw as menacing. She noticed his thick, fleshy lips, half smiling, half sneering, and his curly dark hair, graying at the temples. She marveled at Yasmina's composure, her singular ability to smile and flatter a man whom she knew to be a killer. If Yasmina's hands were shaking, it didn't show on the video.

"I've been in this business long enough that I should know that looks are irrelevant," Jerry said, "but I gotta say, he doesn't look like someone who'd kill his niece. A dirty middle-aged man, maybe. But not a killer."

They watched in silence as Yasmina arranged her wineglasses on the floor and stepped onto the shimmering surface, tracing long graceful arcs across the floor. Jerry stared, wide-eyed, as Yasmina glided across the stage, increasing her speed as she began to move her hips, stomach, and shoulders. He gasped as she picked up a wineglass with her feet, nestling it in her luxurious dark hair and then playfully shaking her head. "Incredible," he whispered.

The music changed abruptly and suddenly Yasmina was brandishing a sword. Gilded and curved, she placed it gingerly on her head and the crowd applauded. The sword tilted back and forth, like a weathervane flapping in the wind. Jeanne jabbed Jerry in the arm. "Don't focus on her chest, Jerry. See how she's making extensive eye contact with someone off camera? Before she was flirting with the entire audience, but now her gaze is focused, intense. It's as if she's telling someone, 'now, do it now.'"

They followed her gaze. It was directed at something—or someone, Jeanne surmised—about thirty degrees to Yasmina's right. For a full thirty seconds, Yasmina's eyes were focused on that spot, unblinking.

"Now look at the sword," Jeanne murmured. "See if you see any reflection."

For a moment, the sword swayed this way and that. But soon it stabilized and a single dark shape began to emerge, wavy and sinuous. The curve of the sword distorted it, the way a Fun House mirror would. And yet the shape was distinctly human.

"That's my guy," she said.

"How do you know?"

"I don't. But in every other frame, the sword is reflecting what appears to be a group of people. That's how people come to Algiers—in groups. It's great for birthday parties, bachelorette parties, that sort of thing. No one comes alone."

Jerry peered intently at the screen. "Except this guy. Is he in Lily's video?"

"Nope. She never swung the camera that far to the side," Jeanne said. "Do you think you can improve the image?"

Jerry nodded slowly. "I'm going to have to call in some favors, but I think I can get you something you can work with." He patted her on the back. "Damn, Twinkletoes. I gotta say you really are good."

Chapter Twenty-Three

Jeanne found the rest of the day both excruciating and exhausting. She should have felt elated—she had only fifty more emails to go until she was finished with doc review for the Somnarvelous case, and her boss had even come by that morning and given her the two thumbs-up sign and a hearty slap on the back. Coming from Jim, that was significant. The day after his wife had given birth to twins, he had come in to work as usual, with the laconic comment, "My wife didn't do too shabby. Only twelve hours of labor." And then he had gone right into the staff meeting.

But it was rather hard to focus on the minutia of a pharmaceutical case—and all the asinine email flirtations between the pharmaceutical reps—while absorbing the shock that her friend, teacher, and idol had faked her own death and quite possibly was complicit in a murder. It was enough to make anyone's head spin on the best of days, and now she was trying to cope on less than two hours of sleep. Her hands shook slightly as she took a sip of her fifth cup of coffee that morning and peered anxiously at the fax machine. Still nothing.

At 1:07 that afternoon, the fax machine spit out a color image and Jeanne raced over to retrieve it. Without looking at the paper, she clutched it to her chest and ran back to her cubicle. "Let's see just who you are," she murmured, smoothing the image with her fingers. Jerry's friend had done an excellent job. The image was still distorted, but it was clear enough to make out his dark close-cropped hair, dark piercing eyes, rimless glasses, and long curved nose. He was clean-shaven and appeared to be Middle Eastern.

Folding the image, she tucked it into her bra and headed for the ninth floor women's restroom.

The meeting with Lily had gone much longer than the normally allotted five minutes. For once Lily was speechless as she tried to make sense of Jeanne's wild night—the bizarre late-night meeting with Dr. Hamza, the sleuthing that had resulted in the discovery that Harding Funeral Home had handled a closed casket funeral for a woman Yasmina's age who also happened to be her client's patient, the pre-dawn huddle with Jerry to re-examine the video, the enhanced image from Jerry.

Twenty minutes later, Jeanne was frantically emailing Vivienne to arrange a 7:00 p.m. meeting at Populo's.

At six-thirty, Jeanne grabbed her purse and snuck out the back. She crossed the National Mall, passing the old-fashioned carousel, now silent, the imposing red Smithsonian Castle, the boxy Air and Space Museum, and the quirky Hirschhorn sculpture garden. Sunken into the ground, the sculpture garden was filled with all sorts of odd steel and bronze contraptions with enigmatic names. She chuckled at the memory of Rodrigo, with his stuffed llamas and waxed chest, and she wondered if he dreamt of taking his place here, amongst a pantheon of angst-filled modernist artists.

The Capitol dome glowed a pale ivory in the moonlight. She had forgotten how awe-inspiring a sight it could be. Past the American Indian Museum she marched, its wavy warm sandstone walls rising like a desert fortress amidst Washington's lush greenery. Rounding the corner, she sped past the enclosed Botanical Gardens, a misty greenhouse filled with palm trees and orchids, and then headed uphill past the House Office Buildings. Young interns, earnest and self-important, scurried out front. She used to be just like them, but now she felt old and jaded. When she got to Pennsylvania Avenue, she turned right, admiring the old brick façades, two hundred-year-old relics converted into stylish restaurants and lounges catering to Capitol Hill staffers, lobbyists, and Congressmen.

At the end of this strip, she spotted Vivienne, who paced in front of the CVS Pharmacy in black stilettos. Her trench coat was unbuttoned, revealing a low-cut red velvet top and long black skirt. She tapped Vivienne on the shoulder and they ducked into the CVS, where they huddled by the feminine products.

"What's the plan?" Vivienne asked.

"All you have to do is pick up where you left off last time. Keep them distracted and ask if they've seen this guy." Jeanne pulled the photo out of her pocket and carefully unfolded it.

Vivienne whistled. "What a hottie."

"Viv, he's an assassin."

"Even so, he's hot." She chewed her lip. "Last time, I told them that Ibrahim was my ex and that I suspected Yasmina was cheating on him with me. How am I going to explain I'm now asking about this guy?"

Jeanne thought for a moment. "The last time you went to Populo's you did so because your husband had lots of receipts from Populo's so you assumed he and his mistress were meeting there. But now you think that maybe he was making payments to someone at Populo's and that person was handing over the money to the mistress."

"You mean like laundering it?"

"Yeah. Maybe you suspect a love child. Maybe he's paying the money to the guy in the picture, and he's giving it to the mistress. Maybe the guy in the photo is the mistress's brother."

"Got it," Vivienne said, and they headed across the street to Populo's.

When they arrived, Populo's was already buzzing with the happy hour crowd. The restaurant was a warm, inviting place with dark paneled booths and a large brick oven, from which beautiful pizzas, with blistered crusts, bubbling cheese, and chunks of crimson vine-ripened tomatoes emerged every few minutes. The sweet scent of basil wafted from the kitchen. "This place smells incredible," Jeanne murmured.

But Vivienne was not paying attention to the hubbub in the kitchen. "Check out the kid at eight o'clock," she said in a low voice. "Skinny pimply kid in the white apron. He's the one I said I'd be very grateful to last time. Probably still my best bet for information."

Jeanne watched as Vivienne sidled up to him, his face lighting up like a Christmas tree when he recognized her. She bent forward ever so slightly, giving him just a peek at her cleavage, and twisted her hair around her finger. Jeanne was impressed with her cunning; Vivienne looked appealingly vulnerable and sweet, rather than desperate. Vivienne reached into her bra and pulled out the folded photo. The kid's eyes were bulging at this point, and he waved away a colleague who tried to ask him a question.

Jeanne couldn't hear their conversation, but it wasn't too hard to guess. Vivienne smiled hopefully at him, pointing at the photo. He looked at it intently for a moment, a glimmer of recognition in his eyes. Vivienne leaned over the counter, and he cupped his hands over her ear. Smiling, she nodded and hastily scrawled a number—almost certainly fake—on a scrap of paper and slipped it across the counter. He beamed.

Jeanne approached and Vivienne pressed a second scrap of paper into her palm. She wandered towards the hostess stand as Vivienne continued chatting with the boy. Unfolding the paper, she read the name: Mike Sellers. Jeanne strolled down the corridor and loitered by the bathroom, keeping one eye on the hostess as she pretended to study the autographed photos that lined the wall. "Incredible pizza," a news anchor with big hair, had written. "Good times, good people," a former mayor had scrawled. As she stared at Jane Fonda's head, Jeanne rummaged in her pockets for a paper clip and then hurriedly unfurled it and twisted it into a hook.

In a few moments, the hostess led a party of five to their table. They were obviously tourists, decked out in baseball caps emblazoned with the FBI logo and "I love Washington D.C." T-shirts. Jeanne leaned against the door marked "Staff Only," and, in a matter of seconds, was able to pick the lock. She had learned the technique while watching re-runs on Matlock and perfected it in high school during search-and-destroy missions of her mother's various liquor hiding places. "Sticky fingers" had been Vivienne's nickname for her one summer.

Pushing the unpleasant memory out of her mind, Jeanne crouched in front of a file cabinet marked "W-2s." In the dim light, she could barely make out the "S-T" written in pencil on a yellowed, peeling label stuck to the second drawer from the bottom. With a flick of the wrist, she picked the lock and then carefully slid the drawer out, grabbed a copy of Mike Seller's W-2, stuffed it in her pocket, and closed the drawer. She crawled back to the door and waited until the sound of two girls giggling outside receded before cautiously, but quickly, opening the door. She loitered by the autographed photos once more, and then hurried to the door where Vivienne waited for her.

"Success?"

Jeanne nodded. "Thanks for getting the name."

"Are you going to have Carlos hook you up?"

"I'll give him a call tomorrow."

Chapter Twenty-Four

Fergus rested his elbows on the table and massaged his temples. Squeezed between a family wolfing down chimichangas smothered in over-processed cheese and a tequila shot-swilling group of women in their forties, Fergus and Jeanne were sharing a pitcher of frozen strawberry margaritas and munching on chips and salsa. It was a particularly boisterous and chaotic Friday night at Cactus Cantina, and Jeanne felt secure in the knowledge that no one could hear their conversation. Garish large-bulbed colored lights were strung along the walls, and a grotesque caricature of a Mexican cowboy, complete with a giant sombrero and gleaming spurs, stared down at them. Jeanne decided that if she were an interior designer, she would call this style Tex-Mex kitsch. And then she would redecorate Vivienne's house with it.

Fergus stared at her. His lips moved, but she could not hear him. He tried again, moving so close to her that she could feel his hot breath in her ear. "Let me get this straight," he shouted, his blue eyes blazing. Jeanne felt herself instinctively pulling away from him. "Yasmina is alive. The charred body is one of Yasmina's client's patients. Yasmina is a psychopath who staged her own death and committed a premeditated murder. You now have a photo of the triggerman and you know his name."

"Well actually—" Jeanne began to protest weakly, but he cut her off.

"Aye, I know. His name is probably not Mike Sellers. So you are going to go visit some underground identification factory—where in addition to the various poor illegal gardeners visiting, there will probably be the odd international drug trafficker—to find out who he really is. And then, without telling the police, you are going to go to his apartment, kick down the door with your" –he looked down—"size seven trainers, hypnotize him with your belly dancing moves right as he reaches for his Uzi, tie him up by his shoelaces, and then wait for Nine News Now to arrive?"

"I wear size seven-and-a-half," she said meekly.

His arm shot up like a rocket. "The bill, please!" he roared.

He marched her down Wisconsin Avenue at a breakneck pace, his hand roughly grasping her arm. Without exchanging a word, they crossed the broad avenue, now choked with traffic, and headed into the moonlit grounds of the National Cathedral. When they reached the secluded Bishop's Garden, he hoisted her up over a low section in the wall and then led her briskly along the brick paths, past rows of English boxwoods.

Jeanne marveled that Fergus knew about the Bishop's Garden, one of her favorite retreats. Designed by Frederick Law Olmstead, the garden was dotted with odd bits of statuary plucked from the medieval cloisters of Europe, wreathed with delicate cherry blossoms in spring, and overladen with sprays of pink and purple perennials in summer accompanied by the intoxicating scent of roses. Out of the corner of her eye, she spotted the Wayside Cross. Celtic in design, it was inscribed with IHS in the center, and a Latin phrase from Psalms along its outer edge. "Our soul is humbled even unto the dust," Jeanne read silently. It was one of those rare occasions on which her college Latin was of any use.

When they arrived at a small wooden bench, Fergus released his grip and, grunting, motioned for her to sit. He paced back in forth in front of her. "Jeanne, what the bloody hell have you gotten yourself into?"

"I wanted to find out what happened to my friend," she said in a small voice.

"And you did!" he exclaimed, exasperated. "You found out she's a bloody psycho who conspired to kill a bloke who happens to be a child-killer and an international terrorist. Case closed. Your friend's alive and apparently doesn't feel the need to let you know her whereabouts. Or even that she's alive. There's no longer any murder to investigate. THERE WAS NO MURDER."

"Except of Ibrahim."

"Who is not a friend of yours. You said,"—he pointed accusingly at her—"that this was all about finding who killed Yasmina. The cops weren't investigating her death as a homicide, but Vivienne's soon-to-be ex-husband put the idea into your head that someone killed her. And now you think that isn't true." He lowered his voice, and it took on the cold, steely tone of an authority figure lecturing a child. She squirmed and looked at the ground. He was not taking the break in the case the way she had hoped. "You do, however, think you have evidence that several crimes were committed. You think Yasmina stole a body and improperly disposed of human remains. You think she falsified records to cover up a crime. You think she committed arson. You think she tipped off Mike Sellers that Ibrahim would be at Algiers that night. And yet you haven't notified the police that any of these crimes have occurred. You also have a photo of the guy who pulled the trigger, and you haven't shared that with police yet."

"Most likely the police already have that photo themselves. They should have imaging experts."

"Not true. They have no reason to believe Yasmina is complicit—they think she's a poor fire victim—so there's no reason for them to key in on the bloke she's making eye contact with." He sat down next to her, and his tone changed from gruff to pleading. "Besides, Jeanne, this is getting dangerous. What if Yasmina finds out you know her secret? Maryam might be in on it, and she might tip Yasmina off. You'd be a loose end she might have to tie up."

Even though Jeanne knew that Yasmina had set a fire that endangered hundreds of lives, she could not bring herself to condemn her friend. "Yasmina's not evil, Fergus. She was just protecting Maryam."

She looked away from him, and a quote from Tolstoy flitted through her mind. *Happy families are all alike; every unhappy family is unhappy in its own way.* He was from one of those happy families, she could tell. She didn't expect him to understand.

She sighed. "Fergus, Yasmina is going to find out I know her secret. I'm going to track her down and convince her to come out of hiding and tell the police what she knows. Leaving out, perhaps, the fact that she collaborated with the killer. We can't let our mystery man run around assassinating people."

He blinked several times and looked up at her, incredulous. "Bloody hell," he whispered. "Why don't you let the cops do their job?"

"Because every time I talk to them, they say I'm imagining things."

"But now you've got new evidence. Maybe they'll believe you this time."

"What evidence? It's all very circumstantial. And what if I'm wrong?"

Fergus grunted. "Well that's a new one. You're not one for admitting you might be wrong."

"There's a tiny possibility I'm wrong," Jeanne said, "and if I am wrong, I'll have dragged my friend's name through the mud for nothing."

Fergus muttered something that Jeanne could not make out under his breath.

"What was that?"

His blue eyes were gray in the moonlight and they stared at her with an unnerving intensity, a mix of determination and fear. "I'm going with you tomorrow. You're going to need some protection."

"From you?" She snorted.

"I was the champion boxer of East Glasgow High."

"Flyweight, I presume."

"Still."

"You don't need to. I've got Carlos."

"Who's Carlos?"

"I guess you could call him an old friend. He's an ex-con. Two years in the slammer, four on the streets. I appreciate the offer—" she clasped his hands in hers and tried not to laugh—"but I think I've got my protection detail covered."

Chapter Twenty-Five

Jeanne struggled to keep pace with her "protection detail." It wasn't that Carlos walked too fast. On the contrary, he sauntered down the street, glancing about as if he were a king surveying his vast dominions. "You've got to walk around like you own the place," he had once explained to Jeanne. "You've got to be on guard for the slightest display of disrespect." After that conversation, she had given him her dog-eared copy of Machiavelli's *The Prince*, and he had returned it to her in a week, complete with notes, penciled into the margins, explaining how Machiavelli mostly had it right, but would have to alter his theories slightly if he were to survive as kingpin of one of the Salvadoran *maras* that menaced the streets of Columbia Heights and Mount Pleasant.

His dominions were quite a bit less grand that the manor houses of England, and yet evidence of the relentless advance of gentrification could be seen even here. The neighborhood was an odd mix: earnest young Salvadoran immigrants snacking on *pupusas* while waiting at the bus stop in their freshly pressed uniforms emblazoned with the logos of swanky downtown restaurants; groups of swaggering Hispanic men, loitering in front of store windows, who whistled at comely young mothers pushing strollers and made barely audible cracks to their gold-toothed companions about her *culo*; preppy Caucasian twenty-somethings pairing designer hand bags with retro-chic outfits from hip consignment shops; and gay men in skinny jeans out walking their Chihuahuas. For the loitering set, there was another dress code altogether: baseball caps worn backwards, jeans so loose half of their boxer shorts were exposed, and shiny new athletic shoes.

In between the stately old apartment buildings, their once-grand Gothic façades somewhat diminished by the swirling litter, cigarette butts, and hunks of dried-up gum, were small bodegas, a grocery and liquor store whose windows were covered with an enormous metal grate, a Laundromat, a smattering of Salvadoran restaurants and bakeries, and the odd high-end coffee shop, café, or florist. Every now and then, Jeanne caught a whiff of urine. But despite the grit, the neighborhood was pleasant and full of life, and she found herself enjoying the walk.

"*Ya llegamos.*" Carlos gave a brief nod and motioned for her to follow him through an unmarked door. Lit by a single light bulb hanging from a string, the tiny entryway was a dingy, depressing place, with yellow-gray walls and chipped linoleum floors. Jeanne quickly scanned the names on the four metal mailboxes: López, Villanueva, Allen, Echeverría.

Carlos's eyes followed hers. "*Arriba,*" he murmured, pointing, and headed up the stairs. They usually spoke in Spanish, and today was no exception. Speaking Spanish had initially been a way for Jeanne to gain his trust, but now it had become their standard way of communicating. She remembered how silent he had been in her GED class two years ago, how he had balked at the idea of taking classes in a jail, especially from a girl from the backwoods of Maine. "What have you got to teach me?" he had once said in an uncharacteristic outburst. "It seems like you could use some lessons from me about how to survive in a big city." Another day he had scoffed, incredulous, when she made an off-handed comment about being a volunteer. "What kind of *idiota* would work for free?" he had asked.

But now they had a relationship based on trust and mutual respect, if not always complete comprehension. Or so Jeanne hoped.

Carlos stopped at the top of the second flight of stairs and put his ear to the door on the left. The door was pock-marked with bullet holes and a brass number

"2" hung, swinging, upside down, from a single nail. Carlos rapped four times on the door. Long, short, short, long.

Jeanne heard heavy, slow footsteps approach, then the sound of a deadbolt sliding out of its slot, followed by the jangling of several chains. Paco was evidently quite security conscious. "*Entre*," said a muffled voice inside.

Carlos turned the knob and slipped inside, with Jeanne right behind him.

An obese middle-aged man in a white undershirt and black sweat pants stood a few feet away, his weapon drawn. A grainy bootlegged version of *Pulp Fiction*, dubbed into Spanish, blared from the TV. The woman doing Uma Thurman's voice sounded as though she had just inhaled helium.

Jean flinched as he took a step towards them, grimacing in pain as his legs, stolid and thick as tree trunks, struggled to bear his weight. But Carlos did not seem concerned in the least. "*Soy yo, Carlos!*" he cried, and the man released his grip, tossing the gun beside the enormous bag of Goya brand plantain chips on the couch, as he smiled in recognition.

He lumbered towards the two guests and then encircled Carlos in his big, beefy arms. "*Sobrino mío.*"

Jeanne raised an eyebrow. Carlos had not told her that Paco, *El Rey de los Documentos Falsificados*, was his uncle. She could hardly believe they were related. While

Paco was flaccid and ungainly, Carlos was agile and muscular, with a broad chest. He was a fine male specimen, as Lily would say, and now, admiring his high cheekbones and big liquid brown eyes, she could hardly disagree. But whenever she was tempted to think of him in that way, she quickly sobered up upon remembering that he was twenty-three and an ex-con.

Carlos introduced Jeanne as his new girlfriend—a *gringa* who didn't understand any Spanish—and Jeanne tried to look the part of the clueless floozy. She smiled blankly and wandered over to the sofa, pretending to watch Uma Thurman stick a needle in someone's heart while in fact she was listening closely to the exchange between Carlos and Paco. Out of the corner of her eye, she saw Carlos unfolding the photo and showing it to his uncle.

Paco said something about making a Bulgarian passport. "Boris Draganov," he murmured. "*Un tipo muy raro.*"

Chapter Twenty-Six

"You forgot to mention Paco was your uncle," Jeanne said as they walked slowly down Eighteenth Street, eyes glued to the address numbers on each establishment.

Carlos shrugged. "I didn't think it was important."

"I hope you're not involved in his business."

"If I were, do you think he'd pull a gun on me? We haven't seen each other too much since I went legit."

She looked at him intently, trying to discern whether this was really true, but his expression was inscrutable.

"You worry too much about other people, *profesora*," he said. "Worry about yourself more."

They locked eyes for an instant, and she had a sudden uneasy feeling that the tables had turned. The distinction between teacher and student had blurred. He was a grown man now, sagacious in his own way, with little education but quite a lot of life experience.

She busied herself by unfolding the W-2 form stuffed in her pocket and squinting at the numbers that sped past. "*Aquí*," she said, pointing at a three-story red brick building crowned by a turret. A rusty bike, bereft of its back wheel, was chained to the handrail that ran alongside the steep flight of concrete steps. There was not a soul stirring.

They ducked into an Ethiopian restaurant across the street and asked to sit by the window. Perched on small wicker stools arranged around a divan, Carlos and Jeanne sipped *tej*, Ethiopian honey wine, as they maintained their vigil. Red chili, garlic, and cardamom wafted through the dining room as the waitresses, tall and elegant in their long white *shamas*, shuffled in and out, laden with heavy trays of lentils, chickpeas, spicy beef *tibs*, and Jeanne's favorite, chicken *doro wat*. The giant boiled egg in the center, sticky with a smoky chili-infused chicken gravy, was her favorite part. Today, she tore off a piece of *injera*, the giant slightly sour pancake Ethiopians use to scoop up all of their food, and tapped on the egg, breaking it in two. "Try it," she said, pushing the other half in Carlos's direction. "*Está rico.*"

"Is he the *maricón?*" Carlos asked, eyeing the rainbow flag that fluttered from the third floor balcony.

Jeanne shook her head. "It says #2 on the W-2. Since there are only three mailboxes, it's got to be the second floor apartment."

"You think he's Bulgarian?"

Jeanne sighed. "I doubt it. And I doubt his real name is either Boris Draganov or Mike Sellers."

Jeanne slouched on her stool, resting her back against the wall. "Do you miss home, Carlos? Do you ever thinking of going back?"

"There's nothing to go back to," he said in a low, even voice, avoiding her gaze. "I'd be dead within a few months."

"The *maras?*"

He snorted. "My old friends. I did a lot of bad things in my past, but people were afraid of me. Now I've gone soft. No one would be afraid of me. And once they realize I'm not scary anymore..." He raised a hand to his throat and made a slicing motion. "Do you miss Maine?"

"No." She considered it more carefully. "I miss the land," she said. "The vast meadows, the wildflowers, the craggy rocks. The connection to something solid and permanent. The change of seasons. The intimate connection with nature. The place I grew up wasn't all concrete and blacktop, yuppies and hipsters, restaurants that are here for a year and then gone, swallowed up by a huge sterile condo building."

"And the people? They are what really makes a place."

"The few friends I had, left. Anyone with any ambition does. There's a gas station, a lumber mill, and a grocery-slash-shoe store-slash-butcher-slash-taxidermist. The latter's run by Old Bob McAdoo. He's very entrepreneurial. You can drop off your freshly caught deer to be butchered while you shop for sneakers and pick up some ice cream and diapers. So if you don't want to work in one of those establishments, or be a farmer, you're out of luck. Most of my friends live in Boston or New York. One's in med school, two are teachers, and one's a lawyer."

He laughed. "Your friends are very different than mine."

"I met mine in Honor Society."

"I guess I could say the same if you consider a *mara* an honor society. After all, if you break the rules..."

Raising a hand to their throats, they both laughed.

"And your family?" he asked.

"My sister lives here."

"Are your parents dead?"

She nodded weakly. It was easier that way.

"Mine too."

They sat in silence for a moment. Jeanne pretended to be interested in a young man arguing with his girlfriend outside. When they moved on, she shifted her gaze to a unicyclist in a red-and-white striped top hat, followed by a skateboarder with pink hair.

She finally got up the nerve to ask the question she had always wanted to know. "What was prison like?" She tried to sound nonchalant, as if she were asking about the weather in El Salvador. The truth was that they had known each other for three years, and it was one thing they had never talked about. She didn't even know what he had done time for; the very first thing they warned volunteers was never, ever to check a prisoner's file. They were some things you did not want to know.

"Boring."

"Boring?" The answer surprised her. She had expected a response like "brutal," "awful," or "dehumanizing."

"There was nothing to do all day. Just watch TV, play cards, argue with the other prisoners, maybe find Jesus. Time went so slowly. Every minute of every day you were aware of the fact that you were one minute closer to dying and you hadn't accomplished anything."

"Were you ever...?" She swallowed.

"Ever what?"

"Raped?"

"It depends what you mean by rape," he said in a soft voice, avoiding her gaze. "The rules are different on the inside. You need to survive."

She took a moment to absorb this. "Did you think about what you did?"

He nodded.

"Were you sorry?"

"Of course."

They sat in silence for a while longer. The unicyclist rode in long, loping circles in the street, and a few cars honked as he weaved around them.

"Do you think the conditions are pretty similar in women's prisons?"

The corners of his mouth curled up into a smirk. "Are you planning on committing a crime?"

"Of course not."

"Well then it doesn't matter, does it?"

"I suppose not," she replied softly.

He licked his fingers. "I've never had Ethiopian food before. It was—"

He broke off suddenly as something caught his eye. Jeanne followed his gaze. Across the street, a tall, well-built man in jeans and a black leather jacket was turning a key in the lock. As he turned around and skipped down the stairs, Jeanne gasped.

"You know him?"

"His name is Rodrigo Robles," Jeanne said without taking her eyes off him. "He's an Argentine artist and a former flame of Yasmina's. And, if I am not mistaken, he is also Mike-slash-Boris's roommate or house guest."

Chapter Twenty-Seven

Jeanne was running across the P Street Bridge when Fergus called.

"How was your afternoon with Carlos?" he growled. He spat out Carlos's name as it were some poisonous substance he was struggling to get out of his system.

"Most informative." She ignored his tone. "Mike Sellers had a Bulgarian passport made for him in the name of Boris Draganov."

"Interesting."

"There's more." She waited for a wailing ambulance to pass. "Carlos and I cased Mike-slash-Boris's apartment. Guess who was coming out the door?"

"Yousef?"

"Rodrigo Robles."

"The chest waxer?"

"That's the guy."

"So what's your theory?"

"Yasmina knew she needed—"

"Wanted—" he interjected.

"—to kill Ibrahim, but she was waiting for the right opportunity. She meets Mike-slash-Boris through Rodrigo. Maybe they are just roommates; maybe Rodrigo is a fellow intelligence agent undercover as a wacky artist. Somehow she finds out that Boris is tracking Ibrahim— maybe she overhears something, maybe she confides in him about her hatred of Ibrahim—"

"Maybe she has an affair with him, just like everyone else."

"She offers to help him assassinate Ibrahim. She agrees to track Ibrahim's movements and keep him abreast by calling him at work."

"So who is Boris?"

"I'm guessing a member of Hamas."

"There is another interpretation, of course," Fergus said. "Ibrahim and Yasmina were having an affair, Rodrigo found out, and he hired—or maybe blackmailed—Boris to kill both of them and stage it as a hate crime."

Jeanne sighed. "I guess anything is possible. I'll check it out."

"And inhale, and exhale, and inhale, and exhale, and wrap yourself in a great big hug and give yourselves a round of applause!"

Jeanne gave herself a half-hearted pat on the back and forced herself to give the group a couple of perfunctory claps. She found the constant touchy-feely self-esteem boosting hollow and manufactured, and she couldn't help but feel that perky Amy, with her six-pack abs and blond ponytail, might be better suited to leading a high school cheerleading team than filling Yasmina's shoes. But Amy was sweet, dedicated, and had great technique, so Jeanne tried to give her the benefit of the doubt.

Jeanne fiddled with her coin belt and slowly, ever so slowly, leaned down to touch her toes, lunge to the right, and then to the left. Out of the corner of her eye, she watched a dozen pairs of bare feet, ranging from milky white to deepest ebony, cross the studio's polished wooden floor, in time to the jingle-jangling of coins.

As the pleasant tinkling sounds began to recede into the corridor, she turned her attention to Amy, who was sliding her Belly Dance Superstars CD into its case. "Great class," Jeanne said, trying her best to sound sincere.

"Oh, well, thank you." Amy twisted her ponytail. "It's hard taking over for Yasmina. She was such an amazing teacher. I can learn the steps, but she felt them. You know? And sometimes I tear up in the middle of the routine. What happened to her is just so upsetting."

"You were close, weren't you?"

Amy nodded and bit her lip. "We didn't hang out too much outside the studio, but then, all we both do outside the studio is work, eat, and sleep. But we were here together so often. I subbed for her; we were in two dance troupes together. We often danced together at the Middle Eastern nightclubs around town." She took a sharp breath. "Including Algiers."

"Did you ever get the sense that she had any enemies at Algiers? Did she have any disagreements with the staff or with customers?"

"No, not at all. Everyone loved her." Amy bit her lip. "Why do you ask?"

"I'm probably being silly and paranoid," Jeanne said, "but there is a chance—a slight, slight chance—that Yasmina was murdered before her body was burned."

Amy's eyes clouded with tears. "Is that what the police said?"

"No, of course not," Jeanne said quickly. "Just my wild imagination." After a pause to allow Amy to regain her composure, she continued, "Was there anyone who paid special attention to her?"

"Yeah, everyone. She was talented and gorgeous."

"Well did she pay special attention to anyone in return?"

Amy frowned and wrinkled her cute little nose. "What are you getting at?"

Jeanne took a deep breath. Amy might not tell her what she wanted to know, but she had to at least ask.

And maybe Amy's expression would tell her everything she needed to know. "Could she have been having an affair with either Ibrahim or Yousef?"

Amy's eyes widened and her jaw dropped in disbelief. "Jeanne! I can't believe you would think such a thing."

"I know, it sounds crazy. I'm just searching for an explanation. Being there and seeing the blood gushing out of Ibrahim was so upsetting. I've been going over and over it in my mind." Looking Amy straight in the eye, she leaned closer and lowered her voice for dramatic effect. "And, of course, it seems selfish, but I've been trying to reassure myself that you or I am not the next target."

She saw that her words had had the desired effect, as Amy recoiled in horror and covered her mouth.

"You don't think...?"

"That there is psycho on the loose who is obsessed with belly dancers?"

Amy nodded, speechless. She scrunched her expertly arched eyebrows close together and little frown lines formed into a row of angry "V"s that pointed towards her platinum widow's peak. Jeanne felt a pang of remorse.

"I doubt it," Jeanne said. "I think it's specific to Ibrahim and Yasmina. I'm just trying to understand the connection."

The little frown lines melted back into Amy's creamy white forehead. "I don't think there was anything going on," she sighed. "I never saw anything unusual. Everything was always very professional—well as professional as things can be at a place where you get paid under the table in cash. To tell you the truth, I only saw Ibrahim a handful of times. And there was nothing going on with Yousef. Yousef and Aisha adore each other. They're the cutest old couple—traditional, of course, but very loving."

"Were you there the night of the fire?"

"I was there earlier in the afternoon, helping Yasmina rehearse. But, before the performance, I had to take off to go and see my niece's school play. Oh!" She clapped her hands to her head. "Sometimes it seems like yesterday. I just can't believe it."

"I noticed that Yasmina had a lot of new costumes and props the night of the fire. They were in a heavy trunk. Did she bring them that afternoon?"

Amy thought for a moment. "I think so—yes, that's right. I believe Yousef helped her. It was quite heavy, Yasmina said." Her eyes widened. "Do you think that's important?"

"Oh, no," Jeanne lied. "I was just curious. Thanks for your time, Amy." She squeezed her arm. "You're doing great and please don't worry. I think what happened at Algiers is an isolated incident."

As she ran down the stairs, her feet sinking into the orange shag carpeting, she was relieved that there was at least one person Yasmina was not having an affair with— at least, according to Amy. She wanted to believe Amy, and there was no real reason to doubt her. But she had to admit that Amy was not the most perceptive person in the world. Maybe Yasmina and Ibrahim had been discrete enough to escape her notice.

Deciding that she needed more confirmation, she called her sister. "I need a favor, Viv."

"More flirting at Populo's?"

"I need you to go on a date with Rodrigo."

"What?" Vivienne sputtered. Jeanne could hear a clanking sound in the background, as if her sister were scrubbing a heavy pot, and she wondered whether the separation from Mitch had also resulted in a loss of her cleaning lady. "I haven't been on a date in almost a decade, Jeanne, and technically, I'm still married."

"To a cheater. You wouldn't be doing anything wrong. You meet him for a drink, pry some information from him, feign a headache, and head on out without so much as a good-night kiss."

"What information would I be prying from him?"

"Oh, just what his relationship with Yasmina was like, what his roommate is like, whether he hired his roommate to kill her. You know—the usual small talk."

"What on earth are you talking about?"

"Carlos and I spotted Rodrigo emerging from the last known address of the man in the video," Jeanne said. "We need to know what his connection is to Yasmina and Ibrahim."

"And you think he's just going to tell me that?"

"You're wily. I know you've got ways of getting the information."

There was a long silence, and Jeanne could tell that she was mulling it over. "But he thinks I'm happily married to an ExxonMobil exec," Vivienne finally said.

"Exactly. An ExxonMobil exec who has just died of a massive heart attack, leaving you with a broken heart in need of consolation and millions of dollars to spend on art."

Chapter Twenty-Eight

At dusk the following Tuesday, on the rooftop bar of the W Hotel, Vivienne reprised her role as a crass but charming Houston socialite while Jeanne hovered nearby. On this occasion, Vivienne was far more subdued than she had been at the gallery. Her cleavage was stowed safely away in a demure long black dress; only her enormous gold hoop earrings and gold-studded cowboy boots hinted at her former exuberant persona.

"It's so nice to see a friendly face at a time like this," she confided to Rodrigo in a soft, plaintive twang, rubbing her fingers across the velveteen cushions. They were reclining on a low bench on the edge of the terrace, which overlooked the Treasury building and the White House. But they paid no attention to the view. "I had a lot of family around right after the funeral. But now the house is so empty...." She trailed off, her eyes misting over, and he nodded sympathetically and patted her arm.

Jeanne kept her eyes on the magnificent view. She did not want to be seen staring. Instead, she leaned her elbows against the railing, swilled the inch of red wine in her glass, and drank in the view like an enraptured tourist. She had to admit that it was beautiful. From the eleventh floor, Washington looked so peaceful, like an enormous expanse of forest punctuated only by a graceful marble monument here and there. The Lincoln Monument was a soft purplish hue in the fading daylight, and the Potomac curved gently behind it. From here, one could not tell that the Potomac was so polluted that male fish were growing ovaries, or that the traffic was gridlocked, or that the District's crime rate was sky high. Everything looked orderly and peaceful.

She pushed her blond polyester locks behind her ears, intent not to miss a word of their conversation, and she pushed her glasses—which she hadn't worn since law school—up the bridge of her nose. Her tight jeans and shiny red top were not the most comfortable disguise, but she couldn't run the risk of being recognized by Rodrigo.

Her sister droned on and on about how lonely her house seemed, taking care to describe its vast size, luxurious trappings, and expensive art. "I find myself wandering into the music room at all hours of the day, just to look at the Renoir," she was saying. "There is something about the expression of the woman that is so enigmatic. I feel as though she is grieving, but she sees a better day right around the corner. I feel more peaceful when I'm in her presence. Our pool and sauna are relaxing, of course, but not as peaceful."

Rodrigo hung on her every word. He wore a thoughtful, concerned expression, his brows knitted together in deep concentration. He didn't look like a killer to Jeanne. But, then again, she hadn't pegged Yasmina as an arsonist.

"Have you ever lost someone you loved?" Her sister's voice was sweet and vulnerable.

Jeanne saw the Argentine nod slowly. He mumbled something that she could not hear.

"That's terrible," Vivienne gushed in a stage whisper. Evidently he had. "But that was years ago. I'm sure an attractive, talented young man like you has found plenty of female companionship in D.C."

He sighed. "I was dating a CPA during the fall. She was amazing. Beautiful. Talented. And an artist too—a belly dancer. But she broke things off right before the New Year. Something about how she was planning on moving soon and didn't want to get more emotionally involved."

Vivienne played dumb. "Did she end up moving?"

Staring down at the floor, he rubbed his hands together. Finally, he looked up and met Vivienne's gaze. "She died actually. In a fire. You may have seen it in the newspaper."

"You don't say! Why, I read about that a couple of weeks ago in the Houston Chronicle. What a terrible crime! And it's still unsolved, isn't it?"

"According to the newspapers, the incident was a hate crime." He shuddered and his long curly hair brushed his shoulders. "It brings back bad memories."

"Bad memories?" Vivienne probed gently, setting her wine glass on the table and leaning closer to him.

"The bombing of the Jewish community center in Buenos Aires. I was nineteen at the time, and my dad's cousin died in the attack."

Jeanne's legs nearly buckled underneath her. Feeling a bit woozy, she grasped the railing. Did this mean Rodrigo was Jewish? She knew that there was a sizable Jewish community in Buenos Aires, but she could not imagine what a Hamas operative would be doing living with a Jew. Unless it was some sort of twisted deep cover. Deep, deep cover.

He was silent for a moment before adding, "I hope the authorities here are less corrupt than the ones back home. Almost twenty years later, not a single person has been convicted. The judge who led the initial inquiry was impeached for allegedly paying a witness to change his testimony and for burning evidence." He laughed bitterly. "Some justice."

He glanced behind him, in Jeanne's direction. She realized that she had been standing there far too long. Retreating to a table next to theirs, she busied herself by flipping through the pages of the *Lonely Planet Guide to Washington D.C.* It was a 1998 version, with a cracked spine and several pages missing, that she had borrowed from the Georgetown Public Library. She doubted anyone would inspect it too closely.

Rodrigo lowered his voice, and Jeanne leaned forward, straining to hear him. "But the good news is that former President Menem was recently charged with obstructing the investigation and hiding the involvement of a powerful Syrian-Argentine businessman. Maybe something will come of that."

They talked about terrorism for a while. Vivienne told him that she had been in Paris working as a fashion buyer on September 11th and had gone to Notre Dame to light candles for the victims. Rodrigo told her about his grandparents, three of whom had died in the Holocaust. Vivienne regaled him with tales of her French ancestors, how they had retreated into the forest rather than being exiled to swampy Louisiana with the rest of the Acadians.

It should have been a bleak, sorrowful conversation, and yet somehow it was leavened with humor and sprinkled with pride. They marveled at the resourcefulness of their ancestors, how they had somehow managed to survive, their idiosyncrasies. "My *grand-mère*," Vivienne laughed, "even kept her coffin under the bed. When the price of lumber crashed, she bought a couple of boards for next to nothing and then nagged *Nonc* Albert until he made her one. And she was sure that the black bear that roamed our yard at night gorging on blueberries was evil *Tante* Marie. She would tip-toe outside in the dead of night with an epidural pinched from the free clinic and try to draw some blood."

Rodrigo just stared at her, incredulous.

"It's an old custom," she explained. "The souls of sinners roam about in black bears. And *Tante* Marie was a sinner. No one ever doubted that. She ran a speakeasy during the Depression and a brothel in an old farmhouse off Rouge Road, behind the railroad tracks."

"Was your grandmother successful?"

Vivienne laughed. "She got some blood, and the bear never came back. So yes, I guess so. But she did end up with three claw marks on her left arm. She was very proud of them. She showed them off in church on Sunday. The claw marks were like confirmation that she had fought the devil and won."

Jeanne was stunned. She hadn't heard Vivienne talk about *grand-mère* or *Tante* Marie in years. Vivienne never acknowledged her Acadian heritage and when people asked her how she knew French, she always said that she had studied the language in college, and then honed it by living in Paris. She never admitted that she had learned it in a rickety trailer half-concealed by a thicket of blueberry bushes on a bend in the St. John's River. It wasn't proper French, and it was filled with all kinds of superstitious creatures and homespun sayings that would leave a Parisian scratching his or her head, but it was French nonetheless.

She realized that except for the accent, there wasn't much of anything that Vivienne was concealing. She had forgotten to talk about Texas or oil money; her rich, dead husband was an afterthought. It had taken a faux date with the possible accomplice of an assassin to bring out her old personality. A thin film of tears clouded Jeanne's vision; she realized how much she had missed the old Vivienne all of these years.

She heard the sound of someone clearing a throat, loud and quite close to her ear, as if someone were gargling right into it. Looking up from her book, she blinked the tears away quickly, relieved that they didn't slide down her cheeks.

There was a gangly teenage boy standing over her. His head was crowned with a mass of frizzy black curls that added at least two inches to his already considerable height, and an army of zits marched across his face. He had a particularly unfortunate pimple on the side of his nose, a huge, red, throbbing mass, topped by a yellowish brown sac of pus. Jeanne remembered her own teenage battle with acne and felt momentarily sympathetic. But she was also supremely irritated. He was interrupting her concentration.

"Yes?"

"You must—" He gulped and stuffed his hands in the pockets of his jeans. "You must be tired, miss. You've been heading through my—you've been—" He looked frantically over his shoulder at a boy about his age who was trying to mouth the words to him. "You've been heading through my run all night. No, I mean you've—"

Jeanne laughed, but not unkindly. "I've been running through your head all night?"

He nodded and turned bright red.

"Well I'm a slow runner. So no wonder it's taking so long."

"You're so pretty," he said. "I guess guys say that to you all the time, huh?"

She shook her head. "To my sister, not to me. And thank you for saying that. You're very sweet." She took another sip of wine and noticed that he was drinking a Coke. "Are you here for a class trip?"

"A debate tournament. I bet you think that's dorky."

She shook her head. Vivienne was asking Rodrigo if he lived alone, and she had to hear the answer. "Let's enjoy the view in silence," she murmured. She smiled, trying to look like a hippy-dippy, New Age cougar. To her relief, he shrugged and sat down.

"I have a roommate named Jacob," Rodrigo said. "He's quiet and polite. We don't interact too much, but sometimes we watch soccer games together. Occasionally we light the Shabbat candles together."

"Is he from Argentina too?"

Rodrigo shook his head. "Israel. We met at the synagogue."

Jeanne looked at them sharply, startled. She forgot that she was supposed to be ignoring them. Could the assassin be Israeli? She had never considered that Yasmina could have collaborated with Mossad. It seemed unthinkable. And yet every sign was pointing to that fact unless, of course, a Hamas operative was posing as an Israeli, even going so far as to join a synagogue.

"Are you all right?" her pimply companion asked. His voice cracked and he fiddled with his collar. "You seem kind of frightened."

"I'm fine," Jeanne said quickly. "I thought I caught a glimpse of my ex-husband, but it turned out to be a false alarm."

He looked dubious, but said nothing. After a few more awkward moments, he got up from the table. "I'd better go. We're going on a nighttime tour of the monuments."

Jeanne bade him good-bye and wished him luck in the debate tournament. She turned her full attention back towards Rodrigo and her sister.

"Well I'm not completely alone," Vivienne was saying. "I have my son Everett. He's two."

"It must be nice to have kids," Rodrigo said wistfully. "I always planned on having a family. But it never happened."

"It's not too late."

"Maybe. But I'm almost forty."

Vivienne snorted. "Sperm lasts forever. You can have a kid when you're eighty."

Rodrigo laughed, and little lines crinkled around his big brown eyes. "So true."

"And my sister Jeanne lives nearby."

"Is she a lot like you?"

"No. She's so much stronger than me. So much more ambitious. Everyone always knew she was going places."

For a minute, Jeanne thought Vivienne had said this for her benefit, but she soon realized that Vivienne had forgotten that she was behind her. Vivienne's Texas twang was even beginning to slip a little, and her "r's" began to fade. Jeanne hoped Rodrigo would not notice.

"I needed a man to protect me," Vivienne said. Her voice quavered, and Rodrigo put his hand on her shoulder. "That's why I married my husband. I was a lonely young woman in Paris without a clue of who I was or what I wanted to do with my life. He gave me an identity and a purpose, even if it was just being his dutiful trophy wife as he climbed up the law firm ladder." She stopped herself. "That's before he joined ExxonMobil, of course." Her twang came back a bit. "And now...he's gone."

Rodrigo rubbed her back gently.

Vivienne blinked back tears and tried to smile. "My sister didn't need a-man, though. She didn't need anyone to protect her. She protected others. She blames herself for what happened to our little sister, but I know she did such a good job protecting her. But you can't be around all of the time. You can't protect against everything."

Rodrigo furrowed his brow. "Who was she protecting your sister from?"

There was a long silence. Vivienne twisted her hair into a knot and secured it in place at the nape of her neck. She opened her mouth to speak, but nothing came out. Jeanne knew what she was going to say, and yet she feared it. It was something they never, ever spoke about.

Vivienne finally spit the words out in a flat, gravelly voice. "Our mother."

Half an hour later, Jeanne paid her eight dollar tab and slipped out of the bar. Deep in conversation, Vivienne did not seem to notice her departure.

She stood in the elevator, furiously punching the button to close the door, tears streaming down her face. She did not want company on the way down.

For once, Vivienne had told the truth. The whole ugly truth. She admitted to being her mother's favorite, to being a simpering sycophant of a daughter, eager to please and loath to disappoint. She had been her mother's *la plus belle*, the embodiment of all of her mother's extravagant schoolgirl dreams. Her mother clung to her fading youth and beauty in a most undignified way, like a drowning woman grasping at a lifeboat; her beauty was the one thing that set her apart from the other lumbermen's wives along their stretch of the river. And when it was gone, she lived vicariously through Vivienne.

And she drank. After a few drinks, she would turn the stereo up all the way and dance around the house, sometimes taking Vivienne for a twirl and maybe, on a particularly good day, even Jeanne or Annie. She wouldn't mind if they ate chocolate for lunch, or even ice cream. That was the best part of having a drunk for a mother. By afternoon, she would be smearing on her makeup, garish and thick, and sashaying in front of the mirror in her Prom dress. Jeanne had once made the mistake of snickering over the four-inch gap in the back. "Just wait until you marry a loser and get fat!" their mother had roared, and Jeanne hadn't been allowed to eat for the next three days, except for the leftover chicken her poor beleaguered father had snuck into her room late at night.

When her mother had to puke, Jeanne was the one she ordered to hold her hair. When she had a hangover and needed someone to watch Annie, Jeanne was the one she made stay home from school. And when their mother was in a particularly bad way, Jeanne was the one who took Annie to their secret hiding place, a humid cave accessed via an old mining shaft, where they pretended to be troglodytes feasting on a wooly mammoth.

Vivienne had told him the truth about Annie too. "She died in a drunk driving accident," she said simply, and when he asked if her mother had been the driver, she nodded yes.

Chapter Twenty-Nine

Jeanne awoke in the middle of the night. She rubbed her eyes and tried to make out the time on her alarm clock. It was three-thirty.

There had been a time in her life when she had often awoken at that time, and she didn't think it a coincidence that the coroner had noted Annie's time of death as 3:34. She had long ago trained her body to stay asleep, but her evening at the W Hotel rooftop bar had evidently reset her internal clock.

Tiptoeing past Scarlett, who was splayed out on the floor beside the coffee table, snoring gently, she opened the closet and reached behind a pile of threadbare pink bath towels until her fingers curled around the edge of a small shoebox. She lifted the box over the towels and then carried it to the windowsill, where she sifted through its contents in the dim light. She could hear the faint hum of Jerry's television and a car alarm wailing off in the distance.

She paused for a moment as she held a photo of her and her father aloft. Dressed in camouflage, they were deer hunting in the woods along the Canadian border. Her eyes fell on the hunting rifle in her hand, which was now at the bottom of old Thibault's well. Shuddering to think what she would have done with it if she hadn't flung it to the bottom, Jeanne quickly shoved the photo back in the box.

At the bottom of the box, her fingers brushed a cheap plastic frame etched with little hearts and the phrase "Sisters Are Forever." The photo inside had faded with age, but the scene looked much as she remembered: Vivienne, resplendent in her pink tutu, and Annie and Jeanne cloaked in the old bearskin that had hung over *grand-mère's* mantle. They stood in front of the pond that lay between *grand-mère's* little old farmhouse and the potato patch, with Morris emerging from the water behind them, the water dripping off his antlers. He was a regular in *grand-mère's* blueberry patch, and they had affectionately named him Morris the Moose. Annie and Jeanne were on a dinosaur-hunting mission, but Vivienne had inexplicably wandered in to turn in a performance as a touring ballerina. Jeanne had informed her that ballet hadn't been invented in cavemen times, but Vivienne had not seemed to care. The show must go on, Vivienne had said.

Jeanne placed the photo gently on the windowsill. It was time for the photo to see the light of day.

*   *   *   *

Much as Jeanne tried, she could not get back to
sleep. At first, her thoughts inexplicably turned to the
Bible. She had always hated the Sunday with the reading
about Leah and Rachel, the ugly daughter and the pretty
daughter constantly in competition. At least, she always
consoled herself, she and Vivienne were not competing
for the affections of a bigamous husband. She had
loathed Mitch from the moment she had caught sight of
him, smirking and raising his martini to his big, fat,
fleshy lips in a café on a cobblestone lane tucked
beneath the Basilica of Sacré-Coeur in Montmartre.
When Vivienne put her hand on the table, gleaming
with an ostentatious new diamond, Jeanne had stuffed
her mouth full of beef tartare, afraid of what would
come out of her mouth if it were empty. She had never
envied Vivienne for marrying him.

But just as Rachel had been jealous of Leah's
fertility, she apparently possessed something that
Vivienne coveted. Ambition. Self-reliance. It came as
quite a shock to her; she had never imagined that
Vivienne envied her in any way.

A man had written the story, of course. Perhaps
Rachel and Leah were not nearly as at odds as portrayed.
Really, when she thought about it, nearly the whole
Bible was written by men. The women did not fare too
well. Eve took the lion's share of the blame for getting all

of humanity expelled from the Garden of Eden; Lot's
wife turned into a pillar of salt; Abraham enslaved
Hagar, slept with her, and then let his wife abuse her
until Hagar had no choice but to flee into the desert.

Hagar.

She crept out of bed and plucked the old family
Bible off her bookshelf. Bound with leather, the pages
were stiff and rippled, and it was so old that the family
tree, full of Pelletiers, Michauds, Daigles, and Martins—
the names of the original hard-bitten settlers—had been
written with a quill and ink.

She was hardly a Biblical scholar, so it took her quite
some time to locate the passage. Silently, she read the
sad story from chapter 16 of Genesis:

*Now Sarai, Abram's wife, had borne him no children. But
she had an Egyptian slave named Hagar; so she said to Abram,
"The LORD has kept me from having children. Go, sleep with
my slave; perhaps I can build a family through her."*

*Abram agreed to what Sarai said. So after Abram had
been living in Canaan ten years, Sarai his wife took her
Egyptian slave Hagar and gave her to her husband to be his
wife. He slept with Hagar, and she conceived.*

*When she knew she was pregnant, she began to despise her
mistress. Then Sarai said to Abram, "You are responsible for
the wrong I am suffering. I put my slave in your arms, and now
that she knows she is pregnant, she despises me. May
the LORD judge between you and me."*

"Your slave is in your hands," Abram said. "Do with her whatever you think best." Then Sarai mistreated Hagar; so she fled from her.

The angel of the LORD found Hagar near a spring in the desert; it was the spring that is beside the road to Shur. And he said, "Hagar, slave of Sarai, where have you come from, and where are you going?"

"I'm running away from my mistress Sarai," she answered.

Then the angel of the LORD told her, "Go back to your mistress and submit to her." The angel added, "I will increase your descendants so much that they will be too numerous to count."

The angel of the LORD also said to her:
"You are now pregnant
and you will give birth to a son.
You shall name him Ishmael,
for the LORD has heard of your misery.
He will be a wild donkey of a man;
his hand will be against everyone
and everyone's hand against him,
and he will live in hostility
toward all his brothers."

She closed the Bible and put it back on the shelf. *Hagar was a whore.* The theory that Yasmina herself had written it had bothered Jeanne ever since she realized Yasmina was complicit in the murder. Was the graffiti meant as a self-indictment? She had, after all, divorced

Dr. Hamza, and slept with both Rodrigo and the puny little funeral director Harding. She had, in essence, prostituted herself to a married man in exchange for access to a corpse. She wore a costume that Islamic fundamentalists considered immodest. And yet, it seemed like such a demeaning action for a woman who, despite her flaws, was remarkably courageous and self-sacrificing. And she was an Arab feminist to boot. Why reinforce the worst stereotypes about Arab women?

But Yasmina was not a Christian, she realized, or a Jew. She would have little use for the Old Testament. She would have looked to the Koran for her ideas about Hagar instead.

What did the Koran say about Hagar?

She knew one person who would know the answer.

Chapter Thirty

"How's your love life? Have things heated up with Braveheart?" Jerry peered at her as he raised a steaming mug of thick, black Turkish coffee to his lips.

"Nothing's going on there, Jerry."

"Well, I can tell you one thing, Twinkletoes. He definitely wants something to happen. I watched him look at you when we were going over those emails last week. I could have told him that the head of Hamas was hanging out in your bathroom, ready to execute us all, and he wouldn't have noticed. He was too busy mooning over you."

"Really, Jerry? Mooning?"

"You heard me, Twinkletoes. Trust me, he's not breaking all kinds of federal laws for his health. He's doing it for you." He took a sip. "And if you were smart, you'd jump on that gravy train. He's a nice kid. Smart too. At least, I think. It's a little hard to understand what the hell he's saying."

Jeanne sighed. "His visa expires in a little over two months."

"So?"

"So he's not staying."

"You don't know that. If he's willing to hack into private bank accounts for you, I think he'd be willing to overstay his visa. Clearly, he's not into following rules."

Jerry extolled Fergus's virtues for a few more minutes, and Jeanne listened politely. Then she cleared her throat, anxious to change the subject. "What does the Koran say about Hagar?" she asked.

"Nothing," Jerry replied. "But she is mentioned in the hadiths, or the oral traditions of Islam which were later written down. In the hadiths, Hagar was the daughter of a king and, after she became pregnant, God ordered Abraham to take her and Ishmael out into the desert as a test of his faith. Soon they ran out of water. Ishmael was near death and Hagar, ever the attentive mother, ran frantically between two hills in search of water. After her seventh outing to look for water, Ishmael struck the ground with his heel and a spring miraculously came forth."

"So, in Islam, Hagar is both loved by Abraham and, in the end, favored by God?"

"Precisely." He swilled his coffee and ran his thick stubby fingers over the table's smooth surface. "Are you wondering why an Arab woman would scrawl 'Hagar was a whore' across a wall?"

287

She nodded.

"I can't say for sure, of course. But the story of Hagar has important political overtones. Muslims believe that Mohammed was a direct descendent of Ishmael and therefore Hagar is, in effect, the mother of all Muslims. The Palestinians view Hagar's flight into the desert at the hands of Abraham, who was of course a Jew, as symbolic of al-nakba—the catastrophe, when they were kicked out of their homes in what is now Israel in 1948."

He took another sip of coffee. "And some left-wing Jews now name their children Hagar."

"Why is that?"

He shrugged. "I suppose it's a way of recognizing how intertwined the history of the two peoples was and always will be."

When Jeanne returned home from Jerry's, Scarlett opened her one eye and looked quizzically at her owner.

"Go back to sleep, Scar," Jeanne whispered, petting her on the head, and Scarlett flopped back down into her bean bag.

Jeanne lay splayed out on her futon, trying to lull herself back to sleep. You have to be in the office in four hours, she reminded herself, and you cannot fall asleep in another staff meeting. She counted sheep and, when that failed (the sheep were milling about in the desert,

nuzzling a dying Ishmael, rather than obediently
jumping over fences), she resorted to trying to name all
fifty state capitals. But when she got to New York, it
made her think of her favorite Jewish deli there, which
made her think about Rodrigo, which made her think
about Yasmina.

Hagar was a whore.
The phrase resounded in her head. She could feel
the blood rushing through her brain; her temples
throbbed and ached. But when she closed her eyes to
dull the pain, she saw images of Yasmina, Rodrigo,
Maryam, and Ari flashing across her eyelids like a
projector run amok. An Arab feminist raised in a refugee
camp, all because Israelis expelled her family three
generations ago, has an affair with an Argentine Jew and
conspires with his roommate, an Israeli intelligence
agent, to assassinate a fellow Arab threatening the life of
a Muslim girl engaged to a Jew.
None of it made any sense.
And yet. Abraham, known as Ibrahim in the Islamic
tradition, had exiled one son into the desert and nearly
killed the other with an axe. Maryam could be seen as a
sacrificial lamb, although she doubted Yasmina would
say that Ibrahim had been commanded by God to kill
her. Abraham had exiled Hagar as well, and now
Yasmina was on the run. She had prostituted herself in a
sense, and yet she had done it all so that Maryam,

perhaps the closest thing she had to a daughter, might live.

Jeanne crept over to Flaca and snapped open her laptop. When Yasmina's Facebook page popped up, she hesitated only a second before posting a comment in the condolences section. "Hagar was not a whore. She protected her family and did God's will. Peace be upon the descendants of Ibrahim and Hagar."

After she snapped her laptop shut, she sat in silence for a moment before going to the windowsill and cradling the photo of her sisters in her hands. She ran her fingers over Annie's round baby-face. "I'm sorry I didn't protect you," she whispered.

As she was putting the photo back in its place, she locked eyes with Vivienne, coy in her pink tutu. The expression was both laughing and accusatory. She supposed that Vivienne had been put out with their refusal to play along with her ballet rehearsal, or perhaps annoyed that Morris the Moose was getting her tutu wet. But now, her expression took on the look of a much deeper, more insightful reproach. "You're right," Jeanne sighed. "I've been too hard on you."

"I promise I'll do better," she whispered as she slid onto the futon and drifted off to sleep.

Chapter Thirty-One

Saturday's technique class was a tough one for Jeanne. They spent part of the time practicing their spins, which had always been her weak point; as hard as she tried, she could not keep her eyes on a single fixed point to stave off dizziness. After three or four turns, she was light-headed and veering off to the left, her veil fluttering around her as though she were a disoriented hummingbird. Amy, perky as ever, reminded her that they were supposed to be spinning in place, not wandering about the room. Jeanne gritted her teeth. It was no use telling Amy that not everyone could effortlessly contort themselves into a human spinning top.

When class was over, she took a moment to recombobulate and then bounded down the stairs, her feet sinking into the orange shag carpeting. At the bottom, she was accosted by Zuleika, who occasionally worked as a receptionist in exchange for free tuition.

Short and round, Zuleika was an apprentice in Jeanne's belly dancing troupe. Jeanne sensed that Zuleika despised her. A couple of times she had caught her staring, and never in a good way. Her black bristly eyebrows were knitted into two angry "V's," her jaw was clenched, and her deep dark irises seemed to be boring a hole in Jeanne's skull. Jeanne hoped that she didn't practice voodoo.

But today Zuleika was all smiles. "Zahira! How are you?"

"Fine." Jeanne eyed her suspiciously. "How are you?"

Her smile faded into a pout. "Not so great," she said. "There's a massive water leak in our apartment. I need to rush home, try to salvage some of my things, and wait for the landlord." She looked hopefully at Jeanne. "Is there any chance you could cover my shift? It's only another hour."

That explained it. She needed something from Jeanne.

Jeanne was tempted to say no, just to spite Zuleika and her evil eye, but she sensed that this was Fate's way of intervening. "What time is Sunny arriving?" She rolled her eyes and tried to look aggrieved. After all, she couldn't seem too eager. That would be suspicious.

"Three o'clock. And she's often a few minutes early."

"Oh, all right," Jeanne said, "but you owe me."

*   *   *   *

For the first few minutes of Zuleika's shift, Jeanne sat primly in the receptionist's chair. She greeted the students trudging in for the two o'clock class, checking them off the registration list. She answered a few phone calls. But soon the students stopped trickling in and the phone stopped ringing.

She looked at the clock and noted the time. She had forty-three minutes to go at most, less if Sunny lived up to her reputation as an early bird.

Her fingers flew to the mouse, scrolling through the files stored on the hard drive. She didn't know exactly what she was looking for, but somehow she sensed that the hard drive might hold the clue to Yasmina's connection to Rodrigo and Boris. The folder marked "Yasmina" was useless, full of flyers for Middle Eastern dance parties called *haflas* and class registration lists. There were several folders that were password-protected, but one in particular caught her eye. It was mysteriously labeled "Abkan."

Jeanne repeated the name silently to herself several times and then, frowning, wrote it on the back of a Starbucks receipt that she fished out from the bottom of her purse. She arranged the letters in different permutations, ripping the receipt as she furiously wrote and re-wrote it, until she at last realized that Yasmina had simply spelled the word backwards.

Nakba. Jerry's words resounded in her ears. *Al-nakba. The catastrophe. The creation of the Israeli state and the displacement of the Palestinians. Hagar as a symbol of al-nakba.*

She glanced at the clock. Twenty-two minutes was not much time to guess the password.

She dialed Fergus and got his voicemail. Drat. She would have to take matters into her own hands.

Her hands shaking, she started with "Yasmina," "Nejla," and "Maryam," but none of these worked. She tried "Rodrigo," and various permutations of his name. She tried "Balata" and "Hamza." Nothing seemed to work.

She wondered if the passcode was in fact a number. But what number?

Opening Internet Explorer, she navigated to Yasmina's Facebook page. A drop of sweat, warm and salty, slid onto her upper lip. Underneath the desk, her feet tapped a frenetic rhythm. Fifteen minutes to go.

The post was buried beneath lots of dance announcements and pictures of her nephew. But at last Jeanne found what she was looking for.

R.I.P. Nejla. Posted on June 20th.

Jeanne's heart thudded in her chest. What was the year?

If Nejla had died when Maryam was six years old, and if Maryam was currently between eighteen and twenty-two years old, Jeanne surmised that Nejla died sometime between 1996 and 2000. She typed

"06201997" in the box, clicked "Enter," and held her
breath. The file opened.

Jeanne's hands shook as she hovered over the
printer, waiting for the last few documents to print. The
printer seemed maddeningly slow today, emitting an
awful screeching sound as the ink eked out in faint
pixelated gray lines.

The door swung open, and Sunny barreled through
the entryway. She peered over her glasses and squinted at
the printer. "Do you need a new ink cartridge?"

"No, thanks," Jeanne replied quickly, adjusting her
bag to better block Sunny's view of the printer.

With a shrug, Sunny launched into a diatribe about
obese people who wear Spandex. Jeanne tried to make
sympathetic noises, although she couldn't help but
notice that Sunny's tummy was oozing out over her
waistband like icing squeezed through a tube.

"Now my neighbor Mrs. Larranaga," Sunny was
saying, "she puts the large in Larranaga. Even her cat is
obese. I'm talking O-B-E-S-E. If there were a 'Biggest
Loser' for cats, Malfoy would be on it. His tummy
brushes the ground when he walks—his fur's even started
to wear away there!"

"Obese cats," Jeanne tut-tutted. She had once read
that, when in doubt, people like it when you just say

their words back to them. "Parroting," the author had called it.

"He has Type 2 diabetes. Mrs. Larranaga has to give him insulin shots twice a day, plus kitty Prozac. Her husband's on insulin and Prozac too, plus their forty-two-old daughter Janice, who lives in the attic with her bulldog Buster."

"Is he on Prozac?"

"Who?"

"Buster."

"Oh, definitely. Everyone in that household is fat, diabetic, and depressed."

"You sure do take a lot of interest in your neighbors," Jeanne said. "How very neighborly of you."

Sunny frowned. For a moment, Jeanne felt as though she could read her thoughts. *Love your neighbor as yourself.* But then she realized that Sunny's gaze was very much fixated on her bag, which was of course shielding the printer.

Settling her glasses back over her bulbous nose, Sunny took a couple of steps towards Jeanne. "What are you printing, anyway? Are you helping Amy with the flyers for Saturday's *hafla?*"

Jeanne placed a clammy hand on the stack of papers. Her pulse was racing, and her mouth was dry. "Stool sample results," she finally managed to squeak.

As the last page printed, she snatched the papers and stuffed them into her bag. She cleared her throat and lowered her voice, trying to sound authoritative rather than terrified. "I may have a parasite," she explained solemnly.

Sunny gasped. "How is that possible?"

"D.C. water," Jeanne said, shrugging. "First they were worried about the lead; now they are worried about a possible parasite that may have hitched a ride with the Brazilian navy during a goodwill cruise up the Potomac." She pointed at Sunny's Nalgene bottle. "You may want to switch to mineral water until this blows over. Just a tip."

Jeanne had not had a chance to read the documents before she hit the "print" button. There hadn't been enough time. Now, as she thumbed through them over a slice of Goober Pie at Kramer Books, the words sent a shiver up her spine. *I know all about what happened in Sharm el-Sheihk. I've got tape-recordings of the conversations between B.L. and H.J. I don't want money, only the freedom of my blessed cousin Marwan.*

Alarm bells were going off in her head as she turned the pages faster and faster, leaving a trail of peanut butter fingerprints across the page, occasionally alternating with a chocolate one from the inch-thick layer of fudge spread across the top of the pie. If the police ever found this stack of print-outs, Detective

Walker might end up here at Kramer Books, questioning the waiters about a woman with a weakness for Goober Pie.

There were a handful of letters, which varied in tone from pleading to threatening, plus a list of initials and twelve digit numbers. Without taking her eyes off the page, she whipped out her phone.

"This is Jerry. Leave a message."

"She set him up, Jerry," she croaked. "She set him up."

Chapter Thirty-Two

"B.L. has to be Binyamin Levin, the Mossad director's deputy," Jerry conjectured. He squinted at the paper, smoothing its edges, before regarding her with a piercing glance. "He does all of the dirty work for the director. He's very effective, well-respected and, of course, feared."

"And H.J.?" Jeanne prodded him.

"Hassan Jabour. He's very powerful within Hamas and is generally their negotiator during prisoner swaps." Jerry swilled his coffee and took a sip. His eyes glazed over and he seemed to be lost deep in thought. "There was some chatter last year about high-level contacts between the Israeli government and Hamas, but the higher-ups never gave the intel any credence. I had my doubts, though. To me, it seems mighty suspicious that Marwan Massoud, whom many believe is the only man that could lead the Palestinians to freedom and ensure a peaceful and stable transition, is never, ever released by the Israelis. But hundreds of dangerous terrorists are."

"So Ibrahim really is related to a terrorist?" Her voice came out in a hoarse whisper.

"Maybe, maybe not. Massoud is a pretty common name. And families in the West Bank are very large. He could have hundreds of relatives."

"Which Yasmina could exploit to her advantage."

"Precisely." He leaned over and tapped the enigmatic list of numbers with his index finger. "And what do you make of this?"

"I just compared them against Fergus's list. They match the bank accounts in Malta, the Cayman Islands, and Lebanon."

"So she set up the accounts in his name too?"

"I wouldn't put anything past her at this point. But there's only one way to find out."

He looked at her expectantly.

"And I'm going to need to borrow your gun."

The steel was cold against the small of her back as she walked briskly down Columbia Road. She was used to slinging a rifle, long and thin, over her shoulder, but this was a different sensation altogether. This gun was short and heavy, and it was intended for human prey. Her heart beat faster each time a shifty-eyed man with low-slung pants crossed their path. Did he know? Could he tell? She felt as though their eyes lingered on her waistband; it was as though they had a sixth sense. "You don't have to come, Jerry." She spoke in a low voice, between clenched teeth. "You can still back out if you want to."

"I may have failed my last poly, been diagnosed with PTSD, and declared unfit to have my security clearance renewed, Twinkletoes, but I am still former Special Ops," he said, and Jeanne detected a hint of wounded pride. "Trust me. You want me in your corner."

"Thanks, Jerry," she murmured, turning away. She did not want him to see the tears welling up within her. So that's why he's always home, she realized. He lost his security clearance. All because he had the audacity to have a conscience, to be traumatized by the horrors of war. And so they got rid of him. No muss, no fuss.

They turned left on Mount Pleasant Avenue, walked a couple more blocks, and passed through an unmarked door. Jeanne motioned for Jerry to follow her up the stairs to the door with the number "2" hung upside down from a single nail. She rapped four times. Long, short, short, long.

She waited for the slow, heavy footsteps, the removal of the deadbolt, and the sliding of the chains. "Entre."

She turned the door knob slowly and motioned for Jerry to slip inside. She pulled the handgun from her

301

waistband, gripped the handle, and followed closely behind.

"*No disparen!*" a terrified deep voice cried from behind the sofa. Evidently he had glimpsed the two guns and realized he had no chance of getting a shot off.

"*No le pasa nada si colabora con nosotros,*" she reassured him, aiming the gun at the top of the sofa, as Jerry maneuvered to cover their flank. "*Levántese,*" she commanded him. She wanted to see his face.

Two beefy hands shot up from behind the couch first. Slowly, his wiry black hair came into view, then his broad face, and finally his overstuffed white undershirt. Jeanne found herself enjoying this. No one ever listened to her, not like this. If only he knew the gun was not loaded.

Jeanne held the gun in her left hand and reached into her pocket with the right. She unfolded the piece of paper and held it out for him to see.

"*Ha estado aquí esta mujer?*"

He squinted, and she realized she was counting on a nearsighted thug to identify Yasmina. How inconvenient. Jeanne advanced towards him, her finger on the trigger. He trembled slightly.

She repeated the question, asking if Yasmina had paid him a visit. "*Disfrazada, quizás?*"

He squinted again and then nodded. Yes, he decided, she had been there in disguise, dressed as a man.

"Y *qué nombre pusiste en los documentos?*" she prodded him.

He struggled to recall the name. She resisted the urge to provide a suggestion; she didn't want to taint the witness, as a prosecutor would say. Especially a witness with a gun pointed at his head. He was liable to say anything to get her to leave, whether true or not. It was the first time her evidence class had ever come in handy.

She and Jerry exchanged a glance. What if Paco's memory failed him? She was sure he didn't keep any written records.

Paco's bottom lip trembled. "Ibrahim," he whispered. "Ibrahim Abu Ali."

Chapter Thirty-Three

"Let me get this straight," Vivienne said as she settled into a lunge. Despite her earlier insistence that she was going to eat ice cream and get fat, she was back to her zumba and power sculpting videos. "Yasmina stole Ibrahim's identity, traveled around the world setting up shady bank accounts in his name, and convinced Mossad that he was blackmailing them to secure his cousin Marwan's freedom?"

"Something like that."

"Is Marwan even Ibrahim's cousin?"

"Maybe distantly."

"And you think she did all of this to protect Maryam?"

Jeanne nodded. "It was a preemptive strike. She knew he killed Nejla, and she knew he would kill Maryam if he found out she was marrying Ari."

"He killed Nejla thirteen years ago," Vivienne said as she tilted her hips in time to the music. She cast a sidelong glance at Jeanne. "Sometimes people can change, you know."

"Like Mom, you mean?" Jeanne could hear her voice rising, shrill and accusatory, petulant like a child. She breathed deeply, trying to recover her zen or her chi, or whatever Lily was always blathering on about. She reminded herself that she had promised to cut Vivienne some slack, and she tried her best to imagine Vivienne as she had been in that picture, resplendent in her pink tutu. But all she saw was the adult Vivienne in her tight black yoga pants, and all she felt was a familiar tightening of the chest and a rising sense of panic.

"Yes, like Mom," Vivienne said softly, "who hasn't had a drink in over a decade, goes to AA meetings twice a week, and feels terrible about what she did." She hit the "off" button and turned around to face her sister. "Was Yasmina really motivated by justice, Jeanne? Or was she motivated by revenge?"

"J-j-justice," Jeanne stammered. "She's been a dancer at Algiers for more than two years and presumably she's known Ibrahim all that time."

"But how long has she known he was Nejla's uncle?"

Jeanne looked down and picked at a loose thread on the sofa. "I don't know."

"How long had she been waiting for an opportunity to kill Ibrahim and fake her own death?" Vivienne pressed. "Months? Years? Corpses the right age and size don't come along every day, nor do sniveling philandering funeral homes directors, or boyfriends who happen to be living with a Mossad agent."

"Her relationship with Rodrigo only began a few months before the murder," Jeanne said defensively. She noticed that her sister flushed at the mention of Rodrigo's name.

"Yes, but what about Mr. Harding?"

"Fergus said the first calls were in late September."

"And the trail of bank accounts from one shady tax haven or terrorist hangout to another? How long did it take to set that up?"

"I don't know." Jeanne sighed before admitting, "I guess I would like to think it was justice."

Vivienne joined Jeanne on the couch and pulled her close. "And I would like to think that Mitch never cheated before this," she said. "But just because you want something to be true doesn't make it so."

Jeanne didn't want to ask how many other paramours her sister suspected. So instead she asked, "What do you think of Rodrigo?"

"He was...nice."

Jeanne wriggled free of Vivienne's grasp and turned to look her sister in the eye. "Nice?"

"Yes, nice." Vivienne's blue eyes locked on Jeanne for a brief moment, then flitted away. Vivienne's pursed her lips into a thin, determined line, as if she didn't trust what would come out of her mouth next. She folded her hands in her lap and finally met Jeanne's gaze. "More than nice, actually. Kind, charming, a good listener."

"Might he be a good actor too?"

Vivienne shook her head. "I don't think so. I really don't think he had any inkling of Yasmina's plans. He didn't seem to harbor any ill will towards his roommate, so I kind of doubt that he was aware of their clandestine meetings. He didn't seem to suspect any affair. He seems like a nice guy. Very genuine." She winced. "Which is more than one could say of me. If he had a good time on our date, it's because he enjoyed hanging out with a recently widowed, self-proclaimed culture vulture as rich as King Midas who parties with sheikhs."

"That *was* the real you. Funny, sweet, self-deprecating. Your funny stories about *Tante* Marie. Your adventures living in Paris as a young woman. That was all you." She cleared her throat and took a deep breath. "You even told him about Mom and Annie. That definitely wasn't part of the script."

"I didn't realize you heard that part. I thought that over-eager teenage boy was still monopolizing you."

"I made him hush up so I could hear."

Vivienne's face darkened. "When did you leave?"

"Right after you told him Mom killed Annie."

"I've never said that aloud," Vivienne admitted, "to anyone. Mitch knew of course, but I never really put it in those terms. Rodrigo just made me feel...free. That's the only way I know how to describe it."

307

Jeanne laughed. " 'Free' is one word for it," she said, and Vivienne blushed. "And based on the look you just gave me, I'm guessing you went off-script at the end of the date too."

Suddenly the twang was back. "What? Little old me? Kiss that tall drink of water?" Vivienne pressed her hand to her heart, and arched her eyebrows in mock outrage.

"I do declare," Jeanne shrieked, hurling a sofa pillow at Vivienne's head, "why Miss Vivienne, you are a brazen hussy!"

An hour later, the brazen hussy and her moralizing younger sister were collapsed on the floor, legs and elbows peeking out from beneath a mound of feathers.

"I can't believe Everett slept through this," Vivienne whispered.

"What's he going to think," Jeanne giggled, "when he finds out his mother and aunt just created a bigger mess than he's ever created in his whole life?"

Vivienne shrugged and burst into laughter. "His momma's done so many loopy things lately, I doubt he'll even notice."

"Are you going on another date with Rodrigo?"

Vivienne shook her head. "I'd like to, but I can't. As awful as Mitch is, I'm still married, and I don't want to do anything that would jeopardize getting custody of

Everett. I don't want any private investigator snapping pictures of me smooching an exotic Argentine artist."

"What did you tell Rodrigo?"

"I told him I needed a little more time to grieve, but that I'd be in touch. I'm hoping that our little investigation will conclude soon, I can get a speedy divorce from Mitch, and six months from now I can give him a call and come completely clean." Vivienne propped herself up on her elbows. "And what about you? Are you going on another date with Fergus?"

"Nope."

"Why not?"

"What do you mean, why not? The first one was a simple favor to get him to do a little hacking for free. I held up my end of the bargain, and he held up his."

"And he's cute and smart and sweet and very, very interested in you. And, as someone who has known you and observed you for twenty-eight years, I can tell you are very, very interested in him."

"He's interesting," Jeanne said evasively. "There are not too many ninety-eight-pound ex-flyweight wrestlers who are genius computer hackers, talk with a funny accent, and wander around in snowstorms in his great-aunt's pink parka. Anyone with a modicum of curiosity would be interested in the antics of such a beguilingly bizarre human being. But I am not interested in dating him."

"*Au contraire*, that's exactly why you would be interested in dating him. You are two of the smartest, nerdiest, most eccentric people I know. You're perfect for each other." Vivienne looked Jeanne straight in the eye. "Don't bullshit me, sis. We both know this has nothing to do with his visa, or the fact you think he's too skinny, or anything else. This has to do—"

Jeanne held up a hand. "Don't say it, Viv. Please don't say it."

"Will you at least think about giving Fergus a chance?"

Instead of answering her, Jeanne just said, "I love you, Viv."

"I love you, sis. Now go get him."

Chapter Thirty-Four

A little after three o'clock, she left Vivienne's with her fingers clutching a manila envelope stuffed with evidence that Yasmina had framed Ibrahim. Her heart should have been heavy, filled with ponderous thoughts of mercy and justice, and yet somehow she felt as though a great weight had been lifted.

Vivienne was right, of course. Her reluctance to date Fergus has very little to do with his expiring visa, and a lot to do with the fact that her last date with a guy she really, really liked had ended at the edge of a potato patch by Pete's Tavern, where sweet math whiz Matt Ouellette had pulled over, wide-eyed, to see if they could be of any use to the first responders at the scene of an accident. The carnage was unbelievable, six dead in all— five Prom revelers and one nine-year-old girl. Jeanne had winced as she saw the lone survivor stumbling towards them, mumbling incoherently, a gash across her forehead, a shard of glass stuck in her arm. "Mother!"

Jeanne had shrieked, "What have you done?" And Matt had recoiled, vomiting in the damp earth beneath them, as Jeanne raced to the wreck smoking in the ditch.

She never even said good-night to Matt. She could not, in fact, even recall him leaving. All she could remember was a horrible howl that filled the night air, searing shuddering sobs that seemed to come from one of the supernatural beasts in *grand-mère*'s tales. They did not sound human in the least. But they were her tears, her sobs. They were the sound of guilt.

If only she had stayed with Annie, if only she had not been so selfish and gone to Prom, if only she had realized that her mother was in an especially bad way that night. If, if, if. She should have realized her mother wouldn't be content to stay home alone on Prom night, but would instead seek solace at Pete's, reliving her glory days with a retinue of washed-up lumbermen, twice-divorced Homecoming queens, and aging football players.

"Poor Matt," she mumbled aloud, and a passerby clad in a gray jogging suit started. "Don't mind me," Jeanne said, "I'm just your local lunatic."

And then she began to laugh. It struck her as absurdly funny, avoiding Fergus just because she had one horrible, awful, no-good, very bad date. The situation wasn't likely to repeat itself—after all, her mother was six hundred miles away, dressed in stripes, and making license plates for twenty-five cents an hour. She wasn't a

threat to anyone or anything, except maybe Jeanne's
sanity.

She broke into a run. Up R Street she ran, past the
beautiful gardens of Dumbarton Oaks and the stately
monuments of Oak Hill Cemetery. She turned right on
Wisconsin Avenue and sprinted past a Turkish
restaurant, a bagel shop, another cemetery, and the local
Safeway. By the time she reached the baseball diamond
towards the top of the hill, she was beginning to run out
of breath.

But she pressed onwards, past the Russian Embassy,
past her own building, cutting into the neighborhood
just before the Cathedral, huffing and puffing her way
up the steps to a familiar beige townhouse. "Fergus!" she
shouted, pounding the canary yellow door so hard she
nearly shook the wreath off. "Fergus! Fer—"

The door opened and she fell forward, nearly
careening into Fergus.

"Steady now," he said, holding her arm and
propping her upright. He peered into her face. "Are you
all right, Jeanne? What happened? Is someone chasing
you?"

She placed one hand on her hip and propped the
other against the door, trying to catch her breath.
"Everything happened and nothing happened," she
panted. Jeanne realized that she was smiling idiotically at
him and he was looking terribly alarmed, but she
continued anyway. The lack of oxygen was doing funny

things to her brain, and she felt slightly woozy, but she knew her courage wouldn't last. "The mysterious phone call was from my mother. She's in prison. She killed six people in a drunk driving accident, including my little sister Annie, who was in the picture you saw, the last time I had a date with a guy I really, really liked. Vivienne was my mom's favorite. I loved Vivienne, but I hated her too. But I don't hate her anymore. And I lied when I said I only liked you as a friend. And I think we should go on a date. A real date. No quid pro quo this time. In fact"—she took a deep breath—"I am asking you on a date. Right now. I am sweaty and out of breath, and I think we should go on a date now before I lose my nerve."

Fergus's mouth hung open for a moment. But then he said, "I once received a mysterious call from the zoo, where my nephew Alastair had climbed into the monkey's enclosure and refused to come out. No one in my family has killed anyone in a drunk driving accident, but my uncle Norbert likes a tipple now and then and my aunt Moira likes a wee dram of whiskey at the most inopportune times, including in church. My sister Rosalind is my mum's favorite. I was honest when I said that I really liked you and yes, even though I haven't taken a shower today, just cleaned the loo, and am in the middle of a very heated game of whist with my aunt's friends, I accept your offer to go on a date right now."

"Can't you at least finish the game?"

Jeanne was startled to hear the quavering, yet
irritated voice cut through the musty air. The voice was
coming from her right. When she swung around, she
was astonished to see Fergus's Aunt Margaret—who
looked remarkably healthy, under the circumstances—
and two elderly friends of hers sitting around a small
wooden table, cards in hands, staring right at her.

"Cheerio, Jeanne, dear," Aunt Margaret said. "And
thank you for speaking up for a change. But you will
have to sit and have a cup of tea while our game finishes.
I was just about to beat Fergus, you see, and that almost
never happens."

An hour later, Jeanne and Fergus were sitting on the
steps of the Lincoln Moment, watching twilight descend
over the Reflecting Pool. It was one of those perfect,
mild March days, with a gentle breeze that rustled
through the gracefully arching avenues of elms, sending
soft shimmering ripples across the pool. The geese
splashed, the squirrels pranced around to the delight of
camera-toting Japanese tourists, and white-haired
veterans, proud yet solemn, were being wheeled around
the marble World War II monument at the far end of
the pool. As far as Jeanne was concerned, all was right
with the world. She felt a trifle smug, as she watched a
few women eye Fergus jealously, and rather lightheaded.

How had she managed to resist his advances for so long? With his muscular arm curled around her and his spicy, masculine scent wafting up her nostrils, he hardly seemed like a ninety-eight pound weakling. In fact, she could not recall a single one of her reasons for not succumbing to his charms sooner.

But then, as she watched a leggy blonde give Fergus an approving look, Jeanne remembered what the bartender at Nanny O'Brien's had said. *Who's your new lady friend, Fergus?* Her spine stiffened as she reminded herself that she had no intention of being the flavor of the month. Jeanne didn't want to be the "new" lady friend, and she didn't want to be referred to a few weeks from now as the "old" lady friend. In fact, she wanted to be a lady friend with enough permanence to merit Sean actually learning her name.

"Fergus..."

"Yes?" Fergus murmured, turning to look deep into her big brown eyes.

Jeanne felt a jolt of electricity shoot through her as the wiry blond hairs on his forearm brushed her wrist and the stubble on his cheek grazed her jawline. It was such a novel sensation, like sandpaper on silk, and yet so human, so intimate. She could feel the tensing of his jaw, the throbbing of his heartbeat, the heat of his breath. But now was not the time to melt like a puddle of chocolate. She was made of sterner stuff, and if he didn't already realize that, he would soon. "What did

Sean mean when he asked if I was your 'new' lady
friend? How many 'old' lady friends are there?"

Fergus's face turned bright red. "Oh, that."

"Yes, that."

"Well, Jeanne, I have a wee confession to make."

"Go on."

"I slipped the bartender five quid to make it sound
like I had a lot of women chasing me."

"Very clever."

"Did it work?"

She slugged him in the arm. "I guess so."

They talked about a great many things. He relived his
glory days as flyweight champion of East Glasgow High
School, waxed lyrical about magical mornings at his
uncle's farm on the Isle of Skye, and explained how to
make haggis in excruciating detail. She regaled him with
tales of Morris the Moose, the secret cave, *Tante* Marie,
and *grand-mère*. And she told him how she had woken up
the morning after the accident at *grand-mère*'s, stayed
there three days, and then left right after the funeral. She
had not looked back even once as she mounted her bike
and sped off on a three-day journey to Moosehead Lake,
where she got a job cleaning rooms at a resort.

"And you've never returned?" She noticed that he
asked this quietly, looking away from her, as if he were
embarrassed.

She shook her head firmly. "Never."

"You must get homesick."

"Not really." As she said this, she realized that she had created her own oddball family out of a bunch of misfits brought together by serendipity. How many people could claim a Filipina grunge band hipster, a Scottish hacker, a tattooed ex-CIA agent, and a Salvadoran ex-con as friends? Not many. "I have my own urban family here," she said with a smile. "I'm lucky. I chose my family."

Fergus didn't say anything for several moments. The moon rose above the Capitol, and his eyes turned lavender in the moonlight. The tourists were gone. "You're a strong woman," he said. "I really admire that. And beneath that tough exterior, you've got a big heart. I know you tried to protect Annie and I understand now why you felt so strongly about vindicating Yasmina."

Jeanne could tell that he was piecing it all together, decoding their earlier conversations, replaying each one in his mind, peeling away the layers of meaning until he was left, at last, with their pure essence. She could tell that he was remembering their conversation in the Bishop's Garden. At the time, she had told him then that Yasmina was protecting Maryam, but he hadn't truly caught her meaning until now.

She cleared her throat. "Yasmina set Ibrahim up." Her voice was suddenly hoarse and raspy. Jeanne found it difficult to say the words aloud; she felt as though she were betraying her idol. Her former idol, anyway. "He wasn't a member of Hamas, or Fatah, or colluding with

318

Israeli intelligence. It's pure coincidence that he and Marwan share a last name. Yasmina just exploited that coincidence. She set up a series of bank accounts to make Mossad think that Hamas was transferring money to Ibrahim. But Ibrahim never saw the money and he probably never knew the accounts existed."

Fergus opened his mouth to speak, but she held up her hands in a silencing gesture. "We were duped. I was duped. I believed what I wanted to believe. What I needed to believe."

"Yasmina spun fantasies wherever she went," Jeanne continued. "To Mr. Harding, she was a fantasy lover. To Dr. Hamza, she was the spark that lit up his gloom. For me, she represented everything I wanted to be: she was confident, exotic, sexy, graceful, uninhibited, passionate, beautiful—"

"You are beautiful," he interjected.

"She was a Mother Goddess, a protector. She succeeded where I failed."

"You didn't fail, Jeanne. You went to a school dance. How could you have known what would happen?"

Jeanne shrugged. "Annie and five of my classmates died. Maryam lived. I let my guard down, let fate take its course, let my selfish desires get the best of me. She sacrificed herself for Maryam."

"But she didn't die. At least according to you."

"That's true," Jeanne said. "But she left her adopted country, her family, her friends, her business, and her studio. That's a lot to give up."

"Are you going to turn her in?"

Jeanne did not answer. Instead, she reached out her hand, pulled him towards her, and dragged him down the stairs to the Reflecting Pool, where she did exactly what Yasmina would have done: jump into the still, quiet waters. Under the watchful eye of a plump spotted owl, she gave Fergus an impromptu belly dance lesson, tilting her hips in a sinuous figure-eight. He lifted up his shirt, exposing his hairy midriff, and tried to follow along, torn between an earnest attempt at imitation and a lusty desire to focus all of his attention on the moonlight dancing across her soft womanly curves. They laughed hysterically, and talked, and touched, and kissed, until a Park Service policeman accosted them in mid-shimmy and threatened them with a citation.

Chapter Thirty-Five

Jeanne felt curiously lightheaded as she turned the key in her lock. Her lips were swollen from Fergus's kisses—so sweet, but so intense (she would need to invest in a case of ChapStick if they were to continue seeing each other)—and her belly ached from laughing so much. They had walked ten miles, dripping wet, all over the District, and yet she felt as though her feet had never touched the ground. They had made the rounds of Dupont Circle, gorging themselves on Larry's ice cream and dancing around the fountain to the beat of a visiting New Orleans jazz band. They had joined the throngs in Adams-Morgan, gyrating to the driving beat of an ebullient eight-piece salsa band wedged into the narrow confines of Havana Village, then munched on Julia's empanadas in the wee hours of the morning. They had traded limericks with a transvestite named Bubbles and Ida, his pet ferret, and sung "It's a Long Way to Tipperary" to a couple of girls from Dublin. They had

321

done all the sorts of things one might do when one was drunk, and yet they hadn't drunk a single drop.

And when they had finally made their way home, through the silent streets of Georgetown, past Vivienne's house, Jeanne had said a silent prayer of thanks. She had made a mental note to send her sister a dozen roses the following day.

She closed the door behind her and tiptoed over to a slumbering Scarlett, who stirred slightly as Jeanne ran a hand through her fur. "Another misfit member of my urban family," she murmured. "My three-legged, one-eyed dog."

She tiptoed to the bathroom, flipped on the light, and rummaged through the medicine closet for a tube of Chapstick. The one she found was old and grimy, with the label half peeled off, but it was still a relief to slather it on her swollen lips.

As she crawled onto her futon and lifted the sheet up under her chin, she glanced at the clock. It was three-thirty.

How impressive. She hadn't been up that late since college.

*   *   *   *

She was awoken an hour and a half later by an insistent ring. It was the call she had been waiting for.

"You figured it out." The voice was deep but feminine, the tone matter-of-fact. There was no hint of surprise or dismay. In the background, Jeanne could hear the call to prayer.

Jeanne swallowed hard and tried to pry her sleepy eyes open. "You're not a whore, Yasmina, and neither was Hagar."

"No," she conceded, "but history is written by the victors. By the West, by Christians and Jews."

"By men."

"Yes, by men. Especially by men."

Jeanne closed her eyes and tried to picture Yasmina. Was she reclining on a divan in a relative's house, or perhaps huddled in a phone booth? Was she wearing a headscarf or even a burqa?

"My people never win," Yasmina continued. "It's never even a draw. My family's olive trees sit behind a security barrier, in the shadow of ugly apartment buildings occupied by Jewish settlers. My family received no compensation and when they protested the confiscation of their land, the settlers burned their mosque. They are nothing but barbarians, mindless zealots who cloak their lust for land in Biblical nonsense."

"You tried to protect Maryam?" Jeanne meant to phrase it as a statement, an affirmation, but to her surprise, it came out as more of a question.

"Of course."

"Why didn't you go to the police?"

Yasmina laughed bitterly. "What good would that do? The official cause of death was appendicitis. Besides, they can't investigate crimes that occurred in another country."

"Why didn't you try to place Maryam in a women's shelter? They could have protected her."

"Maybe, maybe not. But even if they could, what kind of life is that? Why should Maryam have to hide? That's just another way for Ibrahim to win. And besides, there will always be another girl. Another cousin, another niece. People like Ibrahim don't change. I can't protect everyone, all of the time."

"When did you realize Ibrahim was your childhood friend's uncle?"

"The moment I looked up from my audition and caught his beady little eyes roving all over my body. He was always lusting after some woman or another in our refugee camp; I remembered those lips. The awful lecherous curl, like a rabid dog sizing up his prey. For a man so concerned about the honor of his female relatives, he had surprisingly little concern for the honor of his neighbors' wives and daughters."

"So you've known all along."

Yasmina did not respond.

"You are very good at covering your tracks," Jeanne continued. "It's quite a feat to convince Mossad that someone has information damaging enough to the Israeli government to justify blackmail. The shell accounts were genius. How long did it take to set that up?"

"Two years."

Jeanne steadied herself against the windowsill and took a sharp breath. "Maryam only became engaged recently."

Jeanne was silent for a moment. She could hear Yasmina's gentle breathing and the snatches of Arabic conversation in the background. The language was melodious yet guttural, harsh yet beautiful. Kind of like the Middle East, she supposed.

"There's a fine line between justice and vengeance," Jeanne finally said, "but there is a line."

"An artificial construct," Yasmina sniffed. "It's just a line we create to justify our actions. I'm on this side of the line, we tell ourselves, you're on that. It's like the border between Israel and the West Bank. It's one undulating plain of scrubland, but the Israelis draw a line on a map and build a wall. The line goes right through people's homes, through their olive groves, through their ancestral lands, but they don't care. The people on this side of the line are the chosen people of

God; the people on the other side of the line are barbarians."

"So you don't see a difference between justice and vengeance?"

"Not where Ibrahim is concerned."

Jeanne was silent for a moment, and then she said flatly, "I almost killed my mother."

"I know."

Jeanne's mind reeled. How could Yasmina possibly know this? She silently replayed those long midnight talks with Yasmina, stretched out on her couch, drinking hot sweet mint tea. Jeanne had confided in her, told her all about her sordid family past, but she had never, ever told her about the time she had almost killed her mother. Clearly, Jeanne had underestimated Yasmina. Yasmina was not just charming and cunning; she did not rely solely on her feminine wiles. Beneath her beautiful exterior, her charm, and her grace, lay a steely resolve and a fierce intellect. She was methodical and thorough, a better researcher than ten Ph.D.'s put together.

Jeanne had never really known Yasmina; no one had really known Yasmina. But Yasmina had known her. She felt naked, vulnerable, violated. Yasmina knew her secrets, secrets that not even Vivienne or Lily were privy to. And Yasmina knew her dark side, a dark side that, in many ways, mirrored Yasmina's own. It was warm in Jeanne's apartment, but she shuddered nonetheless.

"How?"

"I have my ways." She laughed, and Jeanne suddenly remembered her warmth and kindness. The laugh didn't sound like it came from a cold-blooded killer. "I don't actually know, for a fact, that you almost killed your mother," she clarified, "but I know what happened, and I know you, and I know you would have wanted to."

"But I didn't." Jeanne's voice grew louder and stronger. "I made a choice not to." She stressed the word "choice," and her words resounded in her own words. She had never thought of it that way, had never phrased it that way in her prayers, had never thought to explain it to the priest in the confessional that way. But it was a choice, she realized. It was the harder choice and the stronger choice. She had always felt like a victim, like a pawn in some misanthropic game designed by her mother. But she had in fact been master of her own destiny. A trickle of sweat ran down her forehead and she wiped it on her pajama sleeve. "Why did you choose me?" she asked in a hoarse whisper.

"I think you know."

"It's not because I was the best dancer, was it?"

"You are a terrific dancer."

"But that's not why you chose me. You needed me there that night. You needed me to see you go back towards the fire." Jeanne couldn't bear to say the rest out loud. Yasmina knew that she worshipped her, that even if she had an inkling of her complicity, she wouldn't go

327

to the cops. She looked over at the picture of Annie. Annie, she realized, was Yasmina's insurance policy.

"You always were my smartest dancer," Yasmina said.

"You played me."

"I played a part and you fell for it. Willingly. Just like everybody else."

"And the men in your life?"

Yasmina sighed. "I admired my ex-husband, and I loved Rodrigo."

"You used Rodrigo."

"I used his roommate," Yasmina corrected her. "Rodrigo didn't suspect a thing."

"But you used Rodrigo to get to his roommate."

"On the contrary. I met Rodrigo in a bar, went home with him, and discovered over breakfast the next day that his roommate worked at the Israeli embassy. I knew half of the Israeli embassy staff had ties to Mossad, and it didn't take me long to figure out that he was in as deep as any of them. It was pure dumb luck." She laughed. "Or maybe fate."

"Didn't you find it repugnant to collaborate with an Israeli?"

"Of course. But less repugnant than waiting for Ibrahim to kill Maryam. The Israeli security forces kill hundreds of people every year; that won't change. Why not put their bloodlust to good use for a change? The enemy of my enemy is my friend. Or at least that's what I want him to believe."

"Are you happy, Yasmina? Are you at peace now that Ibrahim is dead?"

"I'm content, I suppose. I doubt I'll ever be at peace though. It's not my nature. Are you happy?"

"Yes."

"Do you regret that you didn't pull the trigger?"

"No."

"I'm glad," Yasmina said in a tone that sounded a bit wistful to Jeanne.

The line went dead. Jeanne just stared at the phone. She even shook it slightly; she felt as though she were in a documentary about Bushmen who are whisked to Manhattan and mesmerized by neon billboards, flush toilets, and freeze-dried bagels. This little silver contraption, small enough to fit in her pocket, had just transmitted the voice of a woman who was not only five thousand miles away, but also legally dead.

Chapter Thirty-Six

Jeanne decided it was useless to try to go back to sleep. Without bothering to get dressed, Jeanne pulled her green and gold William and Mary sweatshirt over her pajamas—blue flannel with happy black-and-white cows frolicking about, courtesy of Aunt Mildred. She shoved her keys and phone in her purse, grabbed the leash, and nudged Scarlett. "Time to get up, Scarlett," she whispered.

Bleary-eyed Scarlett followed her down the corridor and out onto the street, where she hopped along faster than usual, matching Jeanne's determined pace. As they marched down the avenue, Jeanne replayed the conversation in her head. *The enemy of my enemy is my friend. Or at least that's what I want him to believe. You're smart, Jeanne. You always were my smartest dancer. I played a part and you fell for it. Think on it.* Why had Yasmina called her at all? The question gnawed at Jeanne as she flew past the boutiques, oblivious to the looks of bystanders bemused by the woman in the cow pajamas with the one-eyed, three-legged dog.

Why confess at all? Yasmina knew, obviously, that Jeanne had her suspicions based on the Facebook posting, but she could have left Jeanne with a kernel of doubt. But for some reason she didn't want to. Did Yasmina want to bare her soul to the one person who might understand, or was she trying to dissuade Jeanne from going to the authorities by portraying herself as a sympathetic protector?

Or did she actually want Jeanne to go to the authorities?

The thought stopped Jeanne in her tracks. She stood on the corner of Wisconsin Avenue and N Street, leash slack in her hand, with Scarlett staring up at her, confused. Could this be yet another role that Yasmina had created for Jeanne in her twisted, meticulously choreographed drama?

The enemy of my enemy is my friend. Or at least that's what I want him to believe.

Yasmina had collaborated with a shadowy Mossad agent. But could she have been setting him up as well? The Israelis had evidently believed that Ibrahim had evidence of collusion between the Israeli government and Hamas, and they would only have believed that if collusion had actually taken place. Yasmina, or someone she knew, must have had firsthand knowledge of the meeting in Sharm al-Sheikh, Jeanne conjectured. If Jeanne went to the authorities and could prove that a member of Mossad had assassinated an American citizen on American soil to hush up collusion between the Israeli government and Islamic fundamentalists, there would be severe diplomatic repercussions. The ambassador could be recalled; the United States Congress might issue a rare condemnation of Israel, cancel future arms sales, or pressure Israel to freeze the expansion of Jewish settlements on the West Bank. It would be a blow to hard-liners on both sides.

Suddenly, Scarlett lurched to the right, down N Street, hot on the trail of a terrified little squirrel. Hurtling down the sidewalk, Scarlett and Jeanne followed after the bushy tail as it zigged and zagged down the block. The squirrel was out of luck; the narrow townhouses were built close to the street, with nary a tree in sight. Escape routes were far and few between.

"Stop it, Scar!" Jeanne admonished her, but Scarlett paid her no attention. Jeanne hadn't seen Scarlett this excited in years.

Two blocks later, a tree arched over the cobblestone street, its gnarled roots poking through the sidewalk. Jeanne nearly tripped on a loose brick as Scarlett broke into a desperate sprint, nipping at the tail of her prey. But it was not Scarlett's day. The squirrel took a flying leap, dug his claws into the rough bark, and scampered up the trunk. Scarlett was left to sulk about the base, her head hung low.

Leaning against the tree, Jeanne fished a dog treat out of her pocket as she tried to catch her breath. "Your consolation prize," she muttered.

Scarlett sat down, stretching her front paw in front of her like a mutilated Sphinx. Jeanne always thought she looked very wise in that position, more human than canine. She devoured her treat and then looked at Jeanne expectantly.

"Was that a good treat, Scarlett?" Jeanne asked, tugging at the leash. She could see that the Gothic clock tower at Georgetown University read six-thirty-seven. "Now let's get going. I need to go home and shower before work."

To her surprise, Scarlett would not budge. She just sat there, calm and serene, as if she were a queen waiting for her chariot to arrive. Jeanne half expected her to manage a beauty queen wave: elbow, elbow, wrist, wrist.

"Come on, Scar!"

To Jeanne's surprise, Scarlett growled at her. Scarlett had never growled at her before. In fact, she'd never growled at anyone. She was possibly the world's worst guard dog.

As Jeanne considered her options, she looked up and realized that they were standing across the street from Holy Trinity.

She broke into a run and, this time, Scarlett followed. Down the stairwell they raced, to a small white door marked "Rectory." "Father! Father!" she bellowed, pounding on the door with more strength than she ever knew she possessed.

After several moments, she heard the shuffling of feet. The door opened a crack and a sandy-haired young man in gray flannel pajamas poked his head out. He rubbed his eyes. "Yes?"

"I need confession," she blurted out. "Right now."

"Let me change into some clothes."

"No, Father," she said, surprising herself with her own boldness. "I might lose my nerve. Besides, I'm in my pajamas too."

He squinted at the black and white cows. "It must be bad," he said.

"How do you know?"

He laughed. "You just walked through the most fashion-conscious area of the city dressed in that."

He closed the door behind him and motioned for her to follow him into a cozy little chapel with polished wood floors and a simple altar. He sat in the first pew, and she sat in the second one, with Scarlett stretched out at her feet. Turning to face her, he rested an arm on the back of the pew. "Do you know the Act of Contrition?"

"I'm afraid not."

"No problem. Tell me—tell God—what's on your mind."

"I–I–" Her lips failed her. They would not form sentences, or even words; they just trembled. It was humiliating, maddening, and more than a trifle frustrating. How could she ask for forgiveness if she could not even speak? She had held so many secrets inside for so long and now, it was as if they had all been swallowed by her shame.

"Relax, my child," he said, even though he couldn't have been more than a few years older than she. His blue-green eyes were kind, if a little bleary. "Anything you say is in confidence. God loves you, and He wants to forgive you. You wouldn't be here if you weren't ready to ask for and receive forgiveness."

Tears ran down her cheeks, splashing off her nose and chin, landing in a pool on her lap. Her skin was hot and sticky, and her lips tasted of salt. Scarlett whimpered sympathetically and moved closer to her. And still she could say nothing.

"You know," the priest said, "I've heard two murder confessions so far, so you wouldn't be the first. Lots of date rapes, dozens of abortions, affairs, burglaries, muggings. One guy confessed to seven armed robberies, then asked on the way out the door how much we took in during a typical Sunday collection."

She laughed in spite of herself.

"I've heard it all," he said. "I'll buy you a beer at The Tombs if you come up with something new."

She leaned closer to him. "I almost killed my mother," she whispered.

"But you didn't?"

She shook her head. "She killed my little sister in a drunk driving accident. It's so hard to forgive her."

To her amazement, he laughed. "I owe you a beer," he said. "You're the first person to confess to *not* killing someone."

She walked out of the confessional feeling younger and more carefree than she had in years, and a quick glance at her reflection in a shop window confirmed it. Her two little frown lines, which set off her eyebrows like inverted parentheses, had melted away.

He had let her off easy. Ten Hail Marys, twenty Our Fathers, and a promise to talk to her mother the next time she called. She wasn't looking forward to the talk, but at least it would be short. Prison calls were limited to five minutes.

As she and Scarlett made their way back down P Street, she dialed Precinct Number Five. "Detective Walker, please. I have information about the unsolved murder of Ibrahim Abu Ali."

*   *   *   *

Jeanne spent the morning in a hot and airless room, bare except for a small wooden table and three chairs. At first, Detective Walker and her partner, Detective Oates, didn't seem to know what to make of her story.

"You think I'm trying to deflect attention from myself, don't you?" Jeanne asked after three hours of questioning. She squinted at the camera in the corner of the room. The placement was subtle, but the little red light gave it away. She was sure she was being videotaped. "You think I did it, didn't you?"

"Your story does sound pretty preposterous," Detective Walker admitted. She consulted the notes scrawled across her yellow legal pad. "According to you, Yasmina Hariri, whose funeral was a month ago, is alive and well and located somewhere in the Middle East. She recognized Ibrahim Abu Ali as the individual who played a role in her friend Nejla Massoud's death and wanted revenge—"

"I won't guess at her motives. Maryam recently became engaged to a Jewish man, and she may have been trying to protect her from a similar fate."

"So she convinced Mossad that Ibrahim Abu Ali was a Hamas militant intent on blackmailing the Israeli government, tipped off a Mossad agent as to his whereabouts, entered into an affair with a funeral home director, stole a corpse, set fire to Algiers, staged it as a hate crime, faked her own death, and fled the country."

"Right."

"Why should we believe you? This all seems to be based on an alleged phone confession with zero witnesses."

"Not alleged." She flipped open her phone and showed the detectives the call log. "This is the last call I received. I haven't checked the country code, but it's international and I'd bet you anything it's from somewhere in the Middle East."

Looking mildly interested, Detective Oates copied "969" into his notebook. He shrugged. "So you had some friend who's studying abroad call you."

Jeanne shook her head. "I have a friend in Japan and another in France. That's it." She looked him straight in the eye, trying to see if he was wavering in his conviction that she was making it all up. His expression was inscrutable.

"Did you meet Mr. Harding?" she asked.

"No."

"If you'd met him, you'd realize that a woman like Yasmina would never have an affair with the likes of him without some ulterior motive."

He raised his hands and shrugged. "Maybe he's rich, maybe he's good in bed. Who knows? Women do strange things. My ex-wife left me for a flabby guy who drives a hot pink stretch limo and has no savings and no pension."

Jeanne thought for a moment. There was so little evidence she could provide without betraying her

friends; she couldn't admit that Fergus had hacked into
Ibrahim's bank accounts, and she couldn't in good
conscience turn in Carlos's Uncle Paco. "The fact that
she stole a corpse from Harding Funeral Home is just a
hunch," she said. "But it's easy to prove. You could
exhume the body in Yasmina Hariri's grave—if there's
even a body at all—and compare its DNA with the
mitochondrial DNA of her female relatives. I guarantee
the DNA won't match."

"She did work with a lot of dentists..." Detective
Walker grunted. "You must be a *CSI* fan like everyone
else."

"And there's this." She reached into the pocket of
her sweatshirt, pulled out a piece of paper, and unfolded
it before sliding it across the table.

As Detective Walker's eyes scanned the page, her
eyes grew bigger.

"This is from the computer at the studio where
Yasmina taught. All the teachers have access, but the
name is what caught my attention. The file name is
'Abkan', which is 'Nakba' spelled backwards. 'Nakba'
means 'the catastrophe' and it refers to the displacement
of the Palestinian people when Israel was founded in
1948. Yasmina was the only Palestinian teacher at the
studio."

"Circumstantial," Detective Oates said. "Anyone
could have written this. You could have written this."

"The password is '06201997.' The date of Nejla's death."

He raised an eyebrow. "How could you know that?"

"Facebook. Check out Yasmina's page."

"You could have password protected the file yourself. Just to throw us off track."

"You're right," Jeanne said. "But I didn't. I couldn't. This file—and every file like it—was created between 5:30 and 6 p.m. on a Thursday, right before Yasmina's beginner class. I can assure you that, when a law firm pays you by the hour, they keep meticulous records of when you are and are not working. And I am always working until at least 6 p.m."

Detective Oates's upper lip curled slightly and his pen stopped in midair. Their eyes locked. He took out his phone and, without taking his eyes off her, punched in a number. "Carrie?"

The voice on the other end was tinny and high-pitched, the words indistinct.

"I need a warrant to search the computers at the Arabian Nights Dance Studio and exhume the body of Yasmina Hariri." He hung up. "You, missy, aren't going anywhere until this is resolved."

Epilogue

"You should get a Nobel Peace Prize," Father Martin, the sandy-haired priest, said as he tossed a *Washington Post* on the smooth dark wood of a booth tucked in the far corner of The Tombs. "Two West Bank Settlements Dismantled" the headline screamed and underneath a small caption said "Prospects for peace in the Middle East best in past decade."

"That's Yasmina's doing, not mine."

"Don't be so modest. Most amateur sleuthing doesn't result in the fall of an Israeli government, a surge in support for the moderate Palestinian faction, and a peace rally attended by a million Israelis and Palestinians. Of course," he added, "I am obliged to say that pride is a sin."

"Of course." She took a sip of her frothing Guinness. Beer always tasted better when it was free.

"I assume Yasmina's beyond the arm of the law."

"Completely. Uncle Paco confirmed that he forged a Lebanese passport for her." She took another sip. "We have no extradition treaty with Lebanon."

"And what's next for you? More belly dancing? More sleuthing?"

She shrugged. "It's back to business as usual."

"Somehow I doubt that." He leaned towards her. "To whom much is given, much is expected."

"Is that from the Bible?"

He laughed. "Spiderman." He tossed a crumpled twenty-dollar bill on the table. "I'm sure I'll be seeing you in the confessional soon."

"You are?"

He grinned. "I don't think you'll stay out of trouble for long."

ABOUT THE AUTHOR

Maureen Klovers is the author of the memoir *In the Shadow of the Volcano: One Ex-Intelligence Official's Journey through Slums, Prisons, and Leper Colonies to the Heart of Latin America.* A former student of belly dance and Arabic, she lives outside of Washington, D.C., with her husband, Kevin, and their black Labrador Retriever, Nigel.